DESERT FABULOSO

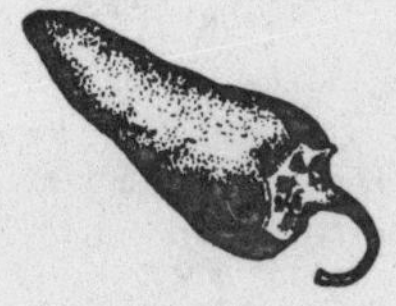

by
Lisa Lovenheim

A PLUME BOOK

NAL PENGUIN INC.

NEW YORK AND SCARBOROUGH, ONTARIO

PUBLISHER'S NOTE

This book is a work of fiction. Names, characters, places, and incidents either are the product of the author's imagination or are used fictitiously, and any resemblance to actual persons, living or dead, events, or locales is entirely coincidental.

NAL PENGUIN BOOKS ARE AVAILABLE AT QUANTITY DISCOUNTS
WHEN USED TO PROMOTE PRODUCTS OR SERVICES.
FOR INFORMATION PLEASE WRITE TO PREMIUM MARKETING DIVISION,
NAL PENGUIN INC., 1633 BROADWAY,
NEW YORK, NEW YORK 10019.

Grateful acknowledgment is made to the following for permission to excerpt from: Pp. 247–248 of *Memories, Dreams, Reflections* by C. G. Jung. Recorded and edited by Aniela Jaffe, translated by Richard and Clara Winston. Revised edition copyright © 1973 by Pantheon Books, a Division of Random House, Inc.

PLUME TRADEMARK REG. U.S. PAT. OFF. AND FOREIGN COUNTRIES
REGISTERED TRADEMARK—MARCA REGISTRADA
HECHO EN HARRISONBURG, VA., U.S.A.

SIGNET, SIGNET CLASSIC, MENTOR, ONYX, PLUME, MERIDIAN and NAL BOOKS are published *in the United States* by NAL Penguin Inc., 1633 Broadway, New York, New York 10019, *in Canada* by The New American Library of Canada, Limited, 81 Mack Avenue, Scarborough, Ontario M1L 1M8

Library of Congress Cataloging-in-Publication Data

Lovenheim, Lisa A.
Desert fabuloso.

I. Title.
PS3562.0863D4 1987 813'.54 86-28529
ISBN 0-452-25927-4

First Printing, March, 1987

1 2 3 4 5 6 7 8 9

PRINTED IN THE UNITED STATES OF AMERICA

To the Earl of Lovenheim
and the Belle of the ball

The Walrus and the Carpenter
Were walking close at hand:
They wept like anything to see
Such quantities of sand:
"If this were only cleared away,"
They said, "it would be grand!"

"If seven maids with seven mops
Swept it for half a year
Do you suppose," the Walrus said,
"That they could get it clear?"
"I doubt it," said the Carpenter,
And shed a bitter tear.

—Lewis Carroll,
Through the Looking-Glass

"See," Ochwiay Biano said, "how cruel the whites look. Their lips are thin, their noses sharp, their faces furrowed and distorted by folds. Their eyes have a staring expression; they are always seeking something. What are they seeking? The whites always want something; they are always uneasy and restless. We do not know what they want. We do not understand them. We think that they are mad."

I asked him why he thought the whites were all mad.

"They say that they think with their heads," he replied.

"Why of course. What do you think with?" I asked him in surprise.

"We think here," he said, indicating his heart.

—C. G. Jung's conversation with a Taos Pueblo Indian, from *Memories, Dreams, Reflections*

PROLOGUE

Historic Architecture

Time was of the essence to the owners of L'Etoile de West, a restaurant slated to open in October. The month was selected to attract cultivated Santa Feans who hungered after novelty during the doldrums season of autumn. The restaurateurs proclaimed that L'Etoile de West was going to be nothing if not novel; its menu would rotate daily, and on weekends local celebrities who fancied themselves gourmet chefs would supervise the preparation of their own *spécialités des Etoiles*. Indeed, three advanced celebrity commitments had been confirmed as early as April. A mystery writer's proposal for Tamales Madeira was tactfully refused, despite his favorable review in *The New Yorker*. Santa Fe newcomer Bradley Roberson III, learning of the rejection, considered it reflective of Santa Fe's provincialism. Himself something of an experimenter in the kitchen, he thought Tamales Madeira might just prove a remarkable taste sensation.

It was anticipated that L'Etoile de West would earn the praise of Santa Fe's Historic Architecture Committee and the chairwoman, Miss Dorothy Cheswick, even before they sampled any dishes (celebrity or otherwise), because none other than Epifanio "Joe" Salazar had been commissioned to construct the restaurant out of his prizewinning adobe bricks. As work progressed, the owners were naturally pleased with the bricks. However, the pace with which the builder laid them indicated that a restaurant might emerge by the next time Moscow hosted the Olympics; slipping a heavy dose of Benzedrine into Joe's thermos of coffee came under discussion as an emergency measure. (The owners might have thought better of hiring the contractor in the first place had they known that the restaurant's precarious beginnings as a stack of adobe dominoes represented Joe Salazar's first go at building an entire building. But the man had come highly recommended by Dorothy Cheswick, who had proclaimed him an "absolute wonder-worker with mud.")

Salazar's adobe was pinkish tan, specked with mineral particles and straw that sparkled golden in the sunlight. It was the golden quality of the bricks that had brought Joe renown. In 1982, he won the Historic Architecture Committee's ¡Viva Adobe! Award, and in the *City Different News* Dorothy Cheswick applauded him further under the headline THE RUMPELSTILTSKIN OF SANTA FE, NEW MEXICO. (Some years later, after observing Salazar make long-overdue repairs to his adobe home, Bradley Roberson III named him the Dirt Man of Alcatraz—an epithet that was never publicized.) Since 1982, Salazar had more construction work than he ever dreamed of. It was no accident that the year he won the ¡Viva Adobe! Award was also the year he made Dorothy Cheswick's fake adobe compound regal with the surrounding addition of his very finest of adobe walls. Walls, lovingly built adobe brick by adobe brick, were Salazar's specialty. Escaping from the hoards at a Dorothy Cheswick Christmas gala one year, Bradley Roberson III found Salazar's wall to be especially poignant. Once he had rid himself of a sickly combination of bourbon, salmon roe, and unmerited applause for his piano playing, the young man leaned against the wall and begged Rachmaninoff's forgiveness for his conversion of a lush concerto into a monolith of hardened mud.

Salazar's golden adobe was an expensive rarity in a city so cherishing hardened mud that most of its structures were fashioned to look as if they were made of it. Smoothing stucco over concrete, the classic means of creating the adobe look, was so economical that even the government could afford to blend in with the Santa Fe style. A long, low, classic fake adobe building housed the archives of the State of New Mexico, and beneath its flat roof was carved: "A Nation That Forgets Its Past Has No Future."

That Winston Churchill's salute to history was etched into wood and not a more monumental substance like stone suggested the weight time brought to bear on the nation's oldest capital city. Perhaps it was New Yorker Bradley Roberson III, remarking at a dinner party welcoming him into the Santa Fe community, who stated it best: "In the time–space continuum," he said, "Santa Fe is light on time and heavy on space. Time is so light here that you can shrug it off to float down that pathetic creek you call the Santa Fe River."

When the Santa Fe estate of a New York heiress was offered up for sale a few years ago, it was discovered that she had shrugged off time in her own way, with hats and shoes. Piles of hat- and shoe boxes, all neatly labeled, filled the apartment rooms where the old woman had resided. "The beautiful black satin sandals that I wore to Bunny's wedding," said one box. "The Lilly Daché sensation at Estelle's bon voyage," said another. A fashion historian hired to assign dates to these accessories found them to span the three decades leading up to the day the eccentric woman's family had shipped her off to the happy haven of Santa Fe, New Mexico. One of the heiress's feathered headbands was bought by a violinist who had made his Carnegie Hall debut at age twelve and now chose to serenade the stars while seated outside the flaps of his hand-sewn tepee. "But the question remains," said Bradley Roberson III, himself a musician (albeit one who had never made an official debut), "whether in Santa Fe you shrug off time, or time shrugs off *you*."

Bradley Roberson III lived in Dorothy Cheswick's beloved Historic East Side, a maze composed of squat, adobe and fake adobe houses, the walls that ran around them, and the narrow streets that ran between them. It was the Historic Architecture Committee's job to police the maze's appearance of having been wrought out of desert earth itself. Violators were promptly crossed off Dorothy's party guest lists and became the subjects of her frequent letters to the editor of the *City Different News*, which always awarded her the satisfaction of seeing them in print.

Dorothy Corazón Cheswick was the daughter of E. Hollins Cheswick, one of the original members of the Santa Fe Colony, a group of artist-settlers who joined forces to enhance the special qualities that had attracted them to the city just after the turn of the century.

A tall, large-boned woman, Dorothy Cheswick walked with a leading thrust of hip that had become more exaggerated with age and helped earn her the nickname Bulldozer. Her hair, gray and pulled back in a wispy ponytail like her mother had worn, was her only soft feature. Her simply constructed vee-necked Navajo tunics, worn tucked into pleated man-styled trousers, added a no-nonsense aspect to her manner, befitting a mover and shaker in a perennial frontier town that needed her direction. Along with stature, she had earned her share of skeptics; the owners of the restaurant L'Etoile de West were not the only ones to question the soundness of recommendations like Epifanio "Joe" Salazar and his mud bricks.

Sylvia Valdez, for example, felt she had Dorothy Cheswick to blame for the Historic Architecture Committee's rejection of her petition to have her street paved. The petition was handily voted down as "a request that would jeopardize the Historic East Side's unparalleled charm merely for the sake of addressing a child-safety issue that, while deserving of consideration, is very temporary in nature." Mrs. Valdez worried about her little boy Stevie's bicycle spills which sent him crashing down on a dirt road peppered with pebbles the size and sharpness of diamonds. Stevie was six, a shaky rider, and more than once Mrs. Valdez had to pick pebbles out of his knees with tweezers. Every time Stevie left the driveway on his bike, his mother whispered a prayer against accidents. Such was the gist of Mrs. Valdez's petition, which seven of her twelve neighbors signed.

The Historic Architecture Committee's action on the petition was swift and hard-nosed. Aiming to soften the blow, Dorothy Cheswick was prompted to write the concerned mother a personal letter.

Dear Mrs. Valdez,

If I am right, I am addressing the lovely wife of one of our most respected New Mexico government officials. Your husband, Robert, has done this state a great service by concentrating his efforts on some of New Mexico's most distinctive "homegrown" features of the economy. I especially cheer his recent efforts to whet investors' appetites for building canneries to package our fabulous chile peppers. It is time for America to get steamed up over chile grown by the people who grow the best there is.

Mrs. Valdez, I know you must be sorely disappointed over the committee's decision regarding the dirt surface of Camino Sin Nombre, and I grant that you must wonder if it was sprouted from the cold hearts of childless people. As the only childless one of the bunch, do allow me to tell you how deeply moved we *all* were by the motive and wording of your petition, which came straight from the soul of a mother's love. In fact, so moved was I by your request that I was launched on a trip down Memory Lane, and I hope that if I let you in on a little bit of my mental journey, you, too, will see why we made the only decision we possibly could.

When I was a little girl, I didn't have a bicycle but used to travel with my father in his jalopy, which provided the jauntiest rides you could imagine. I remember feeling that every bone and organ of my body had been shaken off its hinges as we set out over rocky arroyos until arriving at a vista that made my father stop and set up his easel. The first time my father drove me all the way to Albuquerque and I felt the car hit pavement for the first time, it suddenly occurred to me that our jalopy was something less than a thrill machine but just a thing that was invented to help us get from one place to another. In short, all the fun went out of it. Much later, when I had my first ride in a jeep that was built to handle the bumps of my father's adventurous days, I realized what a challenge he had taken on in braving forth in his jalopy. As for your little Stevie, in learning to ride a bicycle on the dirt surface of one of our city's most charming old streets, he is carrying on the spirit of endurance that can be traced back to Santa Fe's earliest days. I say to him, "Hooray! When you have mastered a ride down that short, bumpy dirt road of yours, then you know you have really mastered the bicycle!"

With fondest wishes,
Dorothy Cheswick

P.S. I saw that your petition was signed by a young man named Bradley Roberson III, who must be among your newest of neighbors. The surprise in seeing his name was a glad one, for I had heard a rumor that he had left us after only a few short months. Do give him a warm hello from me, and tell him I am happy not to have lost one of Santa Fe's most charming new arrivals.

BOOK I

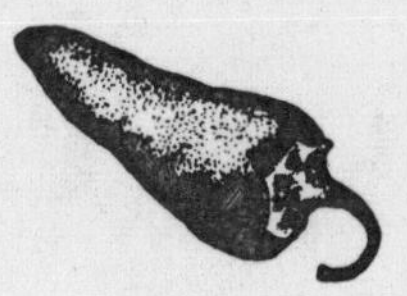

Chapter One

CAMINO Sin Nombre, home to the Valdez family and their neighbor, Bradley Roberson III, was a dirt road off another dirt road in the maze of the Historic East Side. Its distinction lay in the fact that the early name-givers to the streets of Santa Fe found absolutely no way to typify it, and thus called it what they did: Street Without a Name. Nearby was Camino del Monte Sol, Street of Mountain Sun; a bit farther, Acequia Madre, Irrigation Bed; and Alameda, Tree-lined Way. Across town was Camino de las Crucitas, Street of the Little Intersections. Around the corner from Camino Sin Nombre was El Caminito, the Little Street, which explained the problem: There was a word to describe the Camino Sin Nombre, but it was all used up.

The federal buildings were off Washington Avenue, which in its few blocks darted up on the perpendicular from the Plaza until it met the Scottish Rite temple standing huge and pink at Santa Fe's northeast gate. Washington Avenue played host to the compact and friendly city library and an equally compact and friendly supermarket. The library intermittently and with pronounced regret debated the initiation of a fining policy; the supermarket accepted charges and made deliveries. The supermarket also had a respectable selection of wines, and the butcher had been known to steer a shopper toward an obscure and inexpensive vintage that complemented perfectly the prime local sirloin.

With a bank, a gas station, a municipal parking lot, and the post office also situated along its route, Washington Avenue was an errand-runner's oasis in an area of the city where servicing everyday needs—as the Plaza had done—had become an idea that had lived out its time. At the Plaza junction of Washington and Palace Avenues, with a row of galleries and boutiques to the left and a row of Indians selling crafts to the right, function surrendered to charm, and the tourist surrendered his money.

Beyond the Scottish Rite temple, and four too-short miles from Bradley Roberson III, John Aaron, a native of Miami, Florida, lived off Bishop's Lodge Road, which Washington Street became as it neared the resort set on the site of Archbishop Lamy's retreat. Aaron had been tempted to get in on the Plaza property-value boom that sent plebian stores off packing to the new shopping malls, converted gas stations into galleries, and old office buildings into chic arcades. But having moved to Santa Fe more for the many conveniences of Washington Avenue than the encroachment of mirror-countered gelaterias and Ralph Lauren Western wear, John Aaron kept his hands out of commercial real estate and busied them with residential property. And though he had suffered some accusations as to the inflated cost of housing, when his favorite drugstore forfeited its forty-year lease to make room for a leather boutique called PerSuede, John Aaron mourned with a clear conscience.

What he had loved best about the Plaza Pharmacy was the soda fountain. Its yellow-edged placards of savory sodas and BLTs; its worn, green leather stools; and its single-serving boxes of dried cereal gave him, an Easterner, a personal link to the desert-mummified past. All the rest of it—adobe, fake or real, conquistador pageants, Indian dances, a steaming bowl of pork, chile, and hominy—he enjoyed well enough but with reserve. He could not get emotional over the mutation of Santa Fe's skyline; transplants like himself who did he considered merely slaves to affectation. But he was shaken by the closing of the old and sparsely stocked drugstore; he had taught the young Hispanics who worked the fountain how to make an egg cream, and there was a small piece of him there.

Even before he moved to Santa Fe, John Aaron, in his one claim to being a visionary, began to accumulate desert land around the city. In fact, on his first trip to Santa Fe in the 1960s, he bought a few dozen acres off Bishop's Lodge Road. (At the time he had accompanied a decorator friend whose client had bankrolled him to find the very best in Pueblo pottery and Navajo rugs, this client having fallen in love with Southwestern decor while visiting relatives in Phoenix. John was thirty then, recently separated from his wife, and in the midst of what his therapist labeled "an awakening of latency" (and his father labeled "driving a stake through his family's heart").

At the time John's own heart was being chewed to pieces by a gorgeous Cuban bar waiter at the Beach Hotel on Key Biscayne. John would take a room and there perform an act on his knees that, when finished, was thanked with this term of endearment: "I hate your Jewish face." John was trying to forge a healthier relationship with the decorator who brought him to Santa Fe, but the fact that this man raised his legs as readily as if they were filled with helium bored John to tears. He thrived on shock, on the nerve-fraying zap of devastation. His therapist said this was symptomatic of self-loathing, but John felt it was a revolt against the certain prepackaged, freeze-dried death of a Florida retirement community.

"I'm in leisure death camps," John would say over Bombay gin-and-tonics at the poolsides of Key West.

"Too morbid," complained his companions.

He could find no other way to describe the family business, Aaron and Son Developers, a business that engaged in draining swamps, bulldozing through the grasses of the Everglades, laying Astroturf and clustering cheaply built condos around the recreation centers and infirmaries.

It was over an egg cream at a Miami Beach drugstore counter that John had told his father that he was divorcing his wife. "She just doesn't smell right," he subtly tried to explain after "It's not working" had failed to suffice.

"They can treat that problem without chemicals, you know," offered his father. "I read about it. Tell her to eat yogurt. But what am I talking about? What are *you* talking about? Are you telling me that smelling bad is grounds for divorce?"

John decided it was useless to try to own up gently. "I'm telling you that her smelling *female* is grounds for divorce," he said. "That her *being* female is grounds for divorce. Listen, I've given her a case of crabs one too many times, myself—the parting is mutual. Do you understand now? I'm not interested in women, Dad. I like men."

It was their last egg cream together. From then on John's father communicated to him through the family secretary, who took the liberty of condensing his patriarchal rantings into single-word evaluations: critical or fair—but never stable. Then came the heart attack, the bypass surgery, and the mother who ceased being his mother but became a guard against everything his father's heart couldn't stand anymore.

When John's divorce was settled, he sold off all of his Florida holdings, broke ground on a home that would have a full view of the Sangre de Cristo Mountains, and invested in several hundred acres in and around Santa Fe, New Mexico. The desert air, he told his Florida friends (and lovers), would evaporate the smell of death that burrowed in his system. When he moved West, the Santa Fe Opera was just beginning to burgeon into a national institution. The Plaza was a funky promenade for lost ragamuffins who hadn't realized that the decade had changed. And the town's hovering Sangre de Cristos, which turned red—yes, like the Blood of Christ—with each pass of the sun, seemed to stand as giant sentinels wasted at their post, guarding a couple of quaint hotels, a museum, some fledgling galleries, and all that Historic Architecture Committee charm for which John developed an acquired taste.

Why Santa Fe? John Aaron was no artist and thus could not claim that the special intensity of the northern New Mexico sunlight set free the colors and shapes that danced in his head. And he was no writer whose words could flourish among the quiet vistas that called them forth as enticingly as a clean, white sheet of paper. Yet Santa Fe struck him at the same primal level that it has struck many an artist and writer over time.

It was not the city's established homosexual community that lured him, either, although he certainly saw the benefit of living in a town populated by societal outcasts whose eccentricities buoyed them high into the stratosphere. No, what instinctively struck a chord in John was the realization that the market value of Santa Fe's beauty would exceed the heights of its altitude, which was 6,989 feet above sea level. And though it cast something of a lackluster hue to his aura (in a city where auras were read as frequently and fervently as palms), John quickly gleaned for himself the reputation of a highly practical man.

Through mutual acquaintances in Miami and New York John was given entrée into opera circles where he learned that the fastest route to establishing himself in his adopted home was to become a patron of the arts. As a potential collector and contributor to artistic causes, he was fêted with parties and soon had amassed such a large debt of social favors that he was forced to entertain heavily himself. He gave parties for new gallery owners, painters, potters, dancers, artistic directors, and occasionally even for contractors who had a role in keeping Santa Fe art Santa Fe–housed. He entertained for buyers of his old property and sellers of his new property, his graciousness earning him high marks in trade. He wrote home to friends in Miami: "If this is the purgatory to where my father thinks he banished me, its only bane is dinner parties. The plus is that I have become one hell of a cook, but I would love someone who dreams of opening a catering business to come set up shop here."

Indeed John had redesigned his now essential kitchen carefully to accommodate his cramped culinary style. Spices had to be at eye level, and all other ingredients stored as close to arm's length as possible. It was not an airy kitchen, but it was absolutely functional. (His friends called it Mission Control.)

John lived at the end of a street off Bishop's Lodge Road called La Barranca, a romantic-sounding word for a large gully. This gully was full of large and beautiful Santa Fe homes. The noses of the Historic Architecture Committee did not reach into La Barranca, but they would not have sniffed disapprovingly, for the homes were as well in keeping with Santa Fe charm as new, large homes could be. With the interiors, however, the architects had taken obvious delight in their unregulated freedom of expression.

Nor were these homes surrounded by walls; the privacy that walls insured was instead accomplished with enormous plots of land. John's nine acres extended over a terrain whose sand hills rolled out toward the Sangre de Cristos, bordering an area zoned against construction to preserve its visual splendor. Thus he owned his view, majestically displayed through the picture windows that ran from floor to ceiling where his house faced east. John's home was enough of a showplace to have been shot for a *Design ¡Santa Fe!* supplement of the Albuquerque paper, and John took some responsibility for the local celebrity status that his architect had achieved, happily conducting tours of his home. Some sensed a smugness in John's smile when visitors noted that the house represented the architect at his most inspired. Indeed the conical corners and paraboloids that were his trademark lost their impact when later exploded in scale, and his finesse of line was completely lost on the spew of condominiums that composed his Santa Fe swan song before departing for West Hollywood. It was Bradley Roberson III who pinpointed why John himself liked his house so much. Living there was "like living under an open parachute," he said, "but with the secure sense that you would never have to hit ground."

The art that hung on John's flat, windowless surfaces never remained long enough to judge whether or not it had an appropriate home among all those curves, vertexes, and apexes; instead it was rotated into obscurity as frequently as John took new talent under his wing. It was said that an artist had withstood the test of time if he had managed representation in John Aaron's living room for three months running. When accused of being too fickle to claim possession of an art lover's heart, John quipped that a good painting was like a good movie or a good book, or, for that matter, some good ass, and that his enthusiasm for anything grew cold as a corpse the moment he felt committed to enjoying it for life. As for his sexual cavorting, it was frenzied in the fashion of a college dormitory with resident advisers standing by to offer words of wisdom when he complained of fatigue.

It was with no little fascination that the community watched John Aaron go through a number of young Hispanic men as though there were an underground passage leading from his house to the confessional at the Guadalupe Church. Visitors from Los Angeles, Houston, and other distant cities were warned that John's taste was "strictly South of the Border, God knows why." Marissa Goldman, a Santa Fe potter whose ever-piqued interest in men's affairs earned her certain status as an information clearinghouse, knew that it had something to do with a Cuban whom John had left behind in Miami, but the only explanation she received as to why John's young men were never seen at more than two dinner parties before vanishing from the scene was that he found them "lacking in temperament."

"They're too polite," he said. "They seem to want to be adopted."

As far as everyone knew, the only man aside from Bradley Roberson III who came close to lassoing John Aaron's heart was a rodeo rider named Jesús Acosta, whom he met back in 1980 at the Fox Trot bar in Albuquerque. That John had invited a rodeo rider to live with him on La Barranca spurred a false rumor that he was into bondage. (His therapist could have told anyone who cared to ask that it was most decidedly not his body, but his emotions, that John liked to have tied up in knots.)

With as little provocation as a request to chisel horse manure from his boot heels before entering the living room, Jesús Acosta destroyed a half dozen Pueblo pots, two paintings-of-the month, and an Alvar Aalto chair and coffee table before riding off into the New Mexico sunset. John coasted on the drama of this experience for two years, nothing short of karmic, the event "encapsulated the essence of Santa Fe."

By this time John had passed his fortieth birthday, an age some felt deserved sympathy and not condemnation for its tired revelations. But by the time Jesús Acosta had taken off to ride some real bulls, the town had begun to echo John Aaron's own opinion of himself: His wealth, his rotating paintings, his conical corners, and his paraboloidal ceilings were the only glimpses of excitement in the life of an utter bore.

Then, one summer, when even the Santa Fe Opera seemed to have grown weary of its standard repertoire, the Plaza Pharmacy closed. The *City Different News* began to report a new phenomenon, of which John was already well aware: the dramatic slowdown of luxury home construction. The market's saturation point did not threaten John's wealth, but John suddenly found himself faced with an overabundance of idle time. Like the Plaza Pharmacy, real estate development touched something in his blood, reminding him that life did indeed run through his veins. He spoke fondly of his business maneuverings as his "children"; he claimed they brought him as close to parenthood as he would ever come.

That summer an opportunity to expand his interests beyond Santa Fe County came his way like a blessing. When the developers who offered him entrée into the southern part of the state around the resort of Ruidoso proved too brash and Texan for comfort, however, John arranged to become a silent partner. This pleased everyone concerned. The developers had not taken to John, either; his even manner made them wonder how he had earned the label of a wheeler-dealer, and his middle-aged bachelorhood confirmed that Santa Fe was the only southwestern city likely to view him as a respectable tycoon.

At this depressing summer's end, just as John was contemplating with dismay a week's schedule of mandatory social meals, his mother called from Miami to tell him that his father had dropped dead on the Inverarry golf course. She insisted that in death his father forgave all. "He loved you," she proclaimed through her sobs, "even though you broke his heart." Although her husband had gone out in the heat like an idiot, she added, "At least he died doing the thing he loved."

"You know," said John, feeling his throat constrict, "he always resented me for not being a golfer."

"He never hated you for that."

"Well, if not for that, then for all the rest of it. For everything."

John wept as he packed his bags for Miami, and more still when he saw his mother. As long as he cried with her, he discovered, he was spared her pleas as to where she had gone wrong with him, where his father had gone wrong, and why, if he insisted on being homosexual and single, he wouldn't at least move back to Florida. He could live his life and still help her from sinking into terrible loneliness. "I need a son," said the widow of the man who once condemned John's soul to the stinking landfill of the morally dead.

At the cemetery an uncle fainted by the gravesite, causing horror to overtake John's grief, chase away his tears and make him long to run. Burial was too graphic. "I'm going to New York tomorrow," he announced to his mother in the limousine. "You'll be all right. You have your friends." She was powerless to hold him, his mother knew. He patted her hand, and she withdrew it, thrusting it into the bowels of her purse in search of a fresh piece of Kleenex.

On his flight to New York John realized that he had left Santa Fe without having told a soul that he was going, thus standing up three lunch dates, two dinners, and a tennis match. "I stood up six people," he told the stewardess behind the bar of the DC-10 and began to laugh. "I stood up six people. Do you know how that translates into the number of parties to which I will not be invited this year? Where I live the penal code commands an exponential ratio of crimes to penalties." But back in Santa Fe John Aaron's disappearance was actually helping his status. Everyone said it was the most interesting thing he had pulled off in years. And when he returned, days later, accompanied by one Bradley Roberson III, everyone agreed that John Aaron had outdone himself.

Chapter Two

ON April 3, 1958, some hours after Bradley Roberson III was born at Lenox Hill Hospital, his father doused his own body with Taittenger champagne in the Greenwich Village apartment he held under the name of Michael Neumeier. Watching him perform this act of baptism into fatherhood was a man whose come-on at an Eighth Avenue bar was that he was a hit man for the Mafia. In bed, truth to this claim had been quite convincing, but BJ Roberson, or Michael Neumeier (the name the alleged hit man knew him by), could not let out one scream, not even when a lit cigarette came within a hair of his contorted face. The screams lodged in his throat where they were blocked by guilt of such monstrous proportions that the pain of sex meant to salve it that afternoon was no more soothing than the dab of a cottonball.

Fourteen years later when BJ Roberson was diagnosed with cancer, no one understood why the malignancy had selected his stomach for a breeding ground. After Bradley's birth his father often complained of a chronic throat condition but never of an ulcer. A determined smoker, he drank health frappes laced with cayenne pepper every morning for the purpose of clearing his larynx. But though he was able to talk finance and many other topics of the day forcefully, he never could get out many words about his son. Bradley never learned how his father had greeted his arrival, and he was spared his father's suffering in the worst days of his disease. BJ Roberson died instead under his alias—his hit-man phase behind him—nursed in the arms of a poet, his lover of three years.

It was the poet who had intercepted Bradley outside the doors of Juilliard to tell him that his father had not really gone to Mexico to die in the sun, who told him about the apartment, why his father kept it, and under what name. The poet thought that a fifteen-year-old boy should be made to understand why, in facing death, his father had chosen to hide from his family. This was the noble gesture of a man who couldn't bear to elicit sympathy from the people he felt owed him nothing but anger and disdain, the poet explained. He had, in fact, what he considered many healing things to say, and in his feverishness to get them off his chest it did not register that every mention of the name Michael caused Bradley's icy stare to drop another dozen degrees. Thus the poet stood immobilized, his loving memories imploding in a mouth that shut like a trap when Bradley shoved him aside, exclaiming, "My God, you really are too kitsch for words. What do you do, write condolence cards for Hallmark?"

Leaving the poet, Bradley went to the apartment of his piano teacher, who asked him why he was so late. "I was molested on the street," he said, "by my father's lover. He actually thought he was telling me something I didn't know. Can I ask you something? What are you supposed to do when people act so fucking pathetic?"

The instructor had no clear response.

"How dare that asshole," Bradley cried. "How dare he try to use me to keep that bastard's memory alive! Tell me something. Is that what people do? Is everyone full of shit? Are you full of shit? Am I your first budding young pianist? Or am I one of a long line that goes back to the first? 'Oh, Bradley,' you say, 'you play like a dream.' Tell me, you liar. Who's your fucking dream?"

The piano teacher went over to the stereo, removed Bradley's favorite old recording of Glenn Gould's rendition of *The Goldberg Variations,* and hurled it across the room where it smashed against the wet bar. Then, kicking the pieces, he made his way into the bedroom and slammed the door, promising himself that sleeping with his students was a thing of the past.

Bradley fixed himself a gin and tonic. As he drank it down on an S-shaped white sofa, he played over in his mind the first time he had encountered the name Michael Neumeier. Three years earlier he had pulled a book titled *From Ashes: Financing the New Germany* off the Roberson library shelf for the first time. There, inside his father's opus, Bradley found a picture of BJ embracing a classmate from his London School of Economics days. There was a caption: "BJ Roberson and Michael Neumeier, Chairmen of the Board of the World Ltd." And on the back was this handwritten sentiment: "Darling: Alas, a world that will never know. Adieu, M."

Shortly after Bradley's discovery of the photograph his parents were called in by the headmaster at Dalton, who opined that their son's violent outbursts very plainly had to do with something deeper than his recognized genius. The faculty expected a low threshold of frustration in gifted and talented students, and Bradley was among the best of them. Nonetheless Bradley's book report on *Great Expectations* had to be brought to their attention. Twelve-year-old Bradley's paper began: "Deep in the stacks of the Metropolitan Library I discovered this little-known fact about *Great Expectations*. It was that, because of moral nonsense in the days of Victorian England, no one would publish Dickens's book unless he dropped the subtitle. But when I learned what the subtitle was, Charles Dickens's ridiculous story began to make sense to me. This was the full title of the novel, and I hope that my telling it will help everyone else make sense out of this book as well: *Great Expectations, or, Miss Havisham Wreaks Revenge on a Helpless Closet Queen.*"

The headmaster hoped he wasn't stepping out of bounds by suggesting that Bradley was in need of therapy. BJ Roberson thanked him and said he very much agreed. Outside, Cassie Roberson asked her husband what Bradley meant by "helpless closet queen." "God bless you, dearest one," BJ replied, looking askance at his wife. "Surely you know he means me."

On April 3, 1958, when Cassie McDade Roberson awakened after giving birth to her only child and saw the flowers that filled her hospital room, she told the nurse that she felt just like a princess. "You sweet thing," she then whispered to her sleeping baby boy. "You smell like a million gardenias."

That was Cassie.

At home, little Bradley was one among many eye-dazzling treasures in the Roberson town house; Cassie was thankful to her husband for Bradley in the same way she was thankful for the other furnishings he supplied. Nor did it matter to her that Bradley's conception marked the end of her conjugal relations. She had been blessed with a baby as cuddly as a fur coat, and like her chinchilla, she didn't need two.

CASSIE MCDADE WEDS BRADLEY M. ROBERSON, JR., read the banner in the *Times*, two months before sperm met ovum in one of a series of perfunctory stabs at procreation. The marriage notice went on to explain:

> The bride is the daughter of Mr. and Mrs. Lucas McDade of Culpeper, Virginia. She attended the Richmond Secretarial Institute.
>
> The groom graduated from the Groton School and the London School of Economics. His book on postwar advances in West German industry will be published next spring by the Oxford University Press. He is president of Roberson, Smith and Collingwood,

> the international securities firm founded by his father, Bradley Malcolm Roberson, who served as an adviser to the Truman and Eisenhower administrations. The groom's mother, Margaret Sherwood Roberson, is on the board of directors of the Metropolitan Opera.

The marriage ceremony was performed in the Manhattan chambers of a judicial friend of the family. Cassie was a ravishing bride. Her face (the soft curves of her cheekbones, her eyes shaped like half-moons, her mouth puckered permanently since a swarm of newly kissed sailors had departed Norfolk for Korea) had been set aglow at Elizabeth Arden and would never know Maybelline again. Her suit was by Chanel, the skirt immodestly hugging her hips and guiding eyes down to the joining of calf and ankle so perfect that they seemed melted together from a mold God would come to reject upon realizing the scandal it would cause.

At the champagne reception word (albeit whispered) was that Cassie's laugh echoed through the hollow dome of her head and that with a little insulation it would not sound so tinny. By then her hair had been dyed to approximate her natural light auburn shade.

Two months earlier a platinum-blond Cassie had walked into BJ Roberson's office to apply for a clerical position. BJ Roberson's Wall Street office was filled with brown leather furniture and potted palms, and Cassie's first impression of the man who would become her husband was that he smelled like leather and was just as tough. She entered the room in a rayon dress printed top to bottom with large red poppies; standing before him, her white spiked heels sank like golf tees into the dark green carpeting. Cassie asked BJ Roberson if he got his palms from the same place that the Plaza Hotel did. When he fell back into his chair, laughing like an impresario who had just discovered the comic opera of the century, she decided to change her mind about him.

"Are you *staying* at the *Plaza*?" BJ asked when he calmed down.

"Not now, but indeed I have stayed at the Plaza," said Cassie McDade. "Can I ask you what's so funny about the Plaza Hotel? I mean, I broke a nail because a bureau drawer got stuck, and I saw quite a few cracks in the bathroom floor, but is that funny? In my personal opinion the place is a morgue."

Another burst of laughter encouraged her to continue. "Can I ask you something, Mr. Roberson? Is there some law about wearing colors in the offices down here? I got these awful looks from the woman outside, and in my personal opinion, gray and brown are not colors as far as women are concerned. I think it's because they're in those suits that they look so miserable. Can you direct me to a part of town where I can dress in a way that will allow me to look in the mirror and not drop dead from drabness?"

"I'm sorry to say that we are very dull down here," said BJ Roberson. "We lead very tame little lives. Please sit down, Miss McDade, and tell me what angel of mercy sent you here to liven things up. Which dull, gray little man has treated himself to a rendezvous with red poppies in the Plaza Hotel?"

Adjusting her dress, Cassie McDade told him that her personal affairs were none of his business. "Anyway," she said, "what are you hiring, a typist or a nun?"

"A typist, by all means, Miss McDade. But regarding nuns, that does raise a good point. Your *hair*, Miss McDade, is simply awful. Whoever talked you into becoming a blonde should be shot. What are you, really? A redhead?"

Cassie's blue eyes twinkled. "My goodness, Mr. Roberson. You've found me out. Well, I guess you can also tell that underneath all these bright colors is a woman who can really type."

BJ Roberson lit up a cigarette. Cassie accepted another from the pack he proferred, even though, she said, she preferred filter tips. "If you hadn't had the highest score on your typing test, they wouldn't have thought to let you in here, you know," said BJ. "My administrative assistants are sure that I will realize in meeting you that hiring on the sole basis of performance is too rigid a rule. They think I'll reject you out of hand. Now, whoever taught you how to type down in Virginia obviously did a very fine job, Miss McDade. Whoever taught you to dress and select the proper hair color for your complexion should consider a career change. If you want this job, you'll return to your own shade of red to match your milky redhead's complexion, and you will find yourself some other clothes."

"I won't wear awful gray and brown suits," insisted Cassie.

"A wise decision," said BJ Roberson. He pulled three one-hundred-dollar bills from his wallet and handed them over across his desk. "But a deep turquoise, maybe toned down even more with some rust in the tweed, would look marvelous on you. No large prints, Miss McDade. Your eyes are fantastic. Show them off, for God's sake. Don't drown them in prints."

"My eyes are my best feature," Cassie concurred. "You're not the first person to point that fact out to me, but, you know, I'm not sure what I was wearing those other times."

"Trust me. It wasn't a print."

"You sound like an expert, Mr. Roberson. So can you tell me where to get my hair done in this city that won't set me back the price of a new pair of shoes?"

BJ Roberson buzzed his secretary and arranged to have the company billed for a full beauty makeover for Miss

Cassie McDade at Elizabeth Arden. "That one should be good for a few coffee breaks," he said to Cassie with a wink.

"Mr. Roberson!" she squealed. "This is right out of a movie!"

"Which one, Miss McDade? Or do they all run together in your mind?"

Some said it was his status as a Wall Street prodigy that made BJ Roberson thumb his nose at the admiration of the wealthiest of New York's debutantes. Others gossiped that his British education had frozen him in a state of self-importance so stiff that it would take a blowtorch to ignite a hot-blooded pursuit of female companionship. There had been many introductions to women respected for their depth of mind, once it was apparent that beauty did not impress him, but BJ Roberson had snubbed them all. His mother had given him up for a lost cause. "Having a lively debate over American interests in Persia at the club tonight, dear?" she would ask snidely. "Or is it a meeting of the minds over the banana crisis? I hear the banana business is in danger of softening this year."

He took women to the theater, the opera, and the ballet, recognizing the importance of keeping people's prurient interests alive and pointed in the right direction. But even his lawyer advised him that he was not doing enough in that regard. BJ's lawyer was his closest confidant. It was one of many bones of contention between father and son that BJ had broken with the family attorney to choose one of his own. BJ trusted Maurice McPherson implicitly; they shared the same secrets (and, just once, the same bed). Maurice McPherson had married a woman so thankful for a lift in social position that she was content to live with half a husband; she also felt such accomplishment in stimulating a man of his stature that she could ride high for weeks on one good fuck. Maurice McPherson felt BJ should follow his lead. He also told BJ that he should be happy for his newly married friend, Michael Neumeier, who no longer had to maneuver through the streets of London under the shadow of paranoia. "It's not our passions, you know—it's our paranoia that's so lethal," the lawyer said quietly to his client at the Four Seasons. "So we avoid it with a meaningless act to keep society at bay, go about our business, and beat the hypocrites at their own fucked-up game. Plus we keep some needy creature happy with a knockout wardrobe and some glamorous nights on the town."

"It's sinful," BJ Roberson protested. "You'll still be telling me this five years from now, only you won't be able to get the words out because your tongue will be too thick after your fifth martini."

"Well, at least I'll be here. I'm not so sure about you. Have you looked in the mirror lately? Maybe all those trips to Germany have warped your hold on reality. Christ, I'm telling you that I live with myself. I can speak freely in a public place because I have the confidence of a married man, and I don't see that I'm going to have to pay a heavy price for it. I honestly don't."

"But you don't leave any room for anything meaningful. What happens when you fall in love? I'll tell you what: absolute torture. Waking up every morning wondering why you're bothering, because you've locked yourself in a cage where love has no place to lie down with you. I'd rather run scared with love right there beside me. At least I can be titillated by the danger. What is it that will titillate you, Maurice?"

"My God, BJ, you're a money man," the lawyer exclaimed. "Your grasp of the facts makes you one hell of a speculator. There's nothing poetic about the career that's earned you the reputation of the best adviser as to shipping money abroad. So why all this talk of love and danger? For heaven's sake, you know the facts of who you are. You've got to learn to deal with them expediently. You of all people should know that expedience is everything."

When Cassie McDade had left BJ's office, bequeathing to his memory her scandalous, poppy-covered ass, he poured himself a triple Scotch and asked his secretary to hold his calls. He then took pen in hand and finished a letter he had been avoiding for weeks.

The Russian Front
New York City
March 1957

Dear Michael,

I have been meaning to write for days but have been caught up in a battle with my father that may very well cause one of us to leave the company if a compromise cannot be reached soon. He refuses to budge from his position that investments are safe in Cuba. The man is such a disappointment to me.

Michael, Michael, if I go soon, as I plan to, on a factory tour of Bavaria, can you possibly meet me afterward in Berlin? For just a weekend? A day? I know you have a wife now and are striving to keep your "deviant side" in line. You'd be a damn fool not to try, I suppose. But, Michael, I am afraid I'm on the brink of doing something very stupid in this jungle of feigned respectability; I've developed an almost slapstick attitude toward it. I want to take a giant pie and throw it in everybody's face at once—Father's, Mother's, the whole stodgy staff with their stifled whispers. Oh, Michael, see me in Berlin, please! Only you can save me from myself. I need for you to kiss me and tell me I'm an idiot to even think about such things.

I love you, married or pure.

—BJ

BJ Roberson moved Cassie out of the cheap women's hotel where she slept those nights she was unsuccessful at the bars of Manhattan's better establishments, and he set her up in a modest brownstone on Bank Street. He took her shopping for clothes as respectable and flattering as the turquoise-and-rust tweed suit the saleswoman at Saks found for her, and he taught her the finer points of dining at his favorite restaurants.

Office gossip had it that BJ Roberson so wanted to rub his father's nose in Cuba that he had taken up with a commodity that could be sold cheaply on the back streets of Havana. The office situation grew worse daily, as Bradley, Sr.'s threats to resign were met with less and less resistance by partners who had begun to side openly with his son. BJ had to admit that there was deviant pleasure to be gleaned from his new game, if only comic relief from office tension; but Cassie was a game he resolved to keep frivolous—until the reply from England came.

BJ read Michael Neumeier's letter in his office, one hand gripping another triple Scotch, the other shaking so fiercely that it could not hold a cigarette.

The Gulag
Is it Spring 1957?

Dearest BJ,

I enclose a photograph that I found of us the other day when performing yet another "search and destroy" of any incriminating evidence left to my name.

As I watched your latest letter burn, it was as though I, too, was going up in flames, leaving in my place a dutiful zombie. I performed this latest purge in a panic after having my way with a lad near Euston Station where he accepted my offer of £2 for his favors. (When it was over, I asked him for his card.)

Darling, I feel completely ripped apart, and I can't swear before God that I'll be able to hold on. Poor Joanna is at her wit's end over my depressions and asks me to see a psychiatrist. I can't bring myself to tell her that I have been doing just that for the past six months and that I don't know how many more times I can take hearing that my emotional development is still stuck in adolescence and that if I would only work with him, there is a chance that I'll grow up. If I am stuck in adolescence, why do I feel like a decrepit old man?

What to do with your perverse temptation? I can't advise, because nothing rings any more absurd to me now than my own damned existence. But the one thing that I do see clearly is that I cannot meet you in Germany, my petulant, naughty mate. That would do me in as surely as a bullet through the head. If I ask you not to write me anymore, will you understand? I am trying, futile as it seems, to get my house in order. Somehow your talk about Cuba applies to us. It seems that Russia is indeed winning the war.

—M.

After downing a few more drinks alone in his office, BJ Roberson picked up the phone and arranged for the McPhersons to dine with him and his new fiancée, Cassie McDade. Three days later he led into Chez Louis XIV a woman whose diamond shimmered no more blindingly than her glossy, pink lips, and whose nails, once mini-spatulas, had the refined shape of demitasse spoons.

"Virginia's loss is clearly New York's gain," said Maurice McPherson as he gallantly kissed Cassie's hand, provoking giggles of delight. At BJ he winked and said "*Touché.*" But later in the evening when Cassie derided Maurice's views of Eisenhower's high moral fiber with a firm "I bet Mamie drinks martinis while Ike does it to her with his favorite putting iron," Maurice was moved to ask the women to excuse them, "to discuss a pressing legal matter." After Maurice's wife dutifully escorted Cassie to the powder room, Maurice asked his friend and client whether he wasn't carrying a joke a little too far.

"You're questioning my judgment?" prodded BJ.

"Let's be realistic," said Maurice. "She's a bigger scandal than if you were to wear a sign down Wall Street declaring yourself a fruit."

"I see you get my point."

"BJ, you're not going ahead with this."

"Watch me. Now don't worry, dear. I have plans to civilize her."

"Impossible."

"Expedience allows for any possibility, Maurice. I have given her a required reading list. Guess what's at the very top?"

"The bible? It won't do her any good."

"The bible isn't on the list. She wouldn't understand it—not my Bathsheba. No, I'm going to dunk her in O'Hara, but only after book Numero Uno. I'm surprised at you, Maurice, for not coming up with this one yourself, it's so expedient. *Baby and Child Care,* darling. A year from now Cassie will have the pleasing shape of a milk cow, and cowering under the threat of divorce, believe me, she'll be civilized. She'll be as civil as any of Cheever's suburban twats."

"Oh, God," said Maurice, blanching. "BJ, you need an analyst. You just can't do this."

"Here come our lovely ladies, Maurice. And as I said, watch me."

Cassie McDade Roberson was the best dressed indentured servant ever to hold a Bergdorf Goodman credit card, and while pregnancy had deprived her of an hourglass figure, its aftermath returned her to a voluptuousness as civil as Sophia Loren's. For Bradley, his mother was the essence of *la dolce vita* plucked out of context, as if Noel Coward had metamorphosed into Fellini under a laugh-a-minute moon. "Christ turned water into wine," he said. "My mother can turn any fine brandy into the crudest of bardolinos." Bradley made this remark in Italy. Later, in Santa Fe, Bradley had been heard to say that his mother could wander as a homecoming queen into the center of an Indian corn dance, never realizing that she had changed parades. (If he had known her, Bradley might have invoked the name of Mrs. Maude McFie Lansing, a woman who, in 1917, dedicated the opening of Santa Fe's new art museum—an architectural blend of Indian Pueblo and Spanish mission styles—with an operatic French rendition of "La Marseillaise.") For Bradley, metaphors about his mother changed with the territory, but the point they made was always the same: for as far back as he could remember, his mother lived perpetually in the wrong movie.

In an Eighty-sixth Street town house decorated with imposing antique furniture and paintings so prized that they were crowned, not merely framed, in the dark-paneled rooms and stairway, Cassie McDade Roberson was to her young son a burst of color and light. Her heady scent was of perfume blended with cigarettes, and if she smoked too much, it only strengthened little Bradley's fantasy of a sweet-smelling goddess carried from room to room on a cloud. When his nurse would bring him home each morning from the park, Bradley would run to Cassie's room and leap onto the bed where she lay on heaps of pillows reading or watching television, or more often just staring at the walls and humming peacefully to herself. There was already a full ashtray on her night table, and smoke hung above like a gossamer canopy. "Sing my song," Bradley would command as Cassie drew him to her; in turn, she would coo to the tune of "Twinkle, Twinkle, Little Star" the verse she composed when he was a baby:

Cassie's toy and Cassie's joy,
Bradley's Cassie's little boy.
When he smiles upside down,
Cassie tells him not to frown.
Cassie's laughing, gorgeous toy, Bradley's
Cassie's little boy.

Bradley was four when he taught himself to play his song on the piano, and Cassie applauded him in triumph.

"He plays so sweetly for me. Maybe someday he'll play nicely for you, if I ask him to." So Cassie greeted her husband one evening before going to the theater, which they did monthly every season as part of their quota of public appearances.

" 'Sweet' went out with Brahms, dearest. In banging the way he does, he's keeping pace with the trends. What are you wearing?" BJ replied.

"The new Schiaparelli."

"Magenta? No."

"But I've made up for it," Cassie pouted.

"It's inappropriate for the theater."

"How can you say that when it's so dramatic?"

"The point of going to a play, Cassie, is not to compete

with the costumes but to blend in with the public response. Wear the black Chanel."

"I hate it. It makes me look old."

"It makes you look like a proper East Side wife, and that is your role for the evening."

"Bradley likes the Schiaparelli. He picked it out for me," said Cassie. "When he grows up, he's going to write about fashion. He'll tell everyone that magenta is the perfect color for Broadway, and that black is only for funerals."

"Bradley will be a drama critic," countered BJ Roberson. "After living with bad theater for all of his young life, he will surely want to save the world from it."

While his future was being argued upstairs, Bradley struggled in the sitting room with the more immediate challenge of Anna Magdalena Bach. The direction was *allegro,* which Bradley read as "Bang."

Soon after his sixth birthday Bradley managed to get through Beethoven's "Für Elise" without a mistake. The notes that had once frustrated him to the point of anger had at last proved that they loved him. When Bradley reached the age of eight, his father decided that Bradley would be a pianist; his lessons were increased accordingly to three afternoons a week. BJ Roberson counted up the hours that his son would be gone from Cassie's room, with his feet planted on the pedals (and out of Cassie's shoes), his hands at the keyboard (and out of her makeup drawer). BJ hoped never again to hear Bradley suggest to him that his eyes wouldn't look so gloomy if he brushed them with gold shadow.

But after years of training him at Juilliard the staff agreed that Bradley Roberson III would never shine as a pianist, because as studious as he was, he never quite made music. Rather he seemed bent on milking the life out of sonatas, as though he had sentenced an army of notes to hard labor in Siberia.

Chapter Three

> So here I am in Disney frontier town, or is it Venice drained of all its water? I look out every morning on a giant, unshaven face of a landscape that dares me to wake up. Here's how I greet this monster: "Leave me alone," I say. "I have a headache."
>
> —*Santa Fe postcard to Cassie Roberson from her son, Bradley*

BRADLEY Roberson III was a traveler who selected cities as others might select clothes: according to his mood. At his most somber, especially when he was trapped in the notion that he should be sentenced to die by the poison of his crimes against himself, he would pack his many toiletries, a change of underwear, and a long black kimono. Carrying a small piece of hand luggage, he would board a plane for Berlin. There, in what he knew to be his father's favorite city, he would take a room at the Bristol Hotel Kempinski, meticulously wash in the shower, shave and perfume himself, and slip into his kimono. He'd then proceed to obliterate his consciousness with Valium and a bottle of Russian vodka. Performing this ritual in front of a mirror, Bradley would become consumed with the import and finality of what he wrongly assumed was his suicide. When he woke up—as he always did—with a pounding head that cried for vitamins and water, he took it as a sign that he was paroled, that he had not yet reached his limits as an aberration on the planet. "My Time," he would then write Cassie on a hotel postcard, "is not yet Up, *liebchen*."

His survival did not change his perception of Berlin as the perfect place to die, a judgment that he kept no secret. "Every Jew, gypsy and homosexual should do Germany the courtesy of dying there, to help it keep burying the past," he would say to friends. As a result, Bradley's trips to Berlin caused much speculation as to whether anyone would ever see him again. When inevitably friends did run into him later, gracing a bar or table with his lively chatter and face from the heavens, it seemed for a brief moment that all was right with the world.

John Aaron would one day learn that he had saved Bradley Roberson III from a truly spectacular Berlin mood.

Chapter Four

ACROSS the street from the capitol building in Santa Fe was a bar called The Matador. It was a loud and smoky place with much backslapping and backroom political talk, a lot of eyeing—and sometimes more—among burly state officials and women who came to The Matador for a fix of burliness. Robert Valdez was a frequent patron of The Matador, but he always left his wife, Sylvia, at home. And John Aaron dropped by from time to time, having learned from his father that real estate ventures were never harmed by mixing with people of influence.

Even outside the Matador it could never be said that John wore his sexual persuasion on his sleeve, but he was especially conscious of his dress when he went there. In John's closet his Matador shirts were carefully segregated, each a polyester-cotton blend strategically missing a button to expose his stomach whenever he sat down on a bar stool. His Matador jeans never saw the flat of an iron, his Matador watch was set in clumsily fashioned Navajo silver, and his Matador belt was Western-tooled, stitched leather. Boots were another matter. John's Matador boots were snakeskin that shone like silver under the dimmest light. In these boots he was a man who commanded respect.

When, on his second day of exile in New York after his father's funeral, John got wind of a bar called The Wild Bull, he thought it sounded like the place to show off his snakeskin boots. He went to the Christopher Street bar in a pair of dry-cleaned and pressed black Levi's jeans, a black polo shirt, his snakeskins, and a black leather motorcycle jacket bought that day especially for The Wild Bull. He also wore a belt buckle of Hopi silver overlay. At the bar he was chagrined to see that the only other shiny accessories around him were chains that dripped from leather jackets other than his own. He discovered, too, that Santa Fe had fallen behind in the world of nouvelle coifs—not that he would ever think to take a razor to his still-full head of hair.

Though his boots fit him like a glove, in the presence of Wild Bull patrons John shifted in them uncomfortably, feeling overly conservative and overdressed. Disco music blared while videos showed men over whom black leather was skimpily distributed—a belt here, a silver-studded wristband there—mounting each other in a manner suggested by the bar's name.

John sank down in the first available chair, as though

he were shouldering the collective weight of all the chains in the room, and wondered if New Mexico had ruined him for the sophistication of the big city. When he found himself being ogled by a chain-drenched man over fifty who raised a dazzled white eyebrow at his snakeskin boots, John suddenly and sadly wondered where his youth had gone.

"Eureka. A dead ringer for shame."

The voice seeping into his ear from behind was very studied, measured to create the effect of a whisper in a room where a true whisper would be swallowed up by the swirls of sound. It sent a chill down John's spine, causing him to sit up straight and shiver. When he turned, the source of the whisper was no longer behind him but was already on his way to the bar, parting the black leather with a flare of light. Such was the effect that a white silk suit had on the crowd at The Wild Bull that one man asked permission to kiss the young man's robes, while another remarked that things must be awfully dull at Le Cirque, or was it that they had run out of Puligny-Montrachet?

One man who noted that John's mouth had fallen agape from fascination warned him to stop staring or he would turn into a pillar of salt. "The only thing *she* puts out is a heavy dose of mental abuse," he cautioned John. "We tried to have her bounced, you know, but the management absolutely refuses to discriminate against white."

As the young man returned his way with two glasses in hand, John saw that he had the effect of a blasting cap; a public-service campaign had been designed to keep people from getting their hands blown off. When the live explosive handed him a glass of bourbon and invited himself to sit down, John quivered from the honor of having been selected for demolition.

"I want to hear about your eyes," said the intruder.

John shrugged his shoulders back with a tough motion, as though his chains were slipping. "What about my eyes?"

"Why do you tuck them away in the shadows like that?"

"What do you mean? I had nothing to do with it—they came that way."

"That's what *you* say. I say you tuck them away, like you have some shameful secret."

"Fuck you," said John. "I'm not ashamed of anything."

"That's too bad," said the young man, lighting up a cigarette. "Shame is hot. I must be getting rusty; I misread your signals."

"I was just warned about you," said John.

"Really? By whom?"

John strained his neck, then pointed out the man who had warned him about turning into a pillar of salt.

"Oh, him," said the young man. "He's strictly backroom. I wouldn't be caught dead in a back room. Sex shouldn't be served like bad liquor behind the peepholed door of a speakeasy." He sighed. "Look at this place. It's so medieval. I love that you're not wearing chains, you know. But it's too bad about the leather jacket."

"So why are you here?" asked John.

"For the thrill of being illicit by wearing a white suit."

"Come on. There's more to it than that."

"Well, if there is, then that's my own little shameful secret, isn't it? I'll tell you mine if you tell me yours."

"I'm from out of town," said John. "Is that shameful enough for you?"

"Hardly. It isn't even a secret—your boots give you away. That's not an insult, either; I like them. I like them a lot. So does everybody in here, although they wouldn't admit it."

"Why not?"

"Because they're thousand-dollar boots. To admit to liking them would admit to who they are. Do you want to know their shameful secret? They're all Republicans. Outside of here they're strictly Wall Street."

"I find that hard to believe."

"Of course you do. I'm telling you, that's their secret. My deepest secret is that I need another drink. So do you. Excuse me."

The mirror behind the bar allowed John to watch the young man at the same time as he examined his own eyes. They were the same old eyes: recessed, gray, and dull. So was his hair—gray and dull—and his lips were *thin* and dull. His straight nose and strong chin were his best features, but even they were dull. Perhaps it was a law of nature that electricity sought out dead batteries to recharge: it was the only thing that could explain this young man.

"Are you a Republican?" the stranger asked when they returned to their chairs—left vacant, it seemed, because they were now clearly cursed.

"No," said John. "I'm Jewish. Are you a hustler?"

The smirk the question raised was encouraging; it was the closest the young man had come to smiling since he sat down. Not that he needed a smile to help his looks. John tried to find in the smirking face before him some telltale sign that its perfection masked a decaying underbelly promising its imminent downfall. But he had to conclude that here was a fresh work of art that would not need restoring until a distant century.

"No, I'm not a hustler. I'm a numeral. My name is Bradley Roberson III."

"Don't tell me there aren't any numeral hustlers," said John.

"Don't tell me there aren't any Jewish Republicans," said Bradley, quickly finishing off his drink. "This place has warped your consciousness. Let's get out of here."

"I haven't told you my name," said John.

"So what? Is it long and ugly, something like Glotzenblatt? Are you embarrassed about your name? If you are, I still don't buy it as an excuse for those eyes."

"What do you want with me?" asked John, who wished at the moment that he still smoked, because he wanted something to do with his jittery hands besides jiggle his ice cubes.

"If you recall, I said you seem shameful, which I also said I found very sexy. Maybe you'd feel better about yourself if you told me your name. It does seem to be something of a hurdle with you."

His name. Aaron. From Aaronowitz. His father had shortened it. In Miami. For appearances' sake. "My name is John Aaron."

"Feel better now?"

"I am continuing to feel just fine, thank you. Listen, if you're a hustler, go find someone else, will you? You hate back rooms. I hate paying for sex."

"I don't blame you. I'm not all that fond of it, either. Hey, I'm not a hustler. Besides, who said anything about sex, John? I just want to get out of here."

"And go where?"

"Are you at a nice hotel, out-of-towner?"

"The St. Moritz," said John.

"Do you have a view of the park?"

"Yes."

"Lovely. Let's go there. They have a nice bar."

"I don't know if the bar's still open."

"It probably isn't, but they'll open it . . . for me," said Bradley.

"This I'd like to see."

"A man who's easily impressed. Too bad. Come on, let's go."

When they walked outside, John discovered that he was already quite drunk. If he was lucky, his new companion would forget about opening the St. Moritz bar. Room service would do nicely if Bradley wanted to continue his drinking; John would look on because he'd had enough. Besides, he knew the St. Moritz management would bend the rules only if threatened with a scene, and he had no desire to call that kind of attention to himself. He had a fine room, which he hoped to enjoy for a few more days. He eyed Bradley in the cab. Would he cause a scene? he wondered. Of course he would. He had just caused a scene by doing nothing more than wearing a white suit. Causing scenes was probably his life story, thought John. Look at him; he was born for nothing else.

"Don't cause a scene," John said as the taxi bounced down Fifth Avenue.

"What are you talking about?" Bradley was annoyed, John could tell, from having been awakened from a pensive stupor.

"At the hotel. Opening the bar. Don't cause a scene. We can order room service."

"Don't worry. I know the management. At least I think I do. I haven't been there in a while."

"What's your connection?"

"Nothing deliberate. They just like me. I bring in a nice crowd."

"I knew you were a hustler," said John. "I knew it. I really didn't think there could be another explanation."

"That's right. The gang at Lehman Brothers will be very happy to hear that they hang around with hustlers."

"You work for Lehman Brothers?"

"No. But some of the regime were friends of my father's. You see, I'm very well connected."

"Your father's a Republican," John surmised. "Strictly Wall Street."

"No," said Bradley. "Strictly dead. Years dead."

"Mine too." John sighed. "A few days' dead. In Miami. I flew out from Santa Fe for the funeral."

"Bingo," exclaimed Bradley, slapping John's knee. The full-blown smile he gave John showed off his perfect teeth, which, like the rest of him, gleamed white in the darkness.

"Bingo?" John Aaron smiled along with him, as if anyone could resist smiling under the glow of that face.

"The eyes," said Bradley. "The shame."

"No shame," said John.

"You're full of shit."

"Well, then. You owe me one, don't you?" John said.

"Owe you what?"

"Your secret. I'll tell mine if you'll tell yours. Remember?"

"Vaguely. Short-term memory loss. It's an illness that I hold very dear to my heart. But I do vaguely remember this evening at Lutèce, which I still find a memorable restaurant. It's too bad what happened there."

"What was that?"

"I lost a lover," Bradley said.

"I'm sorry."

"Well, it wouldn't have been so bad, you see, if I had, you know, just lost him. It was who I lost him to."

"Who was that?"

"My mother."

"Oh, my God."

"Well, it's not all that horrible. You see," said Bradley Roberson III, "I set it up. That's why I just can't go home tonight. They're there, and I just can't face it. He's a pathetic person, my ex-lover."

"At the very least, he's sexually confused," offered John.

"Worse than that," said Bradley. "He's a hustler. But he's with my mother now, so I guess he has to be called something else. I guess he's a gigolo."

The cab stopped dead at the entrance of the St. Moritz facing Central Park. John was too mortified by the turn the conversation had taken to reach for his wallet, but Bradley was happy to pay. When John still didn't move, Bradley did something that made John cover his eyes: he leaned down and gently kissed the instep of John's snakeskin boot. "So what if your father couldn't stand you?" he said, rising up again. "I think you're wonderful."

BOOK II

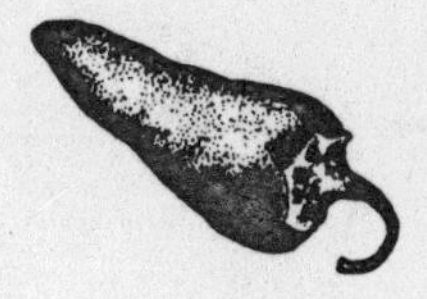

Chapter Five

SYLVIA Valdez was experimenting in her large, modern kitchen on Camino Sin Nombre. She was making *bisco-chitos*—small, pale cookies with the texture of sand and the subtle flavor of anise seed and cinnamon sugar—but she was changing the traditional New Mexican recipe by substituting vegetable shortening for lard. Mrs. Valdez had watched a health program on cable television that told her that cooking with lard was like pouring cement into her family's arteries. Vegetable shortening was not only healthier, said the guest nutritionist; it made flakier pie crusts and did not compete in flavor with added herbs and spices. Mrs. Valdez now had only to look at the consistency of the batter and sniff it to know that the *biscochitos* would not turn out the way she liked them. She sighed with the resolve that certain pleasures must be sacrificed for the sake of her family's health. She was already worried that she had made her son Robby crazy by feeding him too much white sugar; it was obvious that she had learned too late how white sugar turns some children into spinning tops. Robby was a lost cause, but as Stevie had not reacted the same way, she continued using it.

School had been out for an hour, and Robby wasn't home yet. Probably, she thought, he was in his filthy Chevy, drunk on beer, parading at a crawl around the Plaza with his friends, and screaming mean things to people on the streets. There were many who felt that kids like Robby were Santa Fe's number-one problem, she knew. She had talked in confession about Robby and the white sugar, but the priest said that it was the fault of the times that Robby had a mean streak. (He gave her a few Hail Marys to say, though, to make her feel better.)

Her husband, Robert, was over two hundred miles away in Window Rock meeting with the chairman of the Navajo tribe. The city of Gallup was relying on Robert Valdez to talk him out of a boycott of the summer's Intertribal Ceremonial. This was the one event that brought in a flood of tourist dollars to Gallup now that the Interstate was finished; only those careless about watching their gas gauges needed to stop in the town truckers called "Drunk City." Robert had told Sylvia that the threat of boycott was nothing to be taken very seriously, but his position required him to accompany a Navajo state senator. What with federal assistance having been cut to the bone, the Navajo artisan could not afford the loss of tourist dollars any more than could the rest of the town.

Sylvia Valdez felt that the state government gave her husband its most depressing tasks, and she resented that he traveled so much. She thought his frequent absence was making her son Stevie a lonely little boy and her son Robby an even more hopeless case. Over her batter of *biscochitos* with vegetable shortening, she thanked the Virgin for giving her only two children.

"How's your friend?" she asked Stevie, relieved when he walked in unscraped from his short trip next door on his bicycle.

"He's sleeping," Stevie said as he pulled the step stool to the kitchen counter to watch his mother fuss. He grabbed the hair that had strayed out of her Navajo-made silver barrette and tucked it behind her ears; there was nothing worse than finding a strand of hair in a *biscochito*, and besides, his mother's face was beautiful. Sylvia smiled and kissed him.

"So he's sleeping," she said. "*Ee.* Everybody's a lazy so-and-so today."

"He was up before. He's outside now. He's sleeping," Stevie said in defense of their neighbor.

"Well, then, your friend is crazy. The sun will burn him right up, and he'll start to look like an old man. These gringos don't know the strength of the sun, *mijo*. They stay out in it like crazy dogs. You tell him I say he's a crazy dog to lie out in the sun like that."

"He's got lotion on. That stuff smells like your powder. I think he's resting because he watered the grass. He planted the geraniums too. He put them in front of the daylilies."

"I wish you would learn your arithmetic as well as you are learning about flowers. I don't care about his sleeping, little detective. Bradley can sleep all day long. It's none of my business. But let's be good neighbors, no? Let's go tell him that the sun will ruin his beautiful skin. *Ee.* He has such nice skin, that one; he should take care of it."

"He likes the sun," said Stevie. "That's why he's here. He told me. In New York City the sky is gray and creepy. In Santa Fe it's blue and warm and luscious."

"*El cielo esta delicioso? La Madre!*"

"The sky is fabulous," said Stevie.

"*El cielo esta fabuloso? Madre de Dios!*"

Stevie dipped his finger into the mixing bowl and tasted the batter. "Fabulous," he said with a playful and bright smile.

Sylvia yanked the bowl away. "Go wash those hands, Señor Fabuloso."

Stevie climbed down off the stool and ran to the bathroom through the living room cluttered with richly upholstered furniture. With its gaudily framed family photographs and religious figures—some plastic, some genuine antiques from Mexico—its decor was labeled by Santa Fe's decor-conscious as "Mexican kitsch." Sylvia's father was asleep on the large red velvet sofa that overwhelmed his tiny figure. The old man seemed to have shrunken inside his baggy clothes. With clean hands Stevie gently pulled one of his grandfather's socks halfway off his foot and giggled at the private joke. Then he whispered "*Abuelo*" in the old man's ear to see if it would stop his snoring. When his grandfather responded with a loud snort, Stevie ran away.

"Are they done yet?" he asked his mother.

"A tray is in the oven. Hold your horses," she replied.

"I want them to hurry up."

"Patience, *por favor*. Or you'll wait till supper."

"But we have to take some to Bradley."

"I thought you said he was sleeping."

"But we have to wake him up," said Stevie, doing a little dance of frustration, "before he turns into an old man."

Outside, clutching a plastic bag full of cookies in his hand, Stevie mounted his bicycle. The sound of the wheels crunching the stones on the dirt road was the only sound to be heard on dusty Camino Sin Nombre, the Street Without a Name.

It is true that the huge sky above was both as luscious and fabulous as Bradley Roberson III proclaimed it . . . if, in fact, these adjectives are dramatic or delectable enough to describe the essence of Santa Fe blue, a color so deep and sure that the pale sand blushes beneath it, the mountains stand in envy against it, and fair-weather clouds cling to it like downy clumps of dust. Under such blue, the echo of a child's bicycle on a dirt road was a tuneful sound, and the swaying of a carefully held bag of cookies a reassuring sway. It was a child's pure sky blue, and Stevie knew no other. On foot Sylvia also went next door, patting her hair in place and making sure that the buttons of her floral blouse lined up with the center seam of her black pants. In her hand she carried freshly cut lilacs that had just bloomed on the bushes beside her house.

She would tell Bradley that the flowers were for his dining room, whose furniture had arrived by moving van earlier in the week. Sylvia had been glad, even relieved, to see the van pull up next door and the men unload the crates. It had been uncomfortable for her to think of her neighbor living in empty rooms with only a piano bench to sit on while he ate his pizza, which was all he seemed to eat. Sylvia Valdez was such a domestic person that anyone who lived among scattered boxes of pizza seemed otherworldly, like a phantom who would fly off without warning to haunt some other abandoned house.

She remembered when her neighbor had first arrived. The sale of the house that had been vacant next door for so long had surprised her. Even the real estate agent confessed that it was an overpriced dump she used to make anything more expensive shown later on her rounds seem worth the money. Outside, the adobe was cracked and dilapidated; inside, the walls needed repainting—after a good replastering (a job someone had begun in the living room in one spot, exposing a patch of chicken wire before giving up). It was obvious where the previous owners (who'd bought the place as an investment) believed people spent most of their time, for the only renovated space was the bathroom. With its sauna, shower, and Jacuzzi in the bathtub, it was larger than the kitchen. Its walls were bright with Mexican-patterned tile toned down by the handmade *talavera* clay tile on the floor. The floor throughout the rest of the house was brick that had not been properly sealed and showed every spill.

* * *

The day Sylvia had taken around her petition to pave Camino Sin Nombre's surface, she had asked her new neighbor where he was going to start fixing first. Outside, he said offhandedly, confessing that he hadn't given it much thought. Outside, because the Santa Fe spring was warming up nicely, and so it was probably where he'd prefer to be.

"Are you going to repair the adobe yourself?" she asked. He said he intended to leave the walls alone for a while: Where he came from there were more walls than anyone ever cared to see. His thinking leaned more toward planting a garden, he said, for where he came from, gardens were as rare as gold.

"*Ee,* but those walls are in such bad shape." She spoke in a tone that would have made Dorothy Cheswick and her committee proud.

"It's earth," he said, shrugging. "It crumbles. Besides, if I'm going to get my hands dirty, I want to see some instant beautification. What's filling a crack compared to planting a flower?"

Sylvia did not press the matter. He'd signed her petition without reading it, and it wasn't her business if he chose to be indifferent to the upkeep of his own home. "But if you change your mind," she said, "my father can fix those walls for you. Now that he's retired, he won't do nothing except watch TV. It would be nice to get him out of the house for just a little while sometimes. *Ee,* he sleeps too much. It isn't good for him."

To her amazement Bradley bowed slightly and kissed her hand. "Where I come from," he said, "neighbors like you are as rare as platinum." Sylvia blushed, suddenly conscious of the contrast between his overwhelming beauty and their surroundings. He was a marvel. That he had paid for the house in cash also branded him a mystery.

Then a pickup truck pulled up with its bed shrouded

by potted flowers, prompting the first visit from a curious little boy out riding his bicycle.

From that day on, Sylvia and Stevie Valdez formed a privileged audience, sharing delight in the new neighbor who had been sent to Camino Sin Nombre for their private entertainment.

Several weeks later, Sylvia and Stevie, bearing their cookies and lilacs, opened the gate of Bradley Roberson's deadwood coyote fence. As though they were stealing across the moat of an enchanted castle, they maneuvered the obstacle course of strewn gardening tools, hoses, and boxes of daisies, pansies, petunias, and wild strawberry plants waiting to be transferred to the prepared flower beds. Beethoven's First Piano Concerto blasted through the open patio doors from the stereo inside. Their neighbor was shirtless, even though the air was cooling down, and he was fully awake, sitting up in a plastic chaise, and poring over *The Complete Collected Poems and Plays of T. S. Eliot,* which rested in a crease of his dirty, white gardening jeans.

"Hi," said Stevie cheerfully, startling Bradley.

"Stevie! Sylvia!" he exclaimed. "Hi, there. Welcome to my hospital."

"Are you sick?" Sylvia knitted her brow in concern; at the same time she blushed at the movement of his torso.

"Always. Want to hear a poem?"

"Is it clean?" asked Sylvia.

"I guess not," said Bradley. "It can't be. It's about me."

"I don't know," said Sylvia. "I don't know if Stevie should hear."

"I brought you some cookies we baked. Want them?" offered Stevie, holding out the bag in his hand.

"You angels of mercy," said Bradley, reaching for the bag. "What time is it, anyway?"

"I don't know. I think it's dinnertime soon, right Mama?"

"Very soon," said Sylvia. She held out the lilacs. "Stevie says that you have a great big table in your dining room. Did you have a vase, maybe, in one of those crates the men carried in?"

"*A* vase? Many, many vases because you see, I'll have many, many flowers. But, alas, no lilacs. God, I love lilacs. There is nothing in the world that smells as good—they smell as good as these cookies taste. They're fabulous. You came at just the right time. I'm starved."

"Maybe you can eat dinner with us," said Stevie.

"No. No, not tonight, *mijo*," Sylvia said briskly. "We have to go to Tia Grace's house when your brother comes home. *If* he ever comes home."

"Have car, will travel," said Bradley. "Isn't that the way around here? This is the first time in my life I have ever owned a car. And how old is Robby? Sixteen?"

"Cars are trouble," said Sylvia. "That's all I know."

"I just don't understand where he finds a parking space big enough for that thing. I have enough problems with mine, and it's half the size."

"Yours is a good size," said Sylvia. "Robby's is a crazy size. *Ee.* He drives it around with his brain on fire. He never parks it, except maybe in front of liquor stores. I told my husband, you know, not to buy him that thing. Drinking goes with it, that's all I know."

Bradley saw that the six or so beer cans stashed under the chaise had caught her eye and made her anxious; he was not surprised when she told Stevie that they had to go.

"Thanks for the flowers and the cookies," he said.

"Are you going to finish the garden tomorrow?" asked Stevie. "It's Saturday."

"Maybe. I'll sure try. Wanna help me?" He turned to Sylvia. "He loves it, you know, patting the dirt, digging the holes. He's a natural. I'm great at visualizing; it's the doing I have trouble with. Not Stevie. He's a doer, right, kiddo?"

Stevie looked up at his mother hopefully. "We'll see," she said to him. "We'll see what the day looks like when your father gets home. We might go down to Albuquerque and do some shopping."

"Is there really shopping in Albuquerque?" Bradley asked incredulously. He supposed there would be bargains there; the whole city looked to him like a discount house.

"It's the sales, you know," said Sylvia. "Everything is so expensive here."

"I love sales," said Bradley.

"I almost forgot to tell you. Dorothy Cheswick says to say hello to you."

"Who?"

"Dorothy Cheswick. She's the head of the committee that turned down my petition. But it's okay. I don't feel bad about it. Stevie doesn't fall down on the road anymore, do you, *mijo*?"

"I like the bumps," said Stevie.

"She thought you would. She said so in her letter."

"Dorothy Cheswick," muttered Bradley, still trying to remember her. He finally succeeded. "Oh, God," he said. "She made me play the piano at one of her awful parties. It was deadly—the party *and* my piano playing. She called me Santa Fe's very own Liberace, and I almost threw up down the neck of her velvet blouse."

"We have to go now, *mijo*," said Sylvia with some urgency.

"You will come again, won't you?" asked Bradley. "I'm sorry for what I said about Dorothy Cheswick, and I'm sorry for the beer cans, Sylvia. It's the gardening. Under the hot Santa Fe sun. I guess beer goes with that as much as it goes with big, loud Chevys."

"My father drinks beer," said Stevie. "*Abuelo* too. You, too, don't you, Mama?"

Sylvia smiled, her blush even lovelier than before. She felt bad about having lied; they weren't going to her sister's for dinner, but Bradley was the kind of man that neither Robby nor his father would want to have at the dinner table. She would have to explain to Stevie how Bradley was their special friend alone.

Left to himself, Bradley reread Eliot's lines about sickness being the path to health in Planet Earth Hospital. A verse from the *Four Quartets* struck him like a revelation, there in his unfinished garden. He was awed by how the poet had managed to encapsulate the sum total of his life in seventy-five words or less.

"My house is not a hospital, damn it." Three weeks earlier John Aaron had railed a less than fond farewell that had coincided with winter's official exit, the Sante Fe spring having, as usual, jumped its cue and upstaged a tired season well before the equinox. "It is not a rehab center for the deranged."

Bradley had replied with equal contempt. "Fuck it. What do you know? This whole fucking town is a hospital. Life, you guilty-faced faggot, is nothing but a string of hospitals." And now here it was; hats off to T. S. Eliot.

He had not meant to offend sweet Sylvia Valdez. Making a determined move against idleness and debauch, he gathered up the empty beer cans from under the chaise and rose to shower off his sun grease. First he phoned a florist and ordered his neighbor a dozen long-stemmed white roses, adding the words: "No friend of Dorothy Cheswick but, I dearly hope, a friend of yours."

Over the sink in the deluxe bathroom a pair of Dracula teeth hung from the end of a blood-red ribbon. Bradley had bought the teeth for John Aaron's Halloween party the previous fall, his first Santa Fe fall. Sometimes when

John would scream at him through his bedroom door, he had pulled them out to wear in front of the mirror. When John finally threw him out, Bradley had kissed him good-bye wearing the Dracula teeth. In his own house, Bradley continued his sessions in the mirror, feeling the need to remind himself of the kind of person he was. But after his first month alone, when Marissa Goldman told him John was still too weak to stay out after ten, only a few sessions of wearing fangs were needed as a refresher course.

On Bradley's bathroom door was a poster from the musical *Evita,* hung there in honor of his mother, Cassie. He sometimes called her Little Eva as a pet name, though Cassie insisted Bradley had it backwards, since Eva Perón had died of cancer and Juan Perón lived on. There were more differences, certainly, between Eva Perón and Cassie Roberson, such as that Cassie's entire knowledge of South American history was gleaned from seeing *Evita* on Broadway.

As Bradley stepped out of the shower to splash on his second application of cologne for the day, the phone rang. It wasn't Cassie or her hired companion, Franklin Bless-Him-for-Hanging-in-There Petrie (who had recently demanded a raise), because they always chimed right in with a loud hello. This caller said nothing. Bradley sat down on his unmade water bed and fidgeted with his toes.

"Hello?" he probed.

Nothing.

"Hello?"

Silence.

"John? Is this you? Oh, God. Have you really been reduced to this? If you'd only say hello, I might tell you something you want to hear. . . ."

Click.

"Oh, God," said Bradley, and hung up the phone. He

stared at the low ceiling traversed by pine vigas, beams too heavy for the size and height of the room. A claustrophobic would go mad under them. "Damn it," Bradley said, almost at the point of tears. "What is his fucking problem?"

The phone rang again. Bradley composed himself with a cigarette that he pulled from a pack on the floor and then answered bluntly, "What do you want?"

"What do I want? What happened to hello? What happened to 'Marissa, darling, so nice to hear from you at this hour, just as I was debating what in the world I'm going to do about dinner.' "

"Hello, Marissa, I'm sorry. No dinner. Not tonight."

"You can't go on like this, Bradley. *We* can't go on like this. It's Death in Santa Fe since you started this business of living in solitary confinement in the bowels of the city. Notice that I wasn't going to ask you to invite me over. I was going to suggest that you come here and we go off to one of my favorite haunts where no one else is likely to spot us."

"Where's that?"

"Stop 'N Eat in Española. Do they have a chili dog? Do they ever have a chili dog. And onion rings? Better than Metamucil, with or without NutraSweet."

"I was thinking about making myself some eggs. I'm dieting—pizza withdrawal. I'm also cutting down on beer, and eggs go marginally with vodka."

In her circle of friends Marissa Goldman was known as Madonna Gazetta, the town crier whose motto was "All the News that Shits." Living out her self-proclaimed karma of keeping interested parties up to date often resulted in her sustaining enmity between foes, a side effect she would have held in check if only she had been more aware of it. With two phone lines and a hold button, though, it was all she could to to keep her facts straight;

she couldn't afford the assistant she required to edit them for tact.

"He called me today," Marissa announced to Bradley.

"He calls you every day. The surprise is that I think he called *me*."

"He did?"

"I think so. I think it's him who's been calling, not saying a fucking word and hanging up after I've practically started to beg forgiveness."

"John doesn't want you back, Bradley."

"So why does he bother to do this to me?"

"Don't ask me. It doesn't sound like him, if you want my opinion. Not once have I known John Aaron to use the phone for silence. He's a charter member of Kibitzers Anonymous. That's my new idea for a self-help group—do you like it? Or do you think there's a bigger need for Shoppers Anonymous? You know what I bought today? Red chile-pepper Christmas lights. Why? Because they were on sale. What am I going to do with them, for God's sake? I never have a Christmas tree; I just get evergreen with envy about the schmucks who have them. I guess I'll take them to the first tree-decorating party I'm invited to . . . what is it, eight months from now?"

"Marissa?"

"Bradley, sweetheart?"

"Kibitzers Anonymous. Absolutely. Kibitzers Anonymous is what you need."

He heard Marissa light up a cigarette, and he did the same.

"Next week," she dove in again, "he's going to try to reduce his visits to the shrink. Just Mondays and Thursdays. He calls it 'preparing-for-and-recovering-from-the-weekend sessions.' He says weekends are still the hardest, because of the dinner parties and openings when everybody lets him know that without you he's about as exciting as someone on a life-support system."

"I don't want to hear this, Marissa."

"No one is impressed that he's reading Proust, he says. All they can see is that the 'Swan's Away.' "

"Sick, Marissa."

"So, what do you want him to hear about you?"

"About me? How about that I completely alienated my next-door neighbor by relating my state of mind at Madame Cheswick's Christmas party last year; this while I was noticeably drunk on Tecate."

"He'll like that."

"How about that I am so desperate for news of him, I almost agreed to go to a place named Stop 'N Eat in horrible Española for a chili dog and onion rings?"

"This is very good, Bradley. This is excellent."

"I have to get off the phone now, Marissa. My ear is overcooked."

Bradley took a clipper to his toenails and pulled on his clothes—dry-cleaned black Calvins and an Issey Miyake cotton sweater that showcased varied textures in neutral colors. Then he put Beethoven's Pastorale Symphony on the stereo. The sweetness was like a mist of air freshener, which along with his cologne furthered his obliviousness to the rich smell of festering meals overflowing the trash, by now seeming to emanate from every one of the dirty, flaking walls of the five-room house.

Bradley poured himself a bourbon on the rocks, an indoor drink, and then set about fixing a proper supper for himself: an omelet stuffed with horseradish and marmalade. He used to prepare such malicious combinations for Cassie's benefit; now, having acquired a taste for them, he made them for himself. John had always taken his omelets personally, like some culinary punishment for unknown sins, so Bradley now tried to enjoy cooking them as an expression of freedom.

The crates that convinced Sylvia Valdez that her neighbor was a real person had all contained items exclusively earmarked for Bradley's dining room. He had ordered Santa Fe–style furniture—Mexican pigskin chairs, a straight-backed wooden sofa with a Navajo weaving-upholstered cushion, and hand-painted Mexican lamps—that would keep his baby grand piano company in the living room as soon as it all arrived. He would embellish the furnishings with the plants that were crowded together and hanging on for dear life by the hair-cracked plaster window seat.

At John's, two love seats had been displaced to make room for the piano, that Bradley had surrounded with potted tropical trees to give his music resonance. Clear them away, he had said, and his notes would evaporate too soon, like a fine desert rain. John had never liked the plants; they posed an uncomfortable reminder that though he might develop acres upon acres of desert land and mark a hundred of them for an expansive grave, he would always be from Florida and a foreigner. So when Bradley removed the piano, John demanded that he also remove the plants. But at Camino Sin Nombre without John, they missed their daily misting.

Bradley's dining room arrived intact from Eighty-sixth Street. He had summoned it from the house in which he'd been reared with a cruel reminder for Cassie that anything else he might want in the future was his for the taking, according to his father's will. As a result, the Camino Sin Nombre dining room was so jammed with heavily framed miniature Impressionist paintings and English antiques that it resembled a small shop on Manhattan's Upper East Side.

A photograph of BJ Roberson hung on the wall by the Queen Anne breakfront. Rolled up in the breakfront's middle drawer was a silk-screen portrait of Cassie that Bradley had commissioned for her birthday a few years ago but never had framed because she said it made her look like the Bride of Frankenstein. Bradley ate at the head of a George III dining table, a place setting of his mother's cherished Royal Minton china before him. (She'd said that losing the china had hurt the most. When she received a check from Bradley that more than compensated for the loss of everything but the Impressionists, she wrote back about the fun she and Franklin would have playing house mistress and decorator, her loss forgotten.)

Bradley initiated the dinner hour that evening as he had since the day his tableau of rarified Roberson dining had arrived. Raising his omelet-filled fork in the direction of his father's photograph, he exclaimed, "Well, look at this again, darling, we're home."

This said, he tossed a shot of vodka down his throat and set the function of this room in motion. While ingesting his food he attempted to metabolize the far and immediate past that, with bourbon, vodka, eggs, marmalade, and horseradish, was no great treat in seeing out to the other end.

Chapter Six

INSIDE the St. Moritz, Bradley Roberson III had told John Aaron that he had saved him from a Berlin mood. Discovering in his pocket a forgotten gram of cocaine, Bradley also changed his mind about opening the bar. The late hour, he declared, called for the discretion of a private room. John had no sooner opened his door than Bradley was ordering champagne from room service. "To toast our meeting," he proclaimed, sending John's grief flying away as quickly as it had landed on him in the taxi.

John inhaled a line of Bradley's drug, convinced that he had been granted audience with the god of second winds.

"To the end of Berlin moods," John said. "So I guess you won't have me carted off to Auschwitz."

"You won't even have to wear a yellow star," said Bradley, bouncing down on the bed. "You see? I bet you had no idea when you got up this morning that today would be your lucky day. God, I feel great. I can't tell you how wonderful it is to have escaped a Berlin mood. Maybe by morning you'll have gotten me out of my Venice mood and I won't have to ask you to go there with me to keep me from jumping into the Lagoon."

John sat in the satin chair by the bureau to tantalize himself with a gift he feared would electrocute him if he reached for it too soon. "That filthy sewer? Why in the world would you want to do that?"

"It makes me feel close to my mother. I sent her a postcard from Venice once which said, 'The canals, *cara mia*, are you'. Does your mother smell like a harbor in which someone sank a cargo of perfume?"

"My mother doesn't smell like anything," said John. "She keeps the air conditioning up too high. 'Air conditioning,' she says, 'takes the pine out of Pine-Sol, but it keeps the heart ticking.' Maybe my father's heart stopped from lack of an air-conditioned golf course."

"Did it stop just like that?" asked Bradley.

"Just like that. On the fifteenth green. 'It could have been the heat,' one of his foursome told me, 'but I never saw him play such a lousy game.' "

"When was the last time you saw him?"

"Fifteen years ago. I can't say we missed each other. I used to have my mother come to New York. I'd meet her there to take her to the theater. 'Your father, well, you know how he gets through his days,' she'd say with a sigh. And I did know: I could picture it as clearly as I'm seeing you. When pictures are that clear, what are you missing? You miss when your memory plays tricks on you and sends you beautified images of what, in truth, were ugly scenes. My memory never tricked me when it came to my father."

"Fifteen years," repeated Bradley thoughtfully. "Do you know, John, that my meeting you is destiny? That's it. We simply have to go to Venice. We must immortalize this union on the Bridge of Sighs. My father died of cancer fifteen years ago. So how old are you, anyway?"

John looked away for a second and then said, morosely, "Forty-three."

Bradley did a split-second calculation. "Amazing. I'm twenty-eight. I'd say we have found our magic number, John. I'd say we'll be together, you and I, fifteen days, fifteen weeks, fifteen months, or fifteen years."

"I lied, darling. I'm forty-five, and with you around, I don't think I'll make it to sixty."

"Forty-five? Did you say forty-five?" asked Bradley, rising to answer the door. He grabbed the room waiter's shoulders and turned him to face John. "Do you see this man?" he asked. "Guess how old he is. There's a fifty-dollar tip in it for you if you hit it on the nose."

"I dunno," said the waiter. "Forty-five?"

Bradley hugged him and gave him a fifty. "*He* should be giving you this," Bradley said, pointing at John. "Do you see those boots? He tried to fool you."

John's cheerfulness fled as readily as it would from anyone so firmly convicted of looking his age, and Bradley's next words did not comfort him. "What did I say about destiny?" he asked, raising his champagne flute. "Guess how old my father was when he died?"

"I won't answer that," said John. "Cut some more cocaine and tell me what your famous father did on Wall Street that was so wonderful, his friends still put up with you."

"Are you saying I'm unpleasant?" asked Bradley.

"I wouldn't miss your Venice mood."

"Not to worry. It's already gone. Gone with the first taste of this stuff," said Bradley, holding up his glass.

"What kind of mood are we in now?"

"Where did you say you came from?"

"Santa Fe. New Mexico."

"Well, with all these coincidences, John, it should be easy to figure out that I'm in a Santa Fe mood."

"Are you that desperate to leave town that you're ready to go off with anyone who looks like some over-the-hill gringo in a bar?"

"Gringo. That's a Spanish word. Do they speak Spanish in Santa Fe?"

"Some do." John sighed. "You know, we could really get somewhere if you'd stop tossing me your fucking questions. You aren't answering any of *my* fucking questions."

"I heard that's what Jews do. I'm trying to be Jewish."

"If I wanted to be surrounded by Jews and their questions, I would have stayed in Miami."

"Why didn't you stay in Miami? Too many hurtful looks tossed at the dead man's heartache?"

"Jesus Christ," said John. "Fuck. Is it the coke? What is this? What are we doing here?"

Bradley then rose from John's bed which his regal presence had fashioned into a throne, and he walked over to the window. There he lowered his eyes and opened his mouth in an apologetic gesture, pursing his lips just enough to be too tantalizing to bear.

"I think they will love you in Santa Fe," whispered John, who struggled with the temptation to leave his chair and risk another change in Bradley's mood. He stayed where he was, but the mood changed nonetheless.

"Will they, really?" said Bradley with a sudden snarl. "Well, what the fuck do they know?" He walked back to the bed and threw back the covers; immediately he crashed down on his stomach; tucked his hands, palms up, underneath his thighs, and, with the expelling of one long breath, bid adieu to the night.

John finished off the cocaine that lay on the dresser like toothpicks to dislodge despair from his system. After torturing himself with fantasies of prying open the elongated clam that lay before him on the bed, he phoned the front desk. "I need somebody's best judgment," he said into the receiver, "because my own took a hike on me this evening. I can't sleep. It must be almost sunup. Am I asking for it if I go and take a walk in the park?"

"We wouldn't advise it, sir," said a voice as human as could be expected.

"I didn't think so. There isn't any chance of my being able to take a sauna up at the health club at this hour, is there?"

"The health club opens at six-thirty. That's two hours from now, sir."

"Listen," John said, finally pulling the covers over Bradley and feeling obliged to the clerk for liking himself a little better. "I'm a very good friend of Bradley Roberson III. You know, of the Wall Street Robersons."

"How nice for you, sir."

"I don't suppose you ever opened the health club for anyone named Roberson at four-thirty in the morning?"

"No. Not that we can remember, sir."

"Well, fine. I guess I'll just steam up the bathroom and sit in there awhile."

"Steam away, sir."

"Thank you. I will," said John. "Thank you very much. You've been wonderful. Really. Can't seem to stop talking, can I?"

"Well, we don't mind at all, sir. It's pretty boring down here at this hour, as you may well imagine."

"Is it? Well, you should be standing here, that's all I can say. You should be standing here. Oh, my God."

"Sir?"

"I just said 'Oh, my God,' that's all. How do things get so boring and messy at the same time? That's what I want to know. Neat is boring. Like me. I'm very neat. I'm very boring. But this room. My God, you should see it."

"Do you need a night housekeeper, sir?"

"Oh God." John moaned. There was a sudden movement on the bed as Bradley rolled onto his back. "Wait a minute," John said to the desk clerk, as though the clerk were stationed at John's side, watching the spectacle with him.

A twitch of the nose. A flutter of the eyes. A parting of the lips, and a sleeping god called out, *"Help me, Mama. I can't do my shirt up. There's too many buttons and not enough holes."*

"Thank you. Never mind," said John Aaron, hanging up the phone. He undressed, crawled into bed, slid one arm beneath Bradley's head, and with the other stroked the dark stubble on his cheek. "It doesn't matter how you treat people, does it?" he whispered. "Is there anyone in the world who wouldn't want to take you home?"

The next day, Bradley awoke with an insouciance offensive to a man who hadn't gotten a minute's sleep.

"Hi," he said to John cheerfully. "Did you order breakfast?"

It was an odd way to greet a virtual stranger, especially one you hadn't even had sex with.

"I don't know what you like," John responded guardedly, trying to feel his way into a strategy that would at last complete their union.

"It doesn't matter. I'm never prejudiced when it comes to food in the morning."

"It's already afternoon."

"Is it? No wonder I'm starving. Well, you decide. But

be sure to get a decent bottle of champagne." Bradley jumped out of bed. "Excuse me," he said. "I have to take a shower."

John heard him lock the bathroom door and promptly phoned room service, ordering omelets and a bottle of Dom Perignon.

Over breakfast John was moved to ask Bradley if he actually lived somewhere.

"God, I get it," said Bradley blithely. "You really do think I'm a hustler. Oh, well. I thought I told you last night that I live with my mother. We have an East Side town house."

"And you vacation at the St. Moritz?"

"How sad that you don't trust me. And here I was under the distinct impression that I had found a friend."

"I don't think we have much to base a friendship on," said John.

"I must have insulted you last night. I'm sorry. I was a little crazy."

"Well, you weren't what I would call . . . affectionate."

"But we were so drunk. It would have been meaningless."

John delicately wrapped a string of melted cheese around his fork, but his eyes were swallowing his guest. "We're not drunk now," he said.

At this Bradley stood up, his towel tight around him, a cigarette in his mouth. Stopping by the window, he told John he had a lovely view of the park. "The weather looks wonderful," he said. "We should take a walk." He turned around to look at John, who was skimming the rim of his champagne flute with his finger. John seemed to be getting angry, although Bradley guessed the anger was not aimed precisely at him.

"Well?" Bradley asked.

"Well, what?" said John.

Bradley undid his towel. "Well. Come here. Let's be friends."

It was painful for John to be methodical about getting up, to slowly lift the napkin from his lap and then set it carefully down on the little table. Yet John managed it, for precision of movement seemed expected of him. When he reached Bradley ever so slowly, repressing his desire for him was close to an impossible thing. And when Bradley took his head in his hands, it was all John could do to keep from sobbing. It went on like this, with caution and restraint, with the trembling and meticulous examination of a body, until John simply could not hold back anymore.

"It's okay," Bradley comforted when John mourned with tears the deliquescence of their passion on the bed. "Really, it's okay. It's what I do." John looked down at him, pleading for something, and Bradley smiled mischievously. "Let's get cleaned up and go out," he said. "It really is a lovely day, and it's getting stuffy in here."

Saith the sages of modern romance: "Love is nice, but timing is everything." For John Aaron, an estranged son pushed over the brink by his father's death, meeting Bradley Roberson was like landing in a garden lush with all he had planted to embellish his guilt. There was no group in all of New Mexico that so fascinated him (John had once told his therapist) than the Penitentes, the flagellants who dragged crucifixes along the road through ancient towns like Truchas and Peñasco, their feet tortured in sandals hardly suitable for such an arduous mountain climb, their rough robes sanding down the skin and bones of their shoulders as the burden of the cross rubbed against them. "God, do these guys understand what love is," John had exclaimed from the patient's overstuffed easy chair. "It's pain. It's suffering. It's beating yourself over someone who, down to his very roots, is just another human being begging for nothing more than a little goddamn human compassion." And now here was Bradley Roberson III in his arms, making his skin bristle as though he were made of hair cloth, Bradley who in sleep had revealed himself as a helpless two-year-old foundling.

At the Roberson town house on East Eighty-sixth Street, the mama for whom Bradley had cried was sleeping with her head against the chest of her fiftieth birthday present, a man named Franklin Petrie, who was given to her in gift wrapping designed by Giorgio Armani at an intimate table at Lutèce. Cassie had not expected such a delectable surprise, although as she announced at her birthday dinner, when Bradley had asked her what she wanted most to commemorate her glorious half century, she had put in her order for "that gorgeous Mr. Petrie. Why, even his name sounds like a cream-filled delicious something." At this, after taking a sip of birthday champagne, Bradley demurred. "Sweetie, don't boost his ego," he said. "I told him he ran a distant second to your hero Claus von Bülow. I wish Helmut Newton were here to take a picture for *Vanity Fair*."

"I just can't believe it," said Cassie. "You know, Franklin, sometimes Bradley does things that make me think he wants to kill me. Last winter he just disappeared in Europe without leaving me a penny. I couldn't even go out and buy a Christmas tree, let alone a new coat. I'd get these stupid postcards from God knows where, but not one single check. Our maid, Tricia, who I swear is the only maid in America who draws household expenses *and* her salary from her own bank account, took pity on me. Me, the lady of the house, living hand-to-mouth at the mercy of her child's generosity.

"Tricia got me a sweet little tree, and do you know what she put under it for me? Five gift-wrapped boxes, all from my son Bradley. I mean, just beautifully wrapped boxes with perfect bows—and do you know what was in those boxes? An acknowledgment from five different charities that a thousand-dollar donation had been made in my name. Last Christmas I had the privilege of giving to Save the Children, Planned Parenthood, the American Cancer Society, the Fresh Air Fund, and the AIDS Action Committee. One thousand dollars each. Under different circumstances, I would have been overjoyed. But as it was, I didn't have a plug nickel to give to the Salvation Army Santa.

"I said to Tricia, 'I guess, when I go out, I'm supposed to pin these acknowledgments to last year's coat so that I'll get written up in *Vogue* for keeping the Christ in Christmas.' Now tell me something, Franklin Pastry, how is it that for my birthday I've been smiled upon with a dear man like you? Is there something about you that I don't know? Do you have a Vietnam War injury? Did your blood test positive for—"

"Darling," interrupted Bradley, "the only thing Franklin tests positive for is benefiting from supply-side economics. He's his own walking bull market. For me he sold cheap, for you he sold dear, but then, for you he'll have to work for his money. Cassie, with you Franklin is leaping into untried, entrepreneurial waters. So let me leave you at his service, birthday girl. I have to go check out a lead from EF Hutton. They told me there's a hot prospect in leather."

Franklin Petrie had winked his good-bye, and Cassie had blown him a kiss, her eyes beaming with happiness, but a little skewed from confusion over Bradley's benevolence, especially because he had lately been so skimpy with his checks.

Her inheritance from BJ had been tightly held in trust until Bradley reached his twenty-first birthday; by that time it was hoped she would have grown fiscally responsible enough to set Bradley a good example as he himself embarked upon his own financial independence. Once she was handed the control of her half-million-dollar legacy, Cassie Roberson displayed money-management skills so impressive that the store clerks on her tour of high fashion lined up for the chance of assisting in their execution.

It took three years until Bradley, at the age of twenty-four, was posed the same question Cassie had asked his father when she applied for a job? "Do you know where I can get my hair done in this town that won't set me back the cost of a new pair of shoes?" For Cassie, the price of hair treatments and high heels had grown along the same percentage lines as the national defense budget over the years. At the end of her shopping spree she was somewhat surprised to learn that an empty bank account had remained unaffected by the inflation rate, that zilch had the same value in 1981 as it had in 1957.

Bradley would occasionally spend time trying to decipher just who his father was determined to do in by giving Cassie financial freedom. Did BJ expect him to toss her out to wander the streets in tattered Ungaros after she'd squandered her legacy? Or had BJ known that she would suck off his own millions like a baby on demand feeding?

Bradley had played at weaning Cassie, at watching her squirm when he made the bottle disappear, but if this game tormented her, it still didn't serve its purpose of relieving his angst over her steadfast dependency. Finally, in desperation, he had hired for her fiftieth birthday a wet nurse in the form of Franklin Petrie. He had met Franklin in Venice at the home of a socialite who was fast tiring of Franklin's services. Bradley hoped that with a handsome salary and the run of a fine town house (complete with a maid), Franklin might someday realize that life with Cassie was as fine a life as he could hope to achieve, and so would agree to marry her. Bradley pictured them rolling through life together in the perverse, protective bubble of his money, and he planned to be generous, just as long as they went easy on demanding his time.

Even as he left the restaurant Bradley saw little to condemn about his matchmaking and concluded that he had finally done his mother his most noble turn since their relationship had soured years before. Just before arriving at The Wild Bull, however, he had seen the baseness of his gesture; that Cassie had seemed pleased to be handed prepaid companionship compounded his sudden misery.

"What kind of mood are we in now?" John Aaron said, challenging him. Bradley was in a mood to find all of his moods tiresome, one that primed him to attack the defenseless soul reflecting his moodiness. Lucky John Aaron, to have been slouching in his chair at The Wild Bull, sinking under the weight of what? The eyes told the tale. They were the same eyes BJ Roberson had had when sneaking into his son's room at night, when, thinking the boy asleep he whispered, "Bradley, I'm so sorry." Small, recessed eyes, grey and dulled by the gloom and doom that burrowed in the heart. Eyes dulled by the guilt of hurting those they loved. Lucky John Aaron, to have reflected Bradley's mood, given it a name and a place to go. And lucky, lucky Santa Fe, New Mexico.

Chapter Seven

WHAT did Santa Fe know of Bradley Roberson III? Until he moved onto Camino Sin Nombre and Sylvia Valdez began to discuss him with a few of her female relatives and friends, the town's Hispanic community knew absolutely nothing. And with the exception of a Navajo artist for whom Bradley made a present of the Hermès handkerchief pulled in jest from his rear pocket at a cocktail party, the town's few Indians knew just as little. The health-food militants sneered at him for ordering tripe while they were trying to enjoy their vegetarian green chile stew, and the radical feminists (closet smokers or not) never failed to ask him to put out his cigarette when his smoke was blown into their antiporn discussions at Maria's Lunch. The gallery owners loved him because even though he never bought anything, his mere presence lent a first-class ambience to what the absence of the press indicated was a second-rate show. The hairdressers all wished for the challenge of making his looks even more dramatic than they were already, and the waiters drew lots for his table because he tipped like a man who never cheapened his wallet with singles. At the Caballero disco, the libidos he stirred could be measured by the level of feigned disinterest on the part of those he ignored and by the stiltedness of the welcomes afforded the gray-haired real estate man who appeared to control his dance card.

At dinner parties Bradley came across as a one-man

campaign created to challenge everything that any of the guests thought they stood for. If a conversation began to veer from a sublime topic like Japanese ceramics to a more mundane topic like the consistency of the tempura at Fujiyama's, Bradley shifted gears altogether, aiming full speed ahead for the level of the strange. "I think the Santa Fe city government should set up a technological exchange with the Japanese," he'd say. "Santa Feans can teach them how to make sun tea; they can teach enterprising contractors here how to make prefab, passive solar housing in fake adobe. That way maybe Hispanic kids wouldn't have to work at Safeway when they graduate from Santa Fe High."

If someone launched into a racist diatribe against the town's low-riding, slow-driving, vandalizing teens, Bradley would suggest that the host might reform them with a special screening of his fist-fucking video. No one would venture to guess what surprising statements Bradley would find in his silk-lined pockets to pull out in a glorious show of antagonism. And no one understood why such an avid collector of Italian silks never failed to take the side of native New Mexicans, who would still vote the leisure suit the design triumph of the century.

Since in his physical presentation Bradley handily put their casual style to shame along with everything else, people agreed that all in all, as a total package Bradley just didn't make sense. His critics called him Mary Quite Contrary. His fans called him "Bradley Roberson III, a Contradiction in Terms." Legends sprang up about his wealth. Not that he was in any way unusual in this particular regard. One of Santa Fe's art dealers was rumored to have bought into the trade with CIA money paid him for heroin running in Cambodia. It was said of one of Santa Fe's hoteliers that he'd remodeled a ghost ranch with money inherited after the successful murder of his wife. This often happened in small towns where money tended to land suddenly instead of grow. In the overabundance of cafés, people gave their imaginations a field day contriving theories as to where the money landed from.

Some said that they knew for a fact that Bradley Roberson had made a killing in cocaine. Others contested that he was being paid hush money by an actor who'd gone back into the closet to star with Bo Derek. The great majority, however, had decided upon Bradley's arrival that he had no money whatever to speak of, that he was nothing more than an expensive souvenir John Aaron had purchased on his mysterious journey out of town. The great majority believed this because it served to solve the biggest mystery that Bradley Roberson III posed, which was why someone like him had linked up with John Aaron in the first place. They made no secret of their puzzlement, and John was shocked by it; to him, the reason for Bradley's presence in his life was as clear as day: Bradley was obviously on an assignment from God to drive him insane. The question in John's mind as they had traveled from New York was how long the process would take, for he had been shown in their days of getting to know one another in Manhattan how sweetly Bradley's affections could temper the torture he inflicted.

Driving up the highway after they had disembarked at the Albuquerque airport, John knew that Bradley had something to do with the perfect October weather. The Sandia Mountains were out of their smoggy summer haze and stood jagged and gray, like the gates to another planet. To John they were the gates of home where he hoped the man beside him would enliven the dull months of winter. Then there was the outpouring of desert dotted here and there with gas stations and run-down tailings of Indian pueblos. The billboard—"La Fonda *Is* Santa Fe"—caused Bradley to break his silent struggle with his feelings about John and the bleakness that he saw in the landscape.

"Is that what Santa Fe is?" he asked. "Somebody's sand-castle notion of a Grand Hotel?"

"Amazing," said John. "We haven't even gotten there, and you've pegged it perfectly."

"Spain was like this. I took the train once from Barcelona to Granada. I didn't find the Spanish very friendly. Are they friendly here?" asked Bradley.

"Let's say the young ones help to remind people like us that we don't live in Shangri-la. However, they seem to have a pact to stop just short of arson and mutilation."

"Sounds like a balanced environment. I wouldn't know where to turn if no one was held at gunpoint once in a while. How are the Indians?"

"Very water-rights- and money-minded these days. They may have some success in blocking a condominium project that I'm in on. They say that the land isn't theirs, but the water is. And they're not shy about charging a few hundred dollars for a small piece of pottery. I'll take you up to San Ildefonso where the rain dancers weave between the Cadillacs."

"Thar's gold in them thar sand hills," said Bradley.

"Of course there is. The Spanish sell their land, the Indians sell their crafts, and the whites sell anything they can lay their hands on. Capitalism knows no ethnicity, darling, or at least it doesn't here."

"And you? Are you a closet Marxist?"

"I was never a Marxist . . . no," John considered, "I take that back. After my Keynesian economics professor at U Penn dumped me for a drama student, I was a Marxist for three hours when I took his exam, on which, I might add, I got an A. I'm just not one of those hypocrites who claims to love Santa Fe for its spirituality. Do you know what Neil Simon said in *People* magazine? That he loves living so close to the Indians. The guy has his own airstrip, for God's sake. Let's be real."

"So what is it?"

"What is what?"

"What draws people here?"

"Beauty, that's all. And isolation. It's a delicious place to escape the public eye. But then, there's the Santa Fe eye. God, wait till it gets a load of you!"

"What are you doing, driving me into a den of disenfranchised vultures?"

"Heavens, no. They'll adore you. I told you that before. It's me they have trouble with. They think I buy status. Which is true. I do. I don't paint. I don't write. I don't leave anyone reeling on the floor from my brilliant flair for innuendo. I'm a businessman. I buy and sell. In my mind, status is no different from real estate. It's a commodity that gets me out to lunch as often as I want to go. They also don't like me because, until you, of course, I had something of a thing for Latinos, and as far as a lot of *this* group is concerned, we're still living in the days of Pancho Villa. Myself, I am happy to sell any overpriced, stinking piece of desert property to a Texan. Texans should write the book on buying status. The irony is that it's Jews, and not Texans, who are likely to read it."

"Stop the car," said Bradley.

"What?"

"Stop the goddamn fucking car!"

John pulled onto the shoulder of the road. "Are you sick?" he asked. "What's the matter?"

They were ten miles from the exit, halfway up the steep, seventeen-mile incline that told the Santa Fean he was almost home. The lanes were narrow, and John quaked in his everyday brown boots when he saw the flashing lights of the escort for an eighteen-wheeler bearing the sign WIDE LOAD.

"You don't love me," said Bradley. "Why am I doing this if you don't love me?"

"What are you saying? Bradley, this is not a romantic comedy. We can get killed out here."

"You're using me."

"I'm what?"

"What was that speech I just heard about buying status, huh? Jesus, the way you took care of me in New York, I thought you felt something. Fuck it. It doesn't matter. Go ahead. Drive on."

"Not when you feel this way about things. Listen, I think there's some meaning here . . . I mean, between you and me. Two traumatized people don't just fall into each other's laps for no reason. Anyone who's had as much therapy as I have knows that. I didn't bring you here to wear like a new sweater."

"Drop it. It doesn't matter. There's no reason for you to love me, anyway. Christ, I'm paying a zombie to keep my mother company. I'm glad to be of use. Drive. Drive on, Edward, or whatever your name is. The eyes of Santa Fe await us."

John pulled his Mercedes out into the slow lane, unable to do more than fifty in a part of the country where the speed limit was viewed as somebody's idea of a bad joke.

"We don't even have a snowball's chance in hell, you know," said Bradley.

"No," said John. "I don't expect we do. Be quiet now, and let me drive." Suddenly John felt a hand on his crotch and then found his view obstructed as Bradley leaned over and kissed him on the mouth. "Oh, God, that was nice," said John. "But you'd better sit back now. Not even a Mercedes can drive itself."

"Say you love me just a little."

"A lot, Bradley. I love you a lot. But it won't do you any good if you're dead."

He obeyed with a begrudging sigh. "I don't care if I die," he said, "as long as I'm loved."

A beautifully manicured hand on his thigh, John approached the city, convinced he had never seen it so dramatically beautiful. At dusk, with the mountains' aspens gold against the pink-tinted blue; below, dull gold against brilliant beige, the sun streaking it with light and shadow; autumnal Santa Fe was, of course, beautiful on its own. It was only later, at El Ristorante, where it could be said that Bradley Roberson III had any true effect on the scenery or the weather. As the hungry travelers walked into the dining room eddies began to swirl at the tables. "John's got a new one," someone said. "The kid must have really milked his last one. Look at his suit."

An eddy swirled over.

"John. My God, where *were* you? We almost called the police to break your door down, but then Marissa, astute as ever, checked and saw that your car was gone."

"Family business. My father died."

"Oh, no. Sudden?"

"No. Not at all sudden. We're surprised he hung on so long, frankly. He'd been in a great deal of pain, you know. I headed up to New York after the funeral. I'd like you to meet a new friend of mine, Bradley Roberson III." John emphasized the numeral.

Bradley stood up, extending his hand.

"In town for long?"

"Hard to tell. I've just arrived, so I don't really know."

"Well, don't let us lose you too soon. Are you in the arts?"

"No," said Bradley with a cool smile. "I'm completely worthless."

"Fuck you, John," said the visitor. "Imagine, sneaking in an honest one. And a New Yorker! Well, Bradley, you're in for a big change. There's no place in the world like Santa Fe."

"So I hear. A unique crowd."

The visitor delivered the verdict to his table: "He's adorable. It will never last."

Back in the house in La Barranca, John lit a piñon fire in the conical fireplace, and the living room filled with the perfume Bradley had smelled in the air in town. It was too sweet, he thought, like a cover—like John's architectural showplace of a home. Both hid the fact that Santa Fe was not unique at all. Even though he had been warned, it disappointed and depressed him to have found himself in a pit stop on the social circuit; earlier the autumn light of northern New Mexico had given him a glimmer of hope that he was entering a better world. He took a seat in the dark in the far corner of the room. John watched him, struggling to convince himself that whatever was the matter was not his fault this time. "Anything I can do?" he asked, lying down in front of the fire.

Bradley glared at him. John observed how the firelight struck his eyes, making them dance and plead at the same time; it clarified for him how complicated Bradley was. "It's not that I can't stand your friends, John, but can't we just stay home?"

"Ah," said John. "You're having a small-town attack. You took me too seriously in the car. Don't worry. They'll be on the phone about you for a few days, but then the excitement will settle down. It's just that you're the first new face of the doldrums season."

"I didn't come here for people to talk about me. I won't have them talk about me!" shouted Bradley.

A sigh announced John's determination to remain calm. "You can't stop talk, darling. It's a fact of life. You just have to learn to let it be."

"Yes, Mother Mary, 'Let it be, let it be,' " Bradley sang unprettily. "Fuck. There's nothing to let be. It's already gone too far."

"What has?"

"Everything. It should be my epitaph: 'Here lies Bradley Roberson III, born of lies that went too far.' "

John moaned as he stretched out flat on his back and closed his eyes, praying for the right words to come and stave off a drama he simply was not up to after a day of travel over endless rough road. "I'm tired," he finally mustered.

"You see," said Bradley, "you can't handle it, can you? You refuse to see what you really have here, among your artsy walls and postcard scenery. You're hiding out in this movieland town. 'Aren't the mountains fabulous? Isn't life just dandy?' So your father isn't around anymore to tell you the facts. Well, let me be his voice for you, Mr. Diaspora. Let me tell you about life, John. It's fucking putrid the ends that human beings go to, to rip the insides out of each other. We're all a bunch of sadists out for blood, and this place stinks of rotten insides just like everyplace else does."

John let out another moan and rose to his feet. "Listen," he said, "you know where the liquor is. Go fix yourself another drink and wallow as long as you want to, avenging angel. But you read me the script in New York, Bradley. So your father died blissfully of cancer and passed on to you a materialistic half-wit as an albatross to wear around your neck while you grieve among your millions. Believe me, I have heard sicker and sadder stories than yours. I'm going to bed."

"God," screamed Bradley, "won't you face *anything*? One fucking dinner in this Tower of Babel with you and I can see how miserable you really are. Face it."

"There's nothing to face. Listen. I am not involved in this. This is yours to work out, darling, not mine. Take the spare room. You should be alone with whatever it is that brought you here. Let's not fool ourselves that it possibly could have been me."

Bradley stared at the fire. "That's not true," he said blankly.

"Well, I'm tired," said John.

"You don't really care about anything," said Bradley. "That's what you don't understand."

"You, darling, are too drunk to understand anything right now. Take my advice and go to bed."

John left him, and Bradley sat alone, stewing. His eyes took in the room, its precision, its whiteness, its joyless painting of a swimming pool by a David Hockney imitator who'd omitted the sense of humor. He could tell he was in the home of a man whose record collection was restricted by the dimensions of its cabinet.

In a flash it dawned on him why John had favored wild Mexicans and why he had now selected a borderline schizophrenic like himself to grace his home. "It's fucking perfect!" he exclaimed aloud. In a burst of inspiration he pulled a black Magic Marker from John's office desk and ran to the living room. "Hockney lives. This doesn't," he wrote across the swimming pool painting.

After tiptoeing upstairs, he knocked quietly and opened John's door; a cool breeze off the mountains blew through it like an escaping ghost. "I'm sorry," he whispered.

"It's okay, darling," said John. "Are you coming in?"

"Yes. I've decided to be a perfect guest."

"Well, don't expect too much. I'm really exhausted."

"No problem," said Bradley, and then, forcefully and happily, he slammed the door. John let out a startled cry, and arms lovingly reached out through the darkness to soothe him.

In his younger days when he sneaked into the crannies of his secret life in Florida, John had a brief affair with a middle-aged writer who told him that it wasn't growing old he feared so much as the unbearable predictability of his final days. With Bradley, John explored his tolerance for the unpredictable, telling his closest friends he felt younger than he had in years. Youth sprang forth, he said, from his being hurled into states of anguish, only to have his head borne up an instant later by the gentlest of hands that an instant later might stroke him as easily as thrust him to the ground. On the ground he could as likely be kissed as kicked. When he needed a breather from all this, a moment to digest his imbibements from this fountain of youth, he would arrange a dinner party.

John found it tantalizing to see how Bradley could be so consistently civil to him in a crowd while unleashing his venom on unsuspecting guests who were always happy to return again and again for a small dose of what John was daily overfed. John's therapist, a wise woman whose holistic approach to mental health included the art of massage, never bought the youth-instilling angle of why John let Bradley whip him around like he was tied to the propeller of a helicopter. Oh, how she had strived to make him see that he had sufficiently repented for his father's pain so that he would abhor himself no more but finally meet good Job's reward: grow old and full of days.

But, lo, when John sent Bradley from his house, old John grew, but full for weeks only of restaurant cooking.

BOOK III

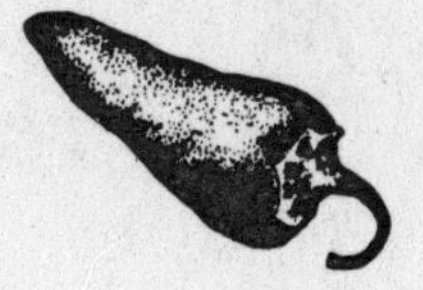

Chapter Eight

Dear Cassie and Franklin,

I know I must have sounded like a Welcome Wagon reject when you phoned yesterday, and I apologize for my rudeness. It really is good to know that you are home safe and sound from the land of Ping-Pong, jade, and mandatory abortions. Tell me, Franklin, do you take the *Socialist Worker* to read over lunch at Le Cirque these days, or did standing amid a billion industrious people set you positively over the edge? I know that in my case, it would be the latter.

But I must tell the both of you that my garden is fabulous, and though I've had some help from my six-year-old neighbor, Stevie Valdez, I can proudly say that it has truly been a labor of love on the part of my own two hands. Oh, Cunégonde, when I think of all the years I wasted at Juilliard, when M. Pangloss could have just as easily set me up with a bonzai master or gotten me an apprenticeship with the Olmstead Society for Urban Landscaping. But then, he never did quite provide the best of all possible worlds, did he?

By the time you receive this, maybe you'll have decided among yourselves where to take off for next. Now that you have done China, might I offer up for a possibility a conducted jungle tour along the waters of the Amazon? Such an adventure would prove deliciously exciting at any time of year and not too perilous, either, since every brochure before me notes that the cost of emergency snakebite kits is included in the fee. Of course, where to next on your mission as worldwide ambassadors of etiquette is entirely up to you. Just let me know to whom I should remit payment, *il va sans dire.*

Darlings, how am I doing covering up my state of mind? I'm a mess, you know. John still refuses to speak to me. God, the man is so unforgiving. I guess you never know what a person is going to take too seriously, although what was I thinking? Who knows? You know me. I'm such a goddamned fascist. The thing is, I don't even know why I fell in love with the man I set out to rule, unless it was just the day-to-dayness of him, or the fact that even his faulty criteria for choosing lovers reflected a mind that managed to impose its own brand of order on its little stakeout in the universe. I suppose it was his patience, too, although to this day I am convinced he never loved me. "Thou shalt not love" was his eleventh commandment. I wonder if it's in the Talmud. Those Hasids in the Diamond District never struck me as the kind of people who get sentimental on Valentine's Day. But what do you know of Hasids—you who aspire to Palm Beach? (The only thing you have in common is that Palm Beach will never let *you* in, either.) Me, I'm thinking of dressing as a Hasid and staging a sit-in in John's driveway until he lets me properly apologize. Problem is, there's nowhere to get the clothes.

So, what do I do to warm my heart that is so cruelly left standing out in the cold? If I were to send a picture, you would know instantly because I am blacker than Tricia, who claims to have only two Caucasians in her family tree. I am sunning even now in this blistering heat and occasionally applying the coolness of my glass of vodka and soda to my neck and armpits. The remedy is losing its effect. If you'll excuse me, I think I'll go swimming at my new haunt. Or should I tell you about it first?

My new hangout is the Bishop's Lodge where I frequent the pool, having paid an extremely reasonable membership fee to the management. I also frequent the bar, which is open to the public. The Bishop's Lodge has been advertised in *The New Yorker* and is quite the Santa Fe resort. From a distance it looks like an alpine monastery. There's a manmade waterfall at the entrance, but none of its exterior features hold a candle to what can be found inside. The lobby and bar are strategically peopled with wooden Indians—these are far from cigar-store noble chiefs but are hunched over and dressed like shabby drunks. Their skin is carved, wrinkled like dried prunes, and their eyes are bloodshot. I've given them all names—Joe, Sam, Billy. Sam is my favorite. He's seated by the fireplace in the downstairs bar where the last time I went, I overheard the shaking tambourines and fervent singing of a revival meeting being held in the next room. There's a hole carved into Sam's mouth so he can smoke, but so far I haven't dared to offer him a drink. I'm not sure the owners would approve if their Indians actually started drinking. But even though no one will serve him, Sam seems to like it there at the lodge. He says it beats the bus station.

Go see the travel agent and phone when you get booked. . . .

—Bradley

As spring gave way to summer, warm to hot, bourbon to gin, John claimed to suffer the December of his years and plunged himself into his business after months of betraying a private vow and living off his principal. His therapist suggested that he try out a new hobby after he insisted that the next dinner party he threw would be in hell. Encouraged to convert a horrific experience into positive expression, John had built onto his house a glass, airconditioned cubbyhole that he christened his "writing studio," bought a word processor, and set about the Santa Fe socially redeeming task of trying to write a novel. "It's a doomed love story, naturally," he would say to anyone patronizing enough to ask, and while he knew he'd never finish it, he hoped the exercise would cleanse him of an unattractive phase of feeling sorry for himself.

But with every siting of the white BMW he had helped Bradley choose as the perfect touring car, and with each bit of news that Bradley continued to waste away as a self-styled monk repenting for his sins, John knew that his condition was terminal. Each hair in his brow that grew in gray he chalked up as another giant step toward the grave.

Badgered by Marissa Goldman and coaxed by his therapist, he tried to rally himself for the opera season by making opening-night dinner reservations at Rancho Encantado two weeks in advance, although he doubted he would follow through with inviting a potential new interest to accompany him. His recovery was too slow. "The hell with fling to fling," he said. "The most I can manage is lunch to lunch."

Indeed, he did not always honor his standing one o'clock lunch reservation on the Palacio Café patio. Sometimes it rained, and sometimes he felt like something other than chicken or crabmeat salad. In the former case a no-show needed no excuses, but John would call in, anyway, as an expression of appreciation that, as wounded as he was, there was still some satisfaction in being a regular in a town full of tourists and transients. Lunch at the Palacio set a few sparks flying in his nearly burned-out lighter of a body when out the patio doors would spring a nimble and attractive Hispanic waiter, and for this, too, he felt obliged to the management.

By opening day of the opera season, the sparks had managed to ignite a tiny flame, and John became determined to fan it by getting himself a date. This he knew would be the first item of discussion when at ten-thirty the phone rang announcing Marissa Goldman's second-cup-of-coffee buzz. "Tell me it isn't true," she answered his not-quite-so-Sad Sack-as-usual hello.

At this John drew a blank.

"Tell me it isn't true, John," Marissa ordered again.

"All right, Marissa. It isn't true."

"Well, thank *God*."

"That's what *I* think."

"So how did a thing like that get around?"

"You know this town, Marissa. *Anything* can get around."

"Some joke, John, you dating that putz Richard Gabrielli."

He had known it would come out eventually. "Marissa?" he prodded, grinning to himself.

"What?"

"It's true."

"Scraping, John," Marissa exclaimed. "That's what everybody says. You're scraping the absolute bottom of the barrel."

"The whole town may say that, Marissa, but half of it is jealous. He may lack character, but what's new? He's gorgeous, and who am I to turn down gorgeous? Gorgeous comes rarely at my age. Besides, as everybody knows, my pride is shot, and for that you can thank your dear, sweet friend, Mr. Roberson, speaking of the absolute führer of putzes."

"I tried him again last night," Marissa volunteered, still

convinced that Bradley was all John really cared to hear about. "Maybe he went to New York. His mother and her friend are due back from that trip he sent them on down the Yangtze River."

"You mean he didn't arrange for their boat to sink? He's not in New York, Marissa. He's not out of town."

"How would *you* know?"

"Because Richard saw him yesterday at the Bishop's Lodge pool. Better. He said Bradley asked him to dinner."

"Well, that's cute, John. Now it all makes sense, doesn't it?"

"Yes," said John. "I suppose it does."

"Well, in spite of what you might think, if Bradley's at the opera—and I doubt he'll be at the opera—he'll be the only jealous one in the crowd. That is, *if* he actually sank as low as you and asked Richard out. I wouldn't trust a word that man says."

"Who said anything about trust? Since when does sex have anything to do with trust, Marissa? Certainly that is a notion that three months ago I was forced to throw out the window."

"All right. So he'll see you at the opera with Richard. *Maybe*. It could be good for him to feel that he's paid off a little more of his debt to you. Maybe he'll sleep better."

"Bradley needs no help sleeping," said John. "If he was Albert Speer, he would have slept through Nuremberg."

"Listen, he's living like a hermit, for God's sake, and you're not convinced he's sorry?"

"Whoever gave him the idea that staying here and sulking would finally attract my sympathy? Was it you, Marissa? Because if it was, have you ever given him a bum steer! Do you know what I dreamed about him last night? I dreamed that he was sipping champagne in some adorable house while being surrounded by emaciated bodies. Does it sound like I'm close to forgiving him? I want him out of here, Marissa. He's making me old."

"Forgive me for saying this, but you brought it on yourself, John. You knew he was unbalanced. And *young*? For the life of me I can't understand why you don't find some handsome, smart, successful man who falls within ten years of your age bracket. I mean, is thirty-five old? No. Thirty-five is not old."

"And Barry?" challenged John. "The twenty-six-year-old Jewish powwow dancer from Taos? Take a look in the mirror and see who's casting stones, Marissa."

"Barry is just a friend."

"You bet he is, but let's not get into it."

"What's that supposed to mean?"

"It means that if I didn't think I'd faint from boredom listening to him talk about the evils of thermonuclear power and the holiness of eagle feathers, I'd be tempted to take him home myself; only, with me he wouldn't sleep in the guest room."

"I'm glad you're so sure, John. Why is it that everybody else insists they haven't got a clue which way he leans?"

"I don't know. You tell me, Marissa."

"He communes with the trees, John. He thinks he's an Indian rainmaker. Standing naked in a thunderstorm is his idea of an orgasmic experience. If you read homosexuality into that, then you are withholding an important treatise from the psychiatric world."

"And I suppose you get some vicarious thrill watching him do rain dances in your living room."

"Call Bradley, John. Just say hello and let him know you don't think poisonous thoughts about him twenty-four hours a day."

"No."

"I just can't believe it about Richard Gabrielli. I don't think you'll get away with it."

"Good-bye, Marissa."

In the kitchen, John poured a tall glass of iced sun tea and garnished it with fresh mint. He was embarrassed for Marissa, and for himself too: two withering grapes clinging to the Santa Fe vine, desperate for anyone to come along and notice that there was juice left in them yet. He couldn't remember the last time that Marissa had a man and refused to believe her tales of one-night stands in La Jolla, Scottsdale, Boulder, and other minor art centers where she toured with her pottery. The cowboy-hat sugar bowl and cowboy-boot creamer set she made out of clay were her most popular items, these followed by pickup-truck gravy boats and sombrero chip-and-dip plates. But that Bloomingdale's had the exclusive on her line in New York was a credential that couldn't shed her extra hundred pounds. (Everyone in Santa Fe agreed, however, that she carried her weight well.)

Back at his word processor in his new writing studio, John put Marissa's plight out of his mind and tried to come up with some clever and snide words about his nemesis, Bradley Roberson III. After some moments of concentration it occurred to John that the most purely despicable aspect of Bradley was his charm, and after sharpening his animosity on the spikes of a yucca plant outside, John recollected Bradley's charm—the deception of its ease and its hard sell of undelivered promise—in this phrase: "A suave, Adonis-like strut." John judged that there was irony in this combination of words and so he went on: "Warren Richardson III left the elevator in the St. Moritz Hotel and walked with a suave, Adonis-like strut to the front desk where he devastated the clerk and people impatiently waiting to register for their rooms with a tirade on the audacity of thinking they could get away with a torn shower curtain in the bathroom, which, by the way, needed repainting." Composing such a long sentence made John thirsty, and he gulped down the rest of his iced tea. Then he looked at his watch, which read noon. He smiled at the reprieve and rose to get ready for his one o'clock appointment at the Palacio Café.

Today he had arranged to lunch with his new friend Max Boorman, who had expressed interest in purchasing some land. Several weeks had passed since the embarrassing spectacle at a Dorothy Cheswick fund-raiser, to which Max had agreed to go only because he lacked a cocktail party on his roster of Santa Fe experiences. At Dorothy Cheswick's gathering for the Friends of the Acequia Foundation (a group dedicated to the repair of a three-hundred-year-old irrigation ditch), Max had flung a potato skin filled with sour cream and red caviar at a man who remarked at his "Nancy Reagan is *not* a Lesbian" T-shirt: "Man, do you have a case of attitude."

What Max had, along with many Santa Feans, past and present, was a trust fund. Not a hugely impressive trust fund but enough of one to afford him a life-style he labeled "Santa Fe minimalist." Unlike John Aaron, he was not susceptible to the label "Santa Fe luncher." Rather, he put social obligations in the category of a troublesome game that interrupted a quiet day on his ratty sofa. With John he opened the game with a joke as a way of easing his transition into the world of homosexual men.

Max Boorman, in his worn Levi's jeans, his unkempt black beard, and eyes that barked like a hyena, was a self-avowed case of burnout at the age of thirty-two. He and John had met in early May when they found themselves neighbors in the public hot tub set in the seclusion of the Sangre de Cristo foothills a few miles out of town. There John toyed with the idea of getting over Bradley, and Max toyed with the idea of replacing a lover lost to a women's collective in the revived ghost town of Madrid. Max was saddened to have been abandoned by the only woman he'd found in Santa Fe who had shared his interest in attack dogs. Thus, like his hot tub neighbor, John, he was more moping than looking, really.

The fact that the two men recognized the utter absurdity of their situation—being uneasy in what was supposed to provide the ultimate in relaxation—prompted them to strike up a chat. John pointed out to Max that everyone in the tub not already caught up in chatter seemed bursting to say something. Did Max think, John inquired, that when a group of strangers found themselves naked together, they used words like clothes, to cover themselves? Would he like to join him in an experiment and climb up on the ledge to see if they'd be pulled into conversation in lieu of being thrown a towel? This they did, evoking the predicted response, and in a burst of laughter, what remained of the barrier posed by their differing sexual preferences was toppled.

"Hey, there, friend. I've got a new one for you" was Max's greeting as he sat down, fifteen minutes late, at John's patio table.

"Oh, boy," said John. He spread his napkin over his summer-weight jeans with a jerky gesture, indicating his annoyance over his guest's tardiness.

"How many Santa Feans does it take to screw in a light bulb?" asked Max.

"Jesus, let me think," said John. First, though, he hailed Ramon, the waiter, with a polite smile and a wag of his finger.

"How's things, Mr. Aaron?" asked Ramon, whose red jacket and black trousers John thought an unfortunate uniform for work outdoors on such a hot day. He cared about Ramon; he cared about anyone who was pleasant to him these days.

"Things are just great, Ramon," John said. "Do you know my antisocial friend, Max? I've dragged him away from his books today by promising him some crabmeat salad. I told him the crabmeat here is fresh, and would you believe he accused me of lying? But he said he'd eat it, anyway. I hope at this late hour you still have some."

"Think so."

"I'm telling you, Max. A hundred huskies died bringing it down here from Alaska."

"How many Santa Feans does it take to screw in a light bulb, John?" asked Max.

"I don't know. Ask Ramon. He's one of the few people I know who was born here."

All eyes were on Ramon, who shrugged without letting his smile slip, a smile John found most engaging and which Max found vacuous. Pure white teeth, low in enamel, which Max correlated with low IQ. The Osmond family would make an ideal case study, he felt.

"Will anybody speak?" asked Max.

"You win," said John. "We're stumped."

"One to screw it in, and four to stop him, because they like the old one."

John and Max ordered their drinks; then John looked over his shoulder and waved at the people he had visited a few minutes ago, letting them know he wouldn't be taking them up on their gracious request to join them in the event that he was stuck with a no-show.

"Do you still have that Nambe property?" asked Max.

"Yup. Just upped the price, in fact."

"Shit. How bad?"

"Fifteen minutes late? Fifteen percent."

"Don't be a bastard. Don't you allow for people who live on Santa Fe time?"

"Not when I'm hungry. And not for people who hurt my reputation by starting food fights when I take them to charity functions."

"I thought you said you liked that kind of ballsiness. Actually I was hoping it would get me a discount."

"Well, maybe so. But that's a piece of ground that I'm not in any particular hurry to sell. It's north, you know, and the trend is north. It's a little gold mine up there in Nambe. What's the matter? Aren't you happy in Arroyo Hondo?"

"My neighbors don't like my trailer. They keep asking me when I'm going to build. My guess is that trailers are still kosher in Nambe."

John shuddered. "There should be a law," he said. "You know dry states? Well, they should have trailer states: Texas, Utah, and New Jersey, and even there, only in restricted areas around butane distributorships."

"Fuck you. I think trailers are great," said Max. "And let me tell you something about my little silver bullet of a home. It'll be one of the first ones picked to go on the maiden Airstream caravan to the moon. Airstreams will tour the universe just as soon as Rand McNally comes out with a road map."

Max cut off his speech when Hank, the old Indian, out on his daily rounds, came through the patio doors. Max liked *his* smile because he correlated toothlessness with wisdom. John thought Hank was positively eerie and was repelled by his daily parade through Plaza restaurants, his gait like a tired mule's, his arm swinging a dozen turquoise necklaces in the offended faces of diners. The Indian's ritual was a mystery to him because not once had he seen him sell anything. Of course, John had been more tolerant before the day Bradley blew a kiss at the Indian's toothless mouth and confessed his desire to take him home for a gourmet meal and then down to Acapulco to teach him snorkeling. "It's so beautiful how he moves," Bradley had remarked. "It's just like he lives in an underwater world." The fascination in his eyes had made John realize Bradley wasn't joking.

"How goes the writing, John?" asked Max. "But need I even ask? It must be going brilliantly on such state-of-the-art equipment."

"You know," John protested with surprising earnestness, "when you accept an invitation to meet a friend, you could have the decency to at least attempt a little civility. It's a foreign word to you, I know, but for God's sake, Max, you don't have to be so fucking snide. If it's putting you out to be here with me, then go. I frequently eat alone."

Hank the Indian wandered over to their table and swung the turquoise necklaces under John's nose. John cringed and shut his eyes, as though he were being visited by the Angel of Death. When Hank wandered off, John blurted, "Fuck it. Where are the drinks? What the fuck is it with the service in this place?"

Having understood John Aaron to be a fairly even-tempered guy, Max wondered what had provoked his anger. He was more peeved than concerned. An hour ago he had been reading Dostoyevski against the resplendent background of *Pavarotti's Greatest Hits* and was not in the mood to witness an anxiety attack in a man he hardly knew. But for the most part he liked John, and so he apologized for nothing and asked him what was the matter.

"It's him," said John, nodding to indicate Hank, who was now exiting the patio. "I just don't understand why they let him in here. It's not just me, you know. He must give almost everyone the creeps."

"Tricultural Santa Fe," Max scoffed. "The Palacio needs him to meet their Indian quota. Lighten up. It's summer."

"And don't make fun of my writing."

"I won't say another processed word about it."

Max then proceeded to say nothing. His silence brought more of John's nervousness to the surface, causing his shoulders to stiffen as though they were being hit under the warm sun by sharp, cold drops of rain. He turned his head away to look again for Ramon; seeing him step out onto the patio with his tray of drinks and crackers provided some relief. When a sip of bourbon only settled Max more comfortably into silence, John was moved to joke to ease the strain.

"I know you'll hate this, Max," he said, "but looking at

you, I'm reminded of one of my ex-lover Bradley's few valid and highly quotable principles: 'Bourbon should never be drunk al fresco.' Even bucolic Southerners drink lighter stuff out on the veranda, Max. Bourbon is so gloomy a contrast to the Santa Fe sunshine. Sorry for being so heavy. I don't know what came over me."

"Obviously your friend Bradley came over you, John. Do me a favor and spare me your heartache. No offense, but I feel like a fucking token in this town. Not that it's so bad. You make it easy as shit to get laid."

"It's all conquest to you, isn't it?" John accused.

Max leaned forward, emptied his remaining bourbon down his throat, and said, "Ho-hum."

"You know, I used to be like you. I used to think there was something pretty superior about the thrill of conquest and the smugness that comes when you realize that you've managed once again to lock out feeling. Maybe I'm the wrong one to be offering you advice, but speaking from my own experience, Max, it's a pretty lousy state of being, in addition to being a dishonest one. Because if you're anything like me, Max, you're really vulnerable as hell. You're asking for somebody to come along and royally destroy you, do you know that? I hope I'm phrasing this so that you understand it, but you're asking to get kneed in the fucking groin. But in the meantime I guess I should pity those poor Santa Fe women, if you are a fair representation of what they have to choose from. I tell my friend Marissa that she's lucky to be alone, with just the two of her."

Max smirked. "I know all about it, John. You're a better human being because you hurt, while I remain an unfeeling slob. How did I know to remind myself on the way here that there's no such thing as a free lunch? Let's change the subject and talk about the opera, shall we? Wait till you see what I'm dragging there. A little waif whose sparkling eyes are daily recharged by the writings of Carlos Casteñeda. She's never heard a note of opera in her life, preferring, of course, the spiritually uplifting monotony of Indian drums."

John comically grabbed his throat, took a big sip of gin and tonic, and said, "Quick. Pass the Aramis." Then he leaned forward and whispered a confession. "Max," he confided, "tonight I am throwing myself to the wolves."

"Do tell," said Max.

"My date is a Mexican."

"No."

"Yes," said John. "And the black word is out already."

Richard Gabrielli had been born Richard Garcia, John explained. Although he was taller than the average Mexican, it was not the reason he had changed his name. He had done it to better his chances of getting a good job in Houston, where he had moved a few years back and had been quick to find a lucrative position in the men's formal wear department at Neiman-Marcus. One of those men who, like Bradley, could be termed fatally gorgeous, Richard Gabrielli met at Neiman's an elderly oil man who died a year later of a heart attack, leaving him a tidy sum of money in his will. Richard returned to Santa Fe and opened a Mexican import shop, keeping the name Gabrielli as a good-luck charm. Richard's shop was the source of the terra-cotta tile that covered the floor of John's new writing studio. Before dining and the opera, Richard was coming by to see what a nice effect the tile lent to the ambience of a writer's space.

"Where's the scandal?" asked Max.

"Everyone thinks he's a crass opportunist. They also say his brain is clogged with semen, and it's nuts to sleep with him because there's no telling where he's been. But to tell you the truth, I don't plan on doing anything. I'm just going to wear him, that's all. Set the tongues wagging, do a little sinister crowd manipulation. That's about all the excitement I can take these days."

When lunch finally arrived, John and Max dug in like two men to whom hunger ranked the most life-threatening disease of the week. As he ate, Max thought about how satisfying it was to live in a place where no one but an adobe contractor was likely to talk about his job over lunch; where if anyone had to have a job, the tendency was to keep it quiet, as if it were akin to having a double agent for a relative.

Max used to have a job back in Washington, D.C. He'd been a lawyer lobbyist for the ASPCA, trying to get legislation passed that would forever take beagles out of the hands of the scientific community. He blamed it on Lyndon Johnson and his twin dogs, Him and Her, that beagles had become a permanent joke of Washington society. When Reagan got elected, he gave up the cause, guessing he'd have better luck winning congressional hearts for canine drug-sniffing squads, the only class of animals for whom he had no sympathy. Save for the rare slip of eating hamburger, and then only if it came from organically raised steers, Max was red-meat free. He had toyed with the idea of joining the New Mexico bar, but so far, after two years in his trailer, he still had too many Russian novels to read to get around to it.

"Where was the love?" John suddenly queried aloud to himself. "Max, there were thrills, but where were our hearts?"

"Must have been a bitch," Max said flatly. "Better luck next time."

Chapter Nine

TUCKED in the back of her vanity drawer, wrapped in tinfoil, and encased in a small cloisonné box was a secret keepsake Cassie McDade Roberson had carried with her from Virginia. The keepsake had been taken from Culpeper to Richmond as an amulet, but in New York it had changed form into something of a magic potion. In actuality it was plain, country dirt, once a heaping tablespoon of it. Over the years, however, it had dwindled down to a scant half teaspoon as it played its role in Cassie's personally conceived fairy tale of her life. Cassie determined that every time she felt badly about the lengths to which she had to go to improve her lot, if she licked the tip of her finger, pressed it to the dirt, and then to the tip of her tongue, like magic she would see why anything she did to keep from going back to it was better than what she'd left. She also believed that the dirt from home was like an hourglass, that when the dirt was gone, leaving her without its magic powers, she would die.

There was something of the hard-core realist in Cassie Roberson; she had the inner knowledge that whatever joy was to be gained from escaping the misery of her childhood, it would be laced with a heaping tablespoon of bitterness. She never once considered that she would live forever. For Cassie, the past was a father whose pleasures in life were whiskey, chewing tobacco, and watching his daughter dress in the morning and undress at night, performances that she let him relish because she felt sorry for him. He had lost a leg as a result of a hunting accident, and there was little for a one-legged man to do for a living in Culpeper, even a once-enterprising man like her father who, forced to abandon his dream of breeding champion quarter horses, spent his day mixing and selling house paint at the local hardware store.

Her mother was the cashier at a trucker's diner just north of Rixeyville—a safe enough distance from Culpeper, she thought, to keep her hometown from talking about why it was that so many teamsters paid her with a twenty and told her to keep the change. Cassie knew about her mother's moonlighting. The woman had told her all about it when she took her to Richmond to shop for a dress that they were both determined would make Cassie the hit of the senior dance. On the road her mother told her that the best things in life come to smart women who have taught their faces to radiate the message that was embossed on throwaway bottles: "No Deposit, No Return." The tragedy of her mother, Cassie realized, was that she saw a winner's circle in the cashier's stool on which she pocketed the chicken feed handed her by the ugly, insignificant lugs who'd had their way with her in the parking lot.

There were numerous dips of the fingertip into the magic Culpeper dirt before Cassie McDade became the property of BJ Roberson. A full quarter teaspoon's worth had measured her embarrassment over having been made to clip and shave all but a heart-shaped tuft of pubic hair in front of a phone company executive who promised her a weekend with unlimited room service at the Sherry-Netherland. Then there was her full-teaspoon boss at the Sharpee Harmonium Company. Wanting to fuck the city that had killed his wife (a rape-murder victim), he'd insisted on taking Cassie from behind in his eighteenth-floor office while her arms flailed in the night air, her upper body being dangled over a window ledge.

It was after the Sharpee Harmonium Company that she was determined to get to Wall Street where she hoped that men let out whatever beastly steam they had on the floor of the Stock Exchange. Did anyone wonder why learning upon their betrothal of BJ's homosexuality had made her laugh at her remaining dirt as though she had seen an evil spirit take flight? She was a bride confident that though die one day she must, she had escaped the danger of dying young. All she had to do to earn a keep that seemed extravagant even by her optimistic standards was to bear a child and occasionally act the loving wife; this was, for Cassie, the stuff of dreams. Her marriage to BJ Roberson transformed her life into a game of guessing what it was that would make the dirt keep disappearing, the hourglass keep running. "Hammerblows and pinpricks," she once reported to Bradley after BJ had physically taken a bow from their lives. "Damn if they don't amount to the same fucking thing. Pain is pain. You know what I mean?"

The human memory is tricky. The same kind of scene on Eighty-sixth Street that had sent his mother, finger ready, bolting upstairs to her vanity drawer, soothed Bradley in its recall on Camino Sin Nombre. It was the kind of repetitive scene that made the photograph of her dead husband the only item from the dining room that Cassie knew she'd never miss.

"So, my boy," said BJ Roberson, presiding over the family meal for nearly the last rare time. (The monster in his stomach had grown large enough that his doctor threatened surgery; a week later he left his family for good.) "I suppose school was consumed with distress over the Kent State massacre. Do you know what I'm referring to, Cassie? Please interrupt if you don't."

"Of course I know," said Cassie. "I know what's going on in this miserable country."

"Well, I'm happy about that. Everyone should."

"We had a discussion in French class," said Bradley, thirteen years old and anxious to express a mature opinion to his father. "About Voltaire. About the flower child as Candide and how Kent State will make everybody reach the same conclusion that he did in the end."

"Fill your mother in on Candide's conclusion, Bradley."

" '*Il faut cultiver notre jardin,*' " said Bradley.

"Translation, please," said BJ, taking a sip of wine.

" 'We must tend to our garden.' In other words, let's be real. The world is a mess, so we might as well just stick to our own business," said Bradley, lifting his own wineglass to his lips.

"Is that what you decided in class today, Bradley? Forget ideals? Stick to what's practical?" asked BJ.

"If you want to save your own skin, I guess. I don't know. It's so depressing."

"Say it again. In French. Would you, Bradley?" asked Cassie.

" '*Il faut cultiver notre jardin.*' "

"What's so depressing about that? It sounds so lovely. French is such a pretty language," Cassie said.

"Jesus Christ, Cassie. It isn't French we're talking about. It's the fucking world. Jesus, are you hopeless," Bradley snapped.

"That's enough," his father said to him calmly. "Let us remember the rules of the dining room. The dining room is where we are civil. I don't care what your psychiatrist says about expressing your feelings. As far as the dining room is concerned, tantrums are for the world outside."

"It's just so stupid that college kids are getting killed, and she's talking about the beauty of French."

"We discuss those things that we are equipped to discuss," said BJ. "Your mother learned to type in school. She did not learn French philosophy as it relates to the conditions of the modern world. She might learn something from you, you know, if you weren't so quick to criticize."

"Well, why don't you buy her an education? You buy her everything else."

"That's enough. Let's change the subject. Cassie, darling, what would you like to talk about this evening?"

"Nothing. I'll just sit here and listen."

"Well, honey, what are you reading? I know you're reading something. I gave it to you."

"*Madame Bovary,*" said Cassie quietly.

"Are you liking it?"

"Yes."

"And does this maybe explain your recent fondness for French?"

"Yes."

"Well, there you are, Bradley. You just didn't give your mother a chance."

Generous. That is how Bradley perceived his father's patience with his mother then, and that is how he perceived it over fifteen years later, his father that long dead and gone. But there had been a time, a very long time, when *generous* was a word Bradley had used to describe his mother's musings over her freshly departed husband.

"Don't scream about him, Bradley," she'd said. "He gave us the best he could, didn't he? He did the best he could at living a deception. Wasn't it good of him to make that man of his suffer his pain with him instead of us? I'm glad he didn't want a funeral. Darling, he spared us a lot of unpleasantness." Another dining room scene, a scene of shattered china, shattered crystal, and a shattered Lalique cameo vase.

"Fuck you," cried Bradley. "He gave us nothing. He gave us a sucky imitation of a human being. He treated you like shit, and he treated me like a fucking piece of glass. Do you want to know why he didn't die of a heart attack? Because he spat his heart out before he married you. Maybe even before you were born!"

"He didn't spit his heart out, Bradley," Cassie had insisted when he had quieted down and focused on the mess of glass he had created. "It was there, but it was broken. Smashed into sharp little pieces. That's why he was so cutting, Bradley. Always I tried to tell myself that I should feel sorry for him. Wasn't it too bad for him that he lost his love? That man, you know, who got married and dropped him, that man whose name he used. It was so hard to keep that in the front of my mind; it was so hard not to hate him. I surely hated him most of the time, but he tiptoed out of our lives so quietly that I think he finally learned to be considerate of our feelings. So now I don't hate him. He left me you, and he left this handsome house for us. So I can be considerate right back to him. I can thank him instead of carrying hatred in my bones. Can't you find it in your heart to do the same?"

"Not on your life," Bradley had replied to his mother's challenge. "I'm not as shallow as you are. You have your things, don't you, Mother? You can wear whatever dress you want whenever you goddamn please now that he's gone, can't you? Boy, you must be happy as a clam. You finally got the answer to your prayers—luxury with no strings attached. Too bad I'm not as lucky as you. I really do wish I could celebrate his death by wearing an orange tie to the Four Seasons, Cassie, but it wouldn't mean a fucking thing to me."

When BJ Roberson left home to die in the Village as Michael Neumeier, Bradley viewed him as a banker who had viciously foreclosed on a petty loan. Now, sitting in his Santa Fe dining room, Bradley missed him. As Cassie had done so many years ago, he rationalized his father's negligence and hostility, ascribing it not to a broken heart, however, but to Cassie's persistence as a target for abuse. Bradley eventually forgave his father for abandoning them, but for Cassie, for an outlook on life that could forgive so easily, he had nothing but contempt.

Had the garden he was fashioning on Camino Sin Nombre sparked the memory of Kent State, Candide, and the dining room? Or had the memory, while inching up from the bottom of the trash heap inside of him, sparked his desire to fashion a garden? He didn't know. All Bradley knew was that he found himself, at the age of twenty-eight, missing his father from where he sat in Santa Fe, New Mexico. More painful, he missed John Aaron, who was across town hating him. It occurred to Bradley that if he sat in the same spot for another fifteen years, he might come to miss his mother too.

Chapter Ten

OF what Richard Gabrielli told John Aaron, this much was true: Richard had indeed seen Bradley Roberson III at the Bishop's Lodge pool. However, the rest of what John had learned from Richard was not true. Bradley had not asked Richard out to dinner. The opposite was true: Richard had asked him. Bradley used to come to ¡Viva Mexico! and order items for his house. Richard had expected him to come back a few more times than he actually did, because the few things Bradley purchased hardly amounted to the completion of a Mexican design statement—that is, unless Bradley was living in a one-room shack, which Richard thought unlikely. He had thought of phoning Bradley once or twice, having kept his number in his file of valued customers, but it went against his grain to operate that way. He preferred to be on the receiving end of phone calls like that, like the one he'd gotten from John Aaron inviting him to the opera.

Even at the pool it had been hard for Richard to swallow enough of his conceit to ask Bradley Roberson out, but he was no longer satisfied with restricting to mere fantasy the idea of parading Santa Fe's most coveted prize before a bevy of tortured faces. Though Bradley had displayed no evidence of interest beyond flashing a smile open to anyone's misinterpretation, Richard Gabrielli delivered his invitation as though its acceptance was a foregone conclusion. Thus it had hit Richard like a boulder when, with that same deceptive smile that painted him as everyone's happy prince, Bradley not only turned him down but requested him to move to the side because he was blocking his sun.

To add even more insult to injury, when Richard returned to his chaise in a stew, he discovered that Bradley had become engaged in conversation with a man who had to be nearing fifty and whose only distinguishing feature beyond his sagging pectorals was a white stripe that looked to be applied to the left side of his crown with a spray can. It was the white stripe that the man and Bradley were discussing. Inquisitive Bradley was informed that the stripe had resulted from a teenage bout with rheumatic fever and had forever dashed hopes of scoring a date with Ponca City's Miss Oil Gusher of 1953. The white-striped man lived in Tulsa now, and he laughed off as ridiculous Bradley's guess that he was a graduate of Oral Roberts U. In Santa Fe for the opera season, he asked Bradley if he would see him at the premiere. When Bradley replied that he didn't have a ticket, he was promptly asked if he would accept one from a stranger.

"When is it?" Bradley asked, and then yawned and stretched his body like a sun-drugged cat. In two days, he was told. "Well, call me then," said Bradley, "and I'll let you know." He wrote his phone number on the cover of the gentleman's copy of the *National Review* and excused himself, saying he had to meet a friend in the bar. "An old Indian," he added, "who only summers in the best places." Bradley then slipped on his white drawstring pants and a feather-light tunic that he'd bought in Greece; packed up his tanning oil, cigarettes, wallet, and dogeared copy of *Querelle* in a mini-backpack, and headed into the lodge. Did he think to wave good-bye to Richard Gabrielli? He did not. He didn't like him; he'd never liked anyone who attempted to trim off his roots by changing his name.

The bartender on the Bishop's Lodge day shift was a woman pianist who liked her new regular enough to play for him at the bar's upright piano when he was her only customer, which, because he usually showed up at an hour when guests were shopping, sight-seeing, trail-riding, or playing tennis, Bradley tended to be. She had so far failed to get him to make good on his one-time promise to play her a Chopin waltz; he insisted that her own mastery of the composer put his to shame. They played "Chopsticks" together once, and one afternoon Bradley played accompaniment to the bartender's singing of a Kurt Weill medley, which she wrapped up by belting in her best Bobby Darin voice, "Look out, Bradley's back." This earned her a warning from the manager, who had been stalking the hallway at the time.

"What do you think our good friend Sam thinks about the Santa Fe Opera?" Bradley asked the bartender as she handed him his usual Wild Turkey on the rocks.

"You'll have to ask him," she said. "I've never heard him say a word on the subject."

"So what do you think, Sam?" Bradley asked, tipping his glass in the direction of the wooden Indian who sat in a permanent daze a few yards away from the bar.

After some moments of pause the bartender asked

Bradley if Sam had anything to say. "He says he wants to smoke on the question," said Bradley. He went over to Sam's table and stuck a cigarette in the Indian's mouth. Then he went back to the bar and said, "He wishes they'd do some Wagner, but he admits that Wagner might shatter the sand hills, as though they were made of fine crystal."

"Are you going to the opening?" asked the bartender, herself nursing a Perrier as she leaned on her elbows and wondered how close Bradley was coming to getting skin cancer.

"I don't know. I've been invited. But the crowd, you know. I don't know if I want to deal with the crowd. It's been ages since I've had to mix with the masses. Although I hear it's lovely, so maybe I shouldn't miss it."

"I love the opera," said the bartender. "There's something almost biblical about the setting, in a Cecil B. DeMille sort of way. I've never witnessed a more rousing sunset as I have out there, with the colors fluttering to the overture of *The Barber of Seville*."

"Nature in Sensorama. Is that what you're saying?"

"I suppose."

"Are you going?"

"Later in the season. Standing room. I have season tickets to the Chamber Music Festival, though. I always buy the poster. God, I love Georgia O'Keeffe."

"She was fabulous," said Bradley. "Did you ever wonder what you'd look like if you got to be that old? God, she was a fantastic-looking old woman."

"I doubt I'll make it that far," said the bartender. "I doubt any of us will. Don't you think the bomb will fall before the end of the century?"

"History teaches us that the brink of total annihilation is as close as we'll come," instructed Bradley Roberson III. "We haven't managed to change any other patterns, so what makes you think we'll change that one?"

"We never had these weapons before."

"Oh, fuck the weapons. They're just sophisticated accessories for men who like to play with G.I. Joe dolls."

"But they're not made of plastic, Bradley."

"Oh? And how do you know? Maybe that's the biggest hoax of all."

"It's because men are ruling the world, you know. If there were more women in politics, there'd be more harmony. Governments are so yang."

"Do you agree with her, Sam?" asked Bradley. "Does she speak to your Indian experience?" He paused. "Sam wonders if you've ever spoken to Margaret Thatcher."

"Why are you making fun of me?" asked the bartender.

"I'm not making fun. I was talking to Sam. He has the wisdom of the ages in him. He speaks right to the soul of man—and woman."

"God help us."

"That's just what he's saying," said Bradley. "God help you, just like he helped the Indian, who understood all about harmony."

"Christ, are you cynical."

"What's that, Sam?" asked Bradley.

"Oh, stop it," said the bartender.

"Sam says I should stop giving you such a hard time. He says I'm ruining his chances of taking you home when you get off work."

"This *is* his home. Who the fuck knows why?"

"Darling, he owns the place, or at least he thinks he does. He lives hopelessly in the past, you know. It's a symptom of throwing in the towel to a higher power, living in the past. When you're still in the game, you spin your wheels, but you maintain the illusion of going forward, otherwise known as progress."

"Want another drink?"

"Need you even ask?"

Bradley drank and smoked quietly for a while, until the

bartender overheard him mutter "the opera" to himself and was moved to start lobbying for his attendance again. "I think you should go," she said. "It might work on you a little bit, music lover. All that musical grandeur under the stars might just make you understand that harmony can be a bigger thing than power, Bradley."

"Well, maybe. I suppose there's something to be said for trying anything once. But if I go, don't expect me to come in here floating along on a cloud of spiritual bliss. I've seen opera before. I've seen stars before. And right now, in my mind's eye, I can imagine them together. Do you know what this vision is saying to me?"

"What?"

"Tell her, Sam."

"Shit," said the bartender.

"It says, 'What next?' "

On opera opening day, Stevie Valdez pushed open the gate of Bradley's coyote fence and peered into a world that never failed to dazzle his eyes with its magic color scheme. He carried with him a few pieces of corn bread left over from lunch with his mother and Aunt Janet, who'd discussed the number of costumes to be repaired by September for the Fiesta. Stevie's father was going to ride a horse as DeVargas this year, and his mother was going to ride on a float with other women dressed lushly in Spanish lace. Although it was only the end of June, Stevie wanted to make sure that Bradley was not going to miss the pageant in which his parents were to play such starring roles. His mother had bragged to her sister at lunch that Stevie had learned to play "Twinkle, Twinkle Little Star" on their neighbor's piano, that their neighbor had said that Stevie learned fast, and that maybe this was a sign that he had some talent. Sylvia was hoping that Robert would agree with her that they should buy a piano and that Stevie should take lessons from a proper teacher when the school year started.

"Am I ever going to meet this handsome neighbor of yours?" Stevie's aunt asked Sylvia.

"Maybe," Sylvia replied. "He comes over here sometimes and helps Stevie with his basketball. But only when Robert is out of town, you know. Robert doesn't like him. I told you what Bradley is. Robert worries about his influence, but he's been here three months, and I don't see anything wrong. *Ee.* He keeps to himself so much, that's all. At night his car is almost always there. No one else's. He says he reads books, writes letters, plays his piano. It's not healthy to spend all that time alone, you know. But a bad influence? I don't think so. He is so nice to Stevie, which is more than I can say for his brother. A terror, that one. He continues to break my heart."

As he did half the time when he came to check on Bradley, Stevie found him sleeping. Bradley was lying in a skinny red bikini on the chaise set out on the garden's small patch of thick green grass. The terra-cotta-tile path Bradley had laid between the flower beds was still stained dark in places, so Stevie knew that Bradley had been watering, although the grass was already dry. Approaching Bradley, Stevie was impressed. His gringo friend had skin shades darker than his own; glistening with sweat and suntan lotion, he seemed as magical as the garden in which he lay. Stevie watched and saw Bradley's lips begin to move. "It's broken. I can't fix it," Bradley mumbled.

"What, Bradley? What's broken?" asked Stevie.

Bradley sat up with a start, popping open blue eyes shaped—like Cassie's—like semicircles, straight across the bottom. "Oh, Jesus," he said.

"What's broken?" Stevie asked again.

"I don't know, kiddo."

"You said something was broken."

"Did I? I guess I was dreaming. If anything was broken, it fixed itself and flew away."

"My mom's heart is broken," said Stevie.

"Why?"

"I don't know. She says it's my brother."

"Ah, yes. The brother . . . Is that bread for me?"

"Yup."

"You're all sweetness, Stevie. You know that?"

Stevie shrugged his shoulders, and the image of his T-shirt of a rock star already out of favor made a little bounce.

"Are you going to be here for the Fiesta?" he asked.

"You mean, in September?"

"Uh-huh."

"God, Stevie. I don't have any idea. I doubt it."

"Are you going away?"

"I don't know. Maybe I'll be here. Maybe not here. I tend to travel in the fall. I don't know why. It's just my way."

"Have you been a lot of places?"

"Many, many places."

"Russia?"

"No. Never there."

"Mexico?"

"Once. No, twice. There are a lot of places by the water. Sometimes I get them confused."

"Someday we're going to Mexico to see the shrine of Guadalupe. My mom says so. Have you been to that shrine?"

"No. I've been to the Mayan ruins, though. The big temples."

"I don't know those."

"Well, you will. You should. They were there before the shrine."

"Can we play basketball today? My dad's in Albuquerque," said Stevie.

"I don't know, kiddo. We'll see how things go after I get moving here a little bit. I have some things to do today."

"Like what?"

"What time is it?" Bradley asked.

"After lunch."

"There's one thing. I have to make myself some lunch."

"We just finished lunch," said Stevie. "We have my aunt. She's going to take my grandfather to the doctor's for his legs."

"What's wrong with his legs?"

"They hurt him at night. They wake him up and he has to walk around. My mom thinks it's from too much sitting, but my aunt thinks maybe his heart is pumping too slow. She's worried it will stop."

"And what do you think?" asked Bradley.

Stevie shrugged. "My dad's going to be DeVargas in the Fiesta," he said. "He's going to ride a horse."

"That's terrific."

"My mom's going to wear a red lace dress and a black mantilla and throw flowers from the back of a pickup truck."

"Sounds like I shouldn't miss it. Listen, buddy, I have to get my day going here. Promise me you won't be hurt if I send you away?"

Stevie nodded, but his dark eyes looked sad.

"Basketball. At four o'clock," said Bradley. "Promise."

And Stevie smiled.

After Stevie was gone, Bradley sat awhile and stared at his feet pressed against the grass, at the hairs growing out of them, and at his uneven toenails, which needed attention. Then he recalled his dream.

It had begun at an outdoor party in a field in Little Tesuque Canyon, a place of rambling Santa Fe ranches, tall grasses, and horses. Bradley had actually been entertained at a birthday party in one of the homes there, in a house with huge rooms and art on the walls three paintings deep. There were works by the likes of Picasso, Ernst, and de Kooning that had made him recall Peggy

Guggenheim's Venice retreat. But in the dream the party was at a simple picnic table set out among the horses and trees beside a tiny creek. It wasn't clear whom the party was for. John was there, and the man with the white stripe whom he had met by the pool. Indian Sam was there too; he sat at the end of a bench, beside some faceless person. There were a lot of faceless people at the party in the dream, and Bradley became very bored and told John that he wanted to leave. That would be fine, John indicated, but he was staying because he was having such a marvelous time. Bradley left the party angry, and thinking to take a shortcut out of the canyon, he turned on foot off the road and headed through the fields toward the canyon wall, a sheer vertical edifice perhaps a hundred feet tall.

It began to snow very hard, and the snow deepened against the canyon wall, which Bradley struggled to climb. Knee-deep in snow, hands groping for something to hold on to, he crawled slowly up the wall, half blinded by the snowflakes that hit his face. He reached the top, finally, and then found himself in his own dining room opposite Cassie, who stared at him as he shook a pocket watch by his ear, trying to make it tick. "It's broken," he said. "I can't fix it." The party had been for him, and the watch had been his present.

"What a lazy asshole," Bradley mumbled to himself as he rose from the chaise to take a shower. With a pima cotton towel wrapped around his waist he was fixing himself a bologna sandwich with Dijon mustard and strawberry jam when the phone rang.

"Is this Bradley?" asked an unknown male voice.

"Mm. Who's this?"

"Um. You don't know me. My name is Steve."

"You're right. I don't know you. How do you know me?"

"I don't. But I'd like to. Maybe. I found your number, so I thought I'd, you know, check it out."

"You *found* my number? Nobody *finds* my number. I'm unlisted."

"You mean you didn't—"

"Who gave you my number?" Bradley snapped.

"It's on the wall . . . in the men's room. I'm at La Fonda. You mean, you didn't put it there?"

"Oh, God," said Bradley, hanging up the phone. It rang again a few moments later. Bradley gave up on eating his sandwich and poured himself a bourbon. The ringing persisted, and in a fit, Bradley grabbed the receiver and shouted into it, "Leave me the fuck alone!"

"I'm sorry if I got you at a bad moment," said the voice, which Bradley vaguely recalled having heard somewhere.

"Who *is* this?"

"It's Paul. Paul Barnett. The Bishop's Lodge pool. Remember?"

"Oh, *Paul*. From Tulsa, right?"

"You got it. Were you in the middle of an argument or something?"

"No. I'm fine. Sorry for screaming," said Bradley, "but I just got off the phone with some creature who found my phone number written on a men's room wall. Can you believe that? First, that some asshole put it there. Second, that somebody is that desperate for company that he actually calls a number he read while taking a shit. God, it's so city. Isn't this supposed to be a small town?"

"A cosmopolitan small town, my friend. I'm calling about the opera tonight," said Paul.

"Oh, God," said Bradley.

"What's the matter?"

"I forgot. We made a date, didn't we? Or did we?"

"We left it up in the air. I suppose you have other plans by now?"

"Oh, no. No plans. It's just that I haven't really thought

about it, about whether I really ought to go or not. There are some people that I've managed to avoid over the past few weeks, and I don't know if I feel up to dealing with them. God, I just don't know where my head is these days. No offense, Paul."

"So you're not going with me?"

"I don't know," said Bradley. "What time is it?"

"It starts at nine."

"I mean, what time is it now?"

"About one-thirty. What on earth does *that* have to do with anything?" asked Paul.

"Well, it helps me to plan, knowing what time it is. Doesn't it help you?"

"I always know what time it is. I wear a watch. Are you okay? Are you on something?"

"No. But I wouldn't mind a Quaalude if you've got any. Kidding, of course. No, it's just the sun, I guess. I'd love to go to the opera with you—that is, if you'll still have me. It has just occurred to me that I've been spending too much time with myself, and as you'll find out tonight, I'm pretty lousy company. I need a jolt. I need to get back on track here," said Bradley, who then finished off his bourbon.

"Well, I don't know if Puccini is very jolting," said Paul, "but it should be a lovely time. You're having dinner with me, of course."

"Oh, of course. Where? What time?"

"The lodge is the easiest place, I guess. Meet you at the bar at, what, six-thirty?"

"Fine. I'll be there. In white. No chance that we'll clash."

"*Me* clash with *you*? Ridiculous. Next to you, everyone just disappears," said Paul.

"You're angry," said Bradley.

"No. I'm serious. And I'll see you. Six-thirty sharp. Buy yourself a watch this afternoon."

Bradley was hungry again when he got off the phone, so he took a few pieces of bologna out of the package and stuffed them in his mouth before repairing to the bathroom to clip his toenails. So he was going to the opera, he mused; they all would be there. With every snip of clippers he counted up the faces he would have to see. John he would have to avoid completely, he supposed. Perhaps he should call Marissa and ask her to stand in front of him all evening to block him from John's view. But he knew it was an impractical request. The question was: Could he bear up under John's heavy look of disdain? Well, maybe he wouldn't go; there was plenty of time to change his mind.

He pulled on a pair of white safari shorts and a pale yellow Calvin Klein undershirt after removing these items from the dry cleaner's plastic wrapping. Around his bare neck he loosely knotted a thin, mint-green tie, hand-painted with postmodern dots, squiggles, and dashes, all balanced to look perfectly random. Sneakers and a pale gray jacket of lightweight linen completed the look, which, to anyone who saw him as he braved the La Fonda lobby and men's room, would say that he was taking the summer completely in stride. Again he wondered what time it was and hoped he would be back by four o'clock to make good on his promise to play basketball with little Stevie. As he stood before the bathroom mirror he was suddenly amazed at how life's little tasks could fill up one's day.

Meanwhile Hank the Indian rested from his rounds over a cup of coffee and a bowl of green chile stew at the Cantina, a dingy place with no handsome waiters, its scratched tables wiped haphazardly with gray, stringy rags that left a film. The Cantina had cheap Mexican food, American sandwiches, and no imported brews. Along with its downtrodden, mostly brown-skinned clientele were 1960s leave-behinds who ate there in open protest of Santa Fe chic. Unluckily for them, the Cantina had lately become an "in" spot for nursing hangovers; just by being there you were punishing yourself for having one. But the hangover-nursing hour was over by the time Bradley Roberson III walked into the Cantina for a beer.

After stopping traffic in the La Fonda lobby, he had done a job on the graffiti in the men's room stall with Magic Marker, covering not only his name but everyone else's as well, in a fit of public service. That he couldn't recognize the handwriting that had signed him "Bradley, Desperate for Love" had made his palms sweat. Hoping to assuage his queaziness by buying something, he went to Daddy's Closet to select a new tie to complete the quiet look he planned for the opera. He picked one of white silk striped with sherbet colors.

It was close to half a mile from Daddy's Closet to his car. (That parking around the Plaza was always impossible in the summer was the major argument put forth in support of a three-story parking garage.) Thus a beer was in order to break up the walk. He chose the Cantina as a safety zone uninhabited by familiar faces, and it gave him perverse pleasure to think that if one of these faces should spot him walking in, the news would be spread as something scandalous. Scandalous his entrance was, the regulars finding him in his sparkling summer outfit a reprehensible invasion on a lineup of clothing against which an army boot-camp uniform would seem crisp.

Instantly a target of the winos' ridicule, Bradley turned to leave; then he caught the eye of Hank the Indian, a character who had floated through some of his dreams in a variety of poses and costumes. The last time Bradley dreamed about him, he was in a tuxedo having dinner with Cassie at Le Cirque in New York. Once Hank had appeared as a harlequin at the Carnevale in Venice. So Bradley tuned out the wolf whistles and shouts of "*Maricón*" to take advantage of the chance to observe this figure in the flesh. He sat a few tables away from Hank, faced him in his chair, and became preoccupied with the manner with which the Indian was going at his chile. Hank inhaled the stewed peppers and swallowed them like one might swallow whole eels. It so transfixed Bradley that he sucked on his bottle of beer like a baby. Then a derelict walked up to him and broke his trance. "Hey, *maricón*," he hissed. "How much to suck your dick?"

Bradley jerked his head to meet the eyes of this Untouchable, who looked like he'd just crawled out of an oil spill. How old was the person inside this creature? Perhaps thirty, Bradley guessed. Thirty and capable of murder. He clung to his old credo that arrogance was the best defense in any circumstance.

"You're spoiling my beer. Could you please go away?" he said.

"Eh, man. Got any change?" asked the wino, whose look of meanness melted into the gaze of the merely pathetic.

"Jesus," said Bradley. "Why didn't you just ask for money in the first place?" He handed over a dollar, then commanded him to leave his presence. The drunk walked back to his pals and showed them his dollar. "Says he'll see you out back," one of them called to Bradley. The winos hooted at Bradley's prettiness and at his cowardly charity. Dazed, Bradley stood to escape. Hank the Indian gave him a wink, wondering if such characters blotted themselves with silk napkins after taking a pee. Soon Hank took his leave, his necklaces dangling at his side, whispering to himself, "This place is getting very strange."

Bradley walked through streets choked with the cars and bodies of visitors to The City Different, Santa Fe, New Mexico, the Tricultural Crossroads of the Southwest. The air around the Plaza felt hotter than its ninety-three degrees. It was said that dry desert heat was easier to take than the muggy heat of the coasts and the plains, but Bradley Roberson was not a bit convinced of this in his sweat-soaked linen jacket and with his cologne losing out to the smells that tailed him from the Cantina. Sitting down in the Cantina had been a horrible mistake. Clearly he was being made to pay his dues for solitude. Even his feet were conspiring against him; getting to his car was taking an eternity.

Some miles from the Plaza, gas stations and other businesses lined a long stretch of Santa Fe highway relegated to serving the basic needs of a small city population. Tourists and some Historic East Side residents were prone to refer to the stretch as "out of town." Here were discount drug and department stores, fast-food restaurants, supermarkets, and lumber yards. Here, too, was sixteen-year-old Robby Valdez making a beer run with his girlfriend, Brenda Sandoval, whose shape gave credence to the falsified ID that said she was twenty-one.

Beer primed Robby's system for a session of yelling obscenities at unsuspecting tourists in the Plaza. On his way there Robby spotted his neighbor, Bradley Roberson III, heading for his BMW—Bradley who stood for everything Robby despised.

The white BMW with the sunroof was the first thing that had clinched Robby Valdez's feelings for his neighbor, even before he met up with him in his own driveway the afternoon he'd earned a *D* as his final grade in English. There he was—the neighbor with the beautiful flower garden, the neighbor who read poetry and pissed Perrier water—sinking a hook shot into *his* basketball hoop and landing on sneakered feet that had probably been born wearing ballet shoes. And then he saw his neighbor actually touch his little brother. More than touch. Bradley had stood behind Stevie, his legs spread, Stevie's legs spread, his neighbor's arms wrapped around Stevie under the guise of helping him aim an underhand free throw. Robby wasn't sure, but he thought what he had witnessed was just possibly a crime punishable by a mandatory life sentence.

Unable to contain himself, Robby leapt out of his Chevy from where it sat out on the street, ran, and busted up the game. After missing his own wild attempt at a hook shot, he slammed the ball into his neighbor's chest. "Are you challenging me to a game of one-on-one?" his neighbor had asked coolly. Robby had spit an affirmative reply. And after Bradley had accumulated four points to his two, Robby hurled the basketball into Camino Sin Nombre, ordered Stevie to fetch it, and in a murderous hiss said to his neighbor, "Get out of here, you motherfucker. You touch my little brother again and I'll cut your fucking balls off."

At this, Bradley took his own turn to spit. "I can see why you're your mother's pride and joy. Your brother needs help with his aim, asshole," he said, and with that he took his leave.

Inside, Robby complained to his parents about Bradley, hoping to rouse their concern and soften the blow of his *D* in English. But he had only to mention his neighbor's name and his mother glared with a fierceness that silenced any objections his father might use against him. "So play basketball with your brother yourself this summer, big shot—that is, when you aren't in school taking English all over again," was all his father said.

"So we like the faggots now," Robby had challenged. "Are they good for the economy, *señor*?" For this he was slapped across the face and sent to his room. He was never told that later, in the privacy of his parents' bedroom, a law was handed down that contact sports were forbidden between Stevie and their neighbor. In actuality, his father would have liked to put a stop to all visits, but the coldness that would have greeted such an edict would have been too much for him to bear.

Responding to Sylvia's contention that their neighbor was a lonely man whom Stevie cheered, Robert Valdez had once braved a look as sharp as an ice pick and said that if queers had been put on reservations instead of the Indians, they would have died out as a breed and their loneliness would not be anybody's problem. As it was, he'd said, catering to their neighbor's loneliness was not his wife and child's priority. A week of powerlessness against the TV's remote control that Sylvia wielded like a weapon in bed had made Robert retract his remarks and vow to try to be more tolerant of a man who paid his taxes just like everybody else.

Perhaps as he leered from his car at his neighbor, who stood awaiting a safe moment to cross over to his parking space, Robby sensed it was not just for himself that he was about to take revenge.

"Watch this," he said to Brenda.

Laughing, Robby gunned his engine when Bradley reached his car. Whizzing by to swerve within a few inches of his neighbor, he saw with glee Bradley's forehead bump hard against the BMW roof as Bradley threw himself into safety.

"That guy's sure cute," said Brenda after Robby turned the corner. "Why'd you scare him like that, you crazy shit?"

"Because he's a faggot," said Robby. "I hate faggots." He yelled this proclamation into the crowd of tourists milling in front of the Indian jewelry peddlers under the portal of the Palace of the Governors on the Plaza. In front of the Polo boutique on San Francisco Street, he yelled, "I hate you fucking preppies, man," and was stopped by the police. When his license was checked and the connection made that he was the son of Robert Valdez of the New Mexico Economic Opportunity Commission, Robby was told to watch his mouth and not bother the tourists.

Chapter Eleven

WHEN John Aaron was a young man learning the ropes of the real estate business and prone to fervent optimism over half-baked deals, his father kept him in check with the adage, "The opera isn't over until the fat lady sings." The expression struck just the right note in John; it depressed him. Unlike his father, John was moved by opera, and he knew it was usually that when the fat lady sang, someone was destined never to sing again, and this person was usually the fat lady. The image of a land purchase personified as, say, Leontyne Price as Carmen, or Joan Sutherland as Tosca hitting the stage floor, her weight crushing the audience's surrendered hearts, which were nestled in the folds of her dress, helped to align John with his father's sentiments and view failed negotiations as a tragedy of gothic proportions. Together they would wallow in mourning, temporarily blind to all the opulence garnered from their habitual success.

The soprano who sang Mimi in the Santa Fe production of *La Bohème* was no fat lady. She was thin and, due to the high altitude, so was her voice. Her performance was admirable for its realism; *La Bohème*'s Mimi was tubercular. But for John, she had unanticipated power. After she had sighed her last sigh and coughed her last cough in the arms of her lover, Rodolfo, the soprano's voice still lingered in John's head, convincing him that the opera was hardly over; the tragedy he sensed was that it never would be.

* * *

On the plane from New York to Albuquerque, with the wine flowing freely in first class, John Aaron had told Bradley Roberson III why sex and room service at the St. Moritz had been the perfect antidote to his father's funeral. When he was growing up, he'd said, his father told him tales of the War, about the day when he and the other troops marched in and liberated Bergen-Belsen. John recalled his father's words. " 'I was a Jewish man,' he said. 'I had a five-year-old son, a boy I tried to use to keep the government from sticking me in the army. But I was one of the thousands with the same excuse. I can never forgive them, either, for making me see what I saw. Imagine. A young father. Can you imagine what I felt,' he asked, 'knowing I had brought you into a world like this? That's it, I decided. One mistake. No more children. Not one more human being will I be responsible for, that they might one day have to witness what I witnessed.'

"On and on like this," said John. "On and on about what an unlucky son of a bitch I was to have been born before he'd seen what humanity was like and had the chance to save me from it. Can you imagine this morbid household? The only thing I knew was that I didn't want to be like him. He was such a humorless creature. And do you know what? He thought that by building tacky apartments for the elderly, he was actually something of a saint. He thought there was no greater contribution to mankind than giving it a clean, overpriced place to die.

"He was angry enough to hit me just once. Do you know over what? I flew home from college for spring break. He hadn't seen me since January, and he creamed me across the face when he opened the door for me, because . . . because, why? . . . because I'd gotten a ride from the airport with a friend who drove a Volkswagen. Can you imagine that? A palm print on my cheek for hours because I rode in a German-made car! I walked right out on him and got a room at a motel. I called my mother and told her that if she wanted, I'd meet her for lunch. I could not believe that the hate in this man's heart ran that deep. It scared me to death.

"My mother met me crying, and talked me into coming home, but I didn't speak to my father for the whole vacation. And do you know he hid from me because he was so embarrassed? Now, Bradley, I by no means have a soft spot in my heart for the Germans. And frankly I don't think your statements about Berlin moods are very clever. But for God's sake, I would rather see the Germans building cars than death factories, wouldn't you? I mean, put Valium in their cereal and put them to work.

"But you know, I tried to imagine the horror that he lived with that was so strong, he couldn't erase it from his memory for anything, and I just couldn't conceive of it. That's why I went home after I graduated and started working for him, even though I found the nature of his business so depressing. You know, this man witnessed the worst horror of the century, and I was not going to turn my back on him. I tried to put aside being gay for his sake. I actually thought it was something that . . . well, I knew it wouldn't go away, I mean, I'd fantasized about it for so long. I guess I just thought it was something that would work itself out. I got married. From the beginning it was an open thing: She knew, she said she'd try to deal, because she loved me and I loved her. And I *did* love her. We used to go down to Miami Beach and watch the old Jews, pretending they were all retired stars. We'd watch their gestures and figure out who they were when they were famous. 'If we find Greta Garbo,' we'd say, 'let's take her to lunch.' We were married for three years, and it almost destroyed her. I think we called it quits just in time.

"I decided to put a stop to all of it, the whole fucking

lie. I told my mother first, and she begged me to keep it a secret from my father. She could handle it, she said. She was strong. But after all my father had been through, it was my duty as his son to protect him from more despair. What are you saying, I asked her? Are you saying that my being gay is going to put me in the category of the Nazis? Is that what I'm going to represent to him? That human garbage that ruined him forever for having a good time?

"I ask you, Bradley, how did I know that in saying this I had hit it on the nose, that I would become like Nazi vermin to him? That a faggot son was right there on a par with the horror of Bergen-Belsen? It was fucking nuts. I cleared out, pure and simple.

"I don't even know if I'm sad he's dead. I won't know until it's not new anymore. I'm sad for my mother, but my father lived for death. He did not live for life. Is it horrible to say that he got what he lived for?"

During their brief life together in La Barranca, Bradley's fits of temper and his alcohol-ignited arsenal of insults had worn on John's sanity, but John claimed to his therapist that the reminder of Bradley's inner pain assuaged his own nerves. Bradley's explosions were provoked by rotten memories, John insisted, and they were always followed by a hug, a kiss, even as small a thing as a smile, which signaled that his moment of rage had disappeared.

"You're a terror," John was sometimes moved to tell Bradley after peace was made. "I should give you away to the Indians." Yet only on the day he referred to as "Bradley's Last Stand" did John begin to tally the cumulative damage that six months of Bradley Roberson III had done to him.

It was during his morning shave on the very first day of spring that Bradley reflected on the dinner party he and John had attended the night before. The host had a

Siberian husky that persisted in poking his snout into John's crotch, undeterred by John's angry pushes and cries of "What does this thing want from me?" When the dog was finally let outside, John exclaimed, "Thank God," and confessed to the other guests his fantasy of changing *curb* on CURB YOUR DOG signs to *shoot*.

In the shower, Bradley was gleefully struck with this revelation: "John is not a dog person, and it's my job to make him one." When, after a late breakfast, John left for his business meetings, Bradley went to the animal shelter, and spying a puppy who was part Doberman and part German shepherd, Bradley considered that it was his job to cure John of his hate for dogs and hate for the Germans in one fell swoop. What man who calls himself a human being, he considered, wouldn't melt from the sight of those desperate eyes? He brought the dog home, put out food and water, and then retreated outside to the hot tub in orchestrating the full impact of surprise. Thus Bradley missed out on seeing John drop his grocery bag filled with two prime filets, fresh asparagus (the first of the season), new potatoes, coffee Häagen Dazs, and two bottles of Château Neuf du Pape when he walked in the door.

The puppy had had full run of the house for close to an hour, time that not only substantiated John's conviction that dogs were God's gift to the carpet-cleaning industry, but also convinced him that had the Germans concentrated harder on perfecting their pedigrees, they indeed could have taken all of Europe, if not the world. But it was not the sum total of the destruction that had made John's wits crumble and his anger swell to the point of ordering the pound to send out a SWAT team. It was not this that finally initiated a drive to send Bradley packing and prompted John to cry at the top of his lungs, "How dare you? How dare you bring that Nazi animal in here!"

In his study John had caught the puppy tearing into a

photo album—too late to prevent the gnawing of a picture of his Miami Bar Mitzvah. The animal had sunk its teeth into a photo of John, surrounded by relatives, beaming as he held up a sign that read TODAY I AM A MENSCH. It documented a rare, happy moment of his youth. What truly ripped John's heart to shreds was that the dog had destroyed the only recorded moment of his father smiling from pride—smiling, indeed, from anything.

On Camino Sin Nombre, the shock of John's anger lingering, Bradley called Marissa Goldman and sobbed into the receiver, "Oh, God, Marissa. Tell me. Where the fuck did I learn to be so inconsiderate and cruel?"

Marissa Goldman had no reply because she didn't know.

Chapter Twelve

The Lord made Adam and Eve ashamed of their nakedness and then gave Eve the job of telling Adam how to dress.

—The Bible according to Cassie Roberson, as told to her son, Bradley

CASSIE Roberson could not be termed a religious woman in the traditional sense. Yet, born into a poverty-gray world that was further blackened by her one-legged father's despair, she grew to perceive color—the reds of the Virginia earth and of lipstick, the purples and oranges of sunsets and taffeta—as nothing less than a precious gift from God.

As a little girl, she cherished the holidays (never a time for celebration in the Roberson home) because of their array of hues; she adored Easter for its pastels, Christmas for glorifying primary shades usually condemned as garish, Valentine's Day for tickling her heart pink. Trying to pass on her love of color to Bradley, she told him a secret fact: that the real chosen people were black; they alone understood the rainbow's vibrancy, created to brighten the bleakest of earthly circumstances.

Bradley would come to love his mother's fervor, until the confusing time of his father's death, which seemed to unleash in her a licentious wildness that, though he had predicted it, frightened him nonetheless. How many days had elapsed before the colors whose intensity competed with the hundred-and-fifty-watt bulbs in her closet were paraded down the streets, beckoning the bedazzled like a beacon guiding ships into safe harbor? Cassie hardly knew. The morgue of a house on Eighty-sixth Street had briefly come alive with lust, while, unknown to her, Bradley stood outside her door, absorbing the fireworks that BJ's death had ignited in her spirit. Unable to tolerate her own emptiness, she found herself careening out of control, not realizing that the decibels of her escape only pushed her son away from her. Bradley's own teenage experimentations with sex had brought on only a crescendo of disappointment that turned him against his partners for having failed him; now she was failing him as well.

When the once steady stream of Cassie's takers thinned out as suddenly as it appeared, as if she were a drug deemed out of fashion and abandoned for the more refined and timeless pleasures of a glass of well-aged whiskey, she thought she'd truly crack from loneliness. And the son to whom she now turned in comfort had grown satisfied, somehow, to see her suffer.

"No use being a peacock when men want doves," she

obliviously declared at last, ushering in her "white period." Perhaps it was an accident that she now mimicked the radiant and simple chic that Bradley, at eighteen, had possessively secured as his own social signature. In white, she followed him to his favorite nightspots, deriding the men at the Oak Room, The Four Seasons, and The Pierre as "high on cash but low on fun." Her middle-aged heels were itching to dance, hardly anxious to dig a grave with the occasional executive who found her still attractive. How oddly content she had felt to loom as Bradley's white shadow at the discos. How giddily she served up her charm, watching in amazement as Bradley's rejects were lured into her corner. She longed to share the joke with him when she actually managed to gather up one of his castoffs, but the victorious winks she tossed over her shoulder as she escorted each one to the dance floor seemed only to harden his features into stone.

It was there, under the disco lights, that Cassie blurred before Bradley like an image in a smoky mirror, leaving him entirely alone, choked with the stale smell of her stubbed-out cigarettes, and embittered that her color had faded.

Chapter Thirteen

SYLVIA Valdez washed the cut on Bradley Roberson's forehead and led him to the back corner of her garden where rosebushes grew high and vines crept up over a trellis protecting a white Mexican fountain. Soothing this overgrown boy eased her conscience over her own crazy son.

Bradley could see that he was being taken to a shrine, a very simple shrine, consisting of the fountain and a plaster statue of a madonna with gold stars painted on the pale blue background of her cape.

Sylvia stood before the madonna, set in a niche between two small spotlights, and told Bradley the story of the Virgin who had filled a Mexican peasant's cloak with roses in winter. "She is my saint," Sylvia told Bradley. "She is my saint of roses. They did not grow well until I put her here, you know. You see here?" She motioned her hand around the garden. "My own little miracle. Stevie loves the story. Robby, he will never listen."

Bradley plucked a red rose and placed it in his neighbor's hair. "Our Lady of Camino Sin Nombre," he whispered, and kissed her cheek.

"Go out front and play with Stevie. He's been waiting all day for you."

"Okay, Holy Mother."

"You stop that," said Sylvia Valdez.

As Bradley headed around to the driveway Sylvia stood in place and watched him. "So beautiful," she whispered to herself. She sucked in her breath and shook her head.

Watching Stevie hug the basketball to him like a pet, Bradley saw a reflection of the love that Sylvia held for the Virgin of Guadalupe. By the time Stevie had enough of basketball, Bradley's mood had plummeted with the memory of his day and the thought of how absent were the forces of devotion in his life. By whom was he awed? To what did he aspire? "I'm tired," he said to Stevie. "I have to go home."

Bradley left Stevie's house and waded through the debris of printed matter on his bedroom floor before flopping down on his water bed. He drifted into sleep with thoughts of taking out his trash, and he dreamed he was toppled by a madonna statue that fell from its precarious position atop an overflowing garbage can. As

Bradley lay on the floor under the madonna's weight, Robby Valdez came bounding into his dream and hoisted up the statue, saying, "You stole my mother."

A ringing awakened Bradley as suddenly as he had dropped off. "*Ee.* What the fuck is this, man?" A threatening voice hauled Bradley into consciousness. The caller was referring to the graffiti he'd discovered in a phone booth at the DeVargas Mall. Scrawled there were the words, "Chicano cum makes my eyes water. Telefoname, hombre. Bradley." The caller was not amused. "I dunno where you live," he said, "but if I find out, you better hope your faggot ass is out of town, 'cause I'll fuckin' cut your head off, man. I'll stick it on a pole and march it around the Plaza, man."

What's happening to me? wondered Bradley. "God, whoever you are, it wasn't me. Honest. Honest to God, it wasn't me. Listen, I will pay you anything to find out who the fuck is doing this to me. Believe me . . ." he pleaded, until he realized that the caller had hung up on him.

His hand shaking, Bradley pulled a cigarette out of his box of Shermans, lit it on his third attempt at striking a match, and finally succeeded in calming his lungs. Exhaling, he took a tally of the people in Santa Fe, New Mexico, whom he believed possessed his phone number. He could think of only two: John and Marissa. He dialed the latter, who put the former on hold to take his call.

"Did you give my number out to anybody, Marissa? Think," Bradley demanded. She would never betray a trust, Marissa replied. "Well, then," said Bradley, "why don't you ask your friend on the other line if he has taken up graffiti as a therapeutic hobby."

"John?" exclaimed Marissa. "John Aaron deface public property? I'm not going to ask him that, Bradley. That's the most ridiculous thing I've ever heard."

"Well, then, why don't you ask him if he's paying somebody to terrorize me?" Bradley said.

"Hold on," said Marissa obediently. She clicked Bradley on again a minute later. "I don't know if you want to hear this," she said, "but he says he threw your number out as soon as I gave it to him, Bradley. He said that just looking at it burned him like a tattoo. I don't believe it, of course. I don't believe it for a minute. I'm sure he just tucked it away."

"Jesus Christ," said Bradley. "When is he going to give it up? Ask him that, Marissa. Ask him when the fuck he's going to stop pretending that I'm the reincarnation of Goebbels. For the umpteenth time, I'm sorry about the fucking dog. It was a bad joke, and now it's an old, dead joke. Tell him the whole fucking world is punishing me for my rotten sense of humor. Tell him that, Marissa."

"Later," she said. "The jerk hung up on me. It sent him up a wall that your voices collided in the same receiver. So what's the deal with your phone number, anyway?"

"Only that somebody's writing it all over town. I've just had my life threatened by an Hispanic who found it in a phone booth. Has anyone ever threatened to behead and impale you? I can tell you, Marissa, it is not a treat."

"Well, don't panic, for God's sake. Listen. I'd love to keep talking, but it's after six, and I've got Barry coming down from Taos for the opera. He's due any minute, and I'm in the middle of a flan."

"It's six already?" asked Bradley.

"Seven after," said Marissa.

"Fuck. I'm supposed to meet somebody at six-thirty."

"Oh? Who?"

"A date, believe it or not. I got invited to the opera by a guest at the Bishop's Lodge. I wasn't sure about going, but I think it's probably the safest place I could be tonight, don't you? I mean, considering it's unlikely that anyone would pull a knife on me there. Marissa, this stranger threatened to put my head on public exhibition. Maybe I should pack. Maybe I should just clear out of town."

"God, are you overreacting. Nobody's going to hurt you, Bradley. Take my advice: Take a Valium."

"I don't have a Valium. I ran out a couple of months ago. Oh, God, Marissa. That's what I need. I need a Valium. Or two or three."

"You'll be at the opera?"

"Maybe. I think so."

"I'll bring you some Valium. Three. I don't trust you with more than that because they're the fives. I'm out of the twos. Where should I look for you?"

"Marissa, darling, I think I can manage to find *you.*"

Robby Valdez had his phone number, Bradley decided. Probably he had made Stevie copy it down, threatening to slash Stevie's throat if he didn't. But when? One day when he wasn't paying attention. When was that? he asked himself and had a ready answer: any minute of any hour of any day of the week. That settled it. He was going to the opera, which for locals like Robby, was as likely a hangout as Burma. But what would he do about John? His finger hesitantly dialed as he embarked on a mission of peace. The two rings, the two stabs in the ear, were hardly all Bradley needed to prepare his case, but that was how John was. Not even sex could restrain him from leaping at the phone when it rang. Sex could be taken up again with a partner who was already there, but a missed call meant missed potential.

"Hi," said Bradley meekly. "It's me."

John was pulling a pair of socks out of his bureau drawer. He put them back and picked up another pair. It helped him now to concentrate on socks.

"Don't hang up," continued Bradley. "Please. Oh, please, John, don't hang up."

The cotton argyles might do well with the gray loafers, thought John. But they were a little worn at the heel. "I didn't give out your precious phone number," he said.

"I know that. I'm sorry. I was in such a state. Somebody out there absolutely hates me. Of course, the first person who came to mind was you. Can we possibly have a very, very short, civil conversation?"

"Possibly, but hardly likely."

"Listen. I read six novels by Philip Roth last month. I love Philip Roth. I loved *The Ghost Writer,* that whole thing about Anne Frank. Tell me you really know that just because I have a soft spot for German mutts doesn't make me a Nazi. Tell me I'm an insensitive asshole who lacks the conviction it takes to be anything at all. Tell me anything you want, but get it over with now because I'm going to the opera and I don't want a scene. I want you to have the satisfaction of having said anything you want to say, but say it now, so when you see me later, you can completely ignore me."

"I can ignore you as easily now as later, if that's what you're after. Hang up, Bradley, and consider yourself ignored by me forever," said John.

"I don't want to go to the opera. I'm going by default. I'm not safe here."

"What's the matter? Is your mother coming to visit?" asked John.

"More, John. I can take it. I can take anything."

"No more. I'm in the middle of getting dressed. Good-bye."

"Wait."

"Oh, leave it alone, Bradley. I'm not going to ruin your good time, all right?"

"No. That's not it. I just need to know what time it is."

"Six-thirty."

"Fuck," said Bradley. "I've got to run. Good-bye."

John slammed his sock drawer shut and hurled the

navy pair he'd chosen to the floor. "Never," he screamed to no one. "Never the last word. Three months, six days, three hours, and still he gets the last fucking word!"

Bradley showered, even though he was running so late. He had to shower. He had to shave, to shake the can of mousse, to mold his hair and face into the model of perfection. Grooming himself was a matter of being fitted with a suit of armor, but even after the final touch, the painstaking knotting and smoothing of his brand-new tie, he felt dented all over. One more thrust against him would bring it crashing down, the armor and himself. The phone rang again, and he dashed out the door.

A vision in white, smelling richly of Paco Rabanne pour Homme, Bradley took to the north road with his sunroof open. The wind gently kissed his face above and below his dark aviator shades. He thought of Paul Barnett's white streak, a mark, maybe, of the holy protection of the gods that would rub off on him if he stood close by. Then he thought of Cassie. Well-traveled Cassie, who thrived against all blows and against all odds. "Oh, Cassie," he heard himself mutter, "blow me a kiss so I can go out there and take a bow."

At the bar he made an apologetic entrance, blaming the telephone for making him an hour late. Paul Barnett was understanding. He'd been having a lovely chat with the bartender, he said, and was only thrilled to see him show up at last.

"Shall we sit over there?" Bradley pointed out wooden Indian Sam's table with one hand and directed Paul with the arm he put around his date's shoulder. "Sam is always desperate for company."

"Horrible decor, these Indians," said Paul, following with a slight hesitation. "Don't you find them strange? Cute that you've named him, though."

"Shh," said Bradley. He covered Sam's ears with his hands. "Don't insult him. He's already had a hard day.

Look at him. He's been through the wars." Bradley placed a cigarette in Sam's mouth and lit it before inhaling his bourbon and motioning for another. "Love your suit, Paul. Calvin Klein, isn't it?"

It was, in fact, a Calvin Klein. "You know," Bradley continued, "Calvin has one of the nicest apartments in New York."

"You've been there?"

"Oh, yes," he lied. "Although he's more a friend of my mother's than of mine. He loves dressing her. You know, she was with him at the Helmut Newton opening. She said it was fabulous."

"Oh, really? Who's Helmut Newton?"

"Who's Helmut Newton? Only *the* paparazzo of the rich and famous. My God, are you that cut off from the leading edge of culture in Tulsa?"

"Do you doubt it? Why do you think I'm here?"

"I haven't a clue, Paul. Why don't you tell me?"

Bradley pulled what was left of Indian Sam's cigarette from his mouth, swept the ashes from the table with his cocktail napkin, lit up for Sam again, and then for himself.

"Are you all right?" asked Paul. "You seem very edgy."

Bradley stared toward the bar and did not respond to the wink of the friendly bartender trying to convey the delight she took in seeing him in action. It surprised her to see how the pressure with which he held his empty glass had bleached his knuckles white. She had another drink sent over to him, and when he took it, he faced his date again. Rubbing the sore on his forehead, he apologized for his inattentiveness.

"I was going to ask you about that cut," said Paul.

Bradley only shrugged and said, "I've had a horrible day, but I won't bore you with it. The rule book says that one should charm new acquaintances. How'm I doing on charm, Paul?"

Noting how quickly Bradley emptied his glass again,

Paul gazed at him sympathetically. "If you don't mind my saying so," he said, "I think we should go ahead on in and eat something."

"Excuse us, Sam?" said Bradley, standing up. "You know," he informed Paul, "they don't allow him in the dining room."

Their footsteps echoed in the corridor that led out of the bar. It was a beautiful night that beckoned people out of doors. The wooden Indians were left to hold court over the remnant cadences of regional dialects inside as, out on the patio, Houston met Hollywood, Denver met Detroit, and San Francisco met Salt Lake City. The lodge was booked for the season. "Lord, how the Indians kill the charm of this watering hole," remarked Paul Barnett as he and Bradley walked through the lobby. "Yes," said Bradley, bending to kiss the Indian he called Billy on the cheek. "Don't they, though?"

Bradley ordered tournedos of beef very rare but sent them back when he cut into the cool, bloody center because he couldn't face it. "I can't decide what I want instead," Bradley explained to the waiter. "How about anything breaded? With ketchup on the side." Paul Barnett gagged on his Veal Oscar when he heard this. "Oh, don't mind me, Paul," Bradley observed. "Don't think about me at all. Why don't you tell me what you did today, starting from the second you left your hotel room—unless, of course, your adventures began in there, behind closed doors."

"Don't I wish?" Paul replied. He told of breakfast in the French Pastry Shop on the Plaza that morning, which had placed him at a window table alongside a man whose torso, bare save for an undershirt, was covered with tattoos. The tattoos, Paul said, included symbols of all the world's religions, even voodoo. The illustrated man noticed his admiration and offered him a guided tour of his right arm, a sampler of the world's tongues. In each language was spelled out what the man proclaimed the secret elixir of life. He lifted up his arm and parted his axillary hair to display in English the word *sweat*. "If you don't sweat, you die," the tattooed man said. Somehow, Paul explained, his *pain aux raisins* tasted a little rancid after that.

After breakfast he toured the galleries, finding many of the pricier paintings not all that different from what could be found in Tulsa's lauded Western art collections. The exception, he said, was that modern place near the museum; there he bought a masterpiece in oil of a cactus being penetrated by a cowboy boot and spur. He would hang this painting in his bedroom.

As Paul watched Bradley pour ketchup over breaded trout with crabmeat mousse stuffing, he decided to forgo a description of the red chile enchiladas he'd had for lunch, preferring to sustain them as a fond memory. He mentioned next the miracle church at Chimayo built over some holy, healing dirt into which hopeless cripples tossed their crutches.

"Did you see the graves?" Bradley interrupted, just as Paul was about to leap into a list of items he had purchased at the Nambeware seconds outlet.

"The what?"

"The graves. Before you reach the church, there are some graves behind a barbed-wire fence. The land is very parched; at least it was when I was there. Parched as could be, with dead wild grasses. But the graves have fresh flowers, even the graves with the simple white crosses. Little neat bundles of flowers, some of them, although there were a couple of large wreaths. Tomorrow you should go back up that road and take a graveyard tour. There is life in those graves, in that holy dirt," said Bradley.

"What's so darn holy about dirt?"

"Only its staying power, Paul. It'll be the last thing to

go, long after your precious oil is gone, you know. Somebody should be working on how to harness the energy of dirt."

"I wouldn't have taken you for a religious crazy, Bradley. Not in a million years," said Paul.

"I'm just telling you a fact. Dirt will outlast us, that's all."

"I don't argue with that. It's the holiness shit. I suppose it has something to do with your trip with the wooden Indians."

"Totally unconnected."

"Well, what in hell's going on here?" asked Paul.

"Beats me," said Bradley. "Other than the fact that my thought process is somewhere between sixty and eighty proof by now."

"Is this a habit with you?"

"What?"

"Three bourbons before dinner."

"No. I was a little early on the third. I usually have that *with* my meal. But you're right. Sorry. Can't help myself. Try to have a good time, anyway."

Paul assured Bradley that he was having one hell of a good time. He felt free in Santa Fe, he said. He was actually going to the opera in the company of an extraordinarily handsome man. In Tulsa, he said, under the lights of the Oral Roberts Prayer Tower and the eagle eyes of fellow oil speculators, he kept his tastes quiet and attended all social occasions with a cooperative woman on his arm.

"So why don't you marry one?" asked Bradley.

"Shit. That's crazy," said Paul. "I mean, some things do change over time, at least they do outside of Tulsa."

"Don't try to tell me you're the only Tulsa oilman who's going to the opening of the Santa Fe Opera. . . ." said Bradley. "Not that I'm trying to make you feel paranoid or anything, but aren't you just a little afraid you'll be noticed?"

"What are you, the Grim Reaper? Jesus Christ!" Paul pushed his plate of food away.

Bradley, feeling a twinge of guilt, served up an alibi for Paul to use in the event he crossed paths with the enemy. "When you were in New York a couple of months ago, you took out the widow of an old friend of yours, an adviser in international investments who died tragically at the young age of forty-five. The poor woman hasn't recovered yet, you see," Bradley revealed. "You try to comfort her in any way you can. She has a son—*moi*—who's as gay as a goose and lives here in Santa Fe, New Mexico. When you mentioned to her that you were coming here for the opera, she begged you to look him up and send her a report because she hardly ever hears from the bastard. He only drops a card once in a while and, very rarely, a letter that's so nonsensical that she worries if he's on drugs. Her son is very, very cruel to her, you see, because he thinks she's a mindless floozy who should be reincarnated as a mink coat cuff."

Paul Barnett saw tears well up in Bradley's eyes and, braving to pat his hand in public, told him he got the point. It was a fine alibi, all right, he said—that is, once the embellishments were edited out. "Is your mother really so awful?" he asked.

"No," mumbled Bradley. "She's like the graves in a way. Holy as dirt."

Eighteen hundred and seventy miles and two time zones away, at ten forty-five in New York City, Cassie Roberson and Franklin Petrie were leaving the ballet. They had watched Balanchine stiffly, like the few other couples in the audience who had entered Lincoln Center not on speaking terms—silent for no other reason than that they were bored with one another's company.

Earlier in the day Cassie had hurled Kodak boxes of slides and delicate pieces of Chinese porcelain at Franklin over the matter of his hiring a live-in houseboy from Cambodia whose second language sounded to Cassie like a dolphin's version of English. She hadn't minded Franklin's extended excursions away from her in Beijing, she had argued, but this was different. Not even her husband had paraded his lovers under her nose, to say nothing of putting them on the household payroll. Cassie declared that even Bradley would be able to see that it was all too cruel and get her somebody else. "He promised me royalty once," she cried. "He promised me a bankrupt lord of England. Oh, God, why did he ever give me you?" She had covered her ears to block out the inevitable, oft-repeated answer to her oft-repeated question.

"Because, darling," said Franklin Petrie, interrupting himself to duck a flying ginger jar, "he thinks we're a perfect match. And he enjoys playing God, doesn't he? Why, I bet he's the burning bush of Santa Fe, New Mexico."

At the Bishop's Lodge, Bradley sipped his Tia Maria and stared at Paul Barnett's hair, which now brought to mind a redheaded skunk. He couldn't help picturing Cassie with a similar stripe in her red, Loving Cared–for tresses that she left long in stalwart protest against asymmetrical cuts. Did he smell potential matrimony in the air, like he had smelled in Venice upon his introduction to Franklin Petrie? Would Paul and Cassie's hair clash? Paul wasn't so bad—he was rich, and his Oklahoma accent was rather charming. Bradley then realized that he'd really had too much to drink, because in reevaluating Paul Barnett, he had found himself considering that Cassie deserved someone better.

BOOK IV

Chapter Fourteen

SANTA Fe was situated off State Highway 84, which, heading north, wound its way through the foothills of the Rocky Mountains. Save for towns like steel-jawed Española whose cars (and their drivers) caused a few accidents and were the butt of many racist jokes in Santa Fe cafés, the highway rewarded most major climbs with a pleasantly scenic spot. There was Velarde, famous in autumn for its peaches, apples and *ristras*, the strung cascades of red chile peppers. There was Taos, once home of that peach of an Indian scout, Kit Carson, and writer D. H. Lawrence. The town's brutal history was part of its mystique, for even with its art galleries, the Taos plaza still looked like it was beaten with the bare fists of the frontier. Side trips off the highway caused a few to ponder hidden secrets, like what went on underground in the Pueblo Indian kivas, or behind the number-coded doors of the research laboratories at Los Alamos. There was an ashram of white-turbaned Sikhs outside of Española who traveled to Santa Fe for work as hotel guards, vegetarian chefs, and Mercedes and Volvo mechanics.

And, of course, well-covered by the Arts and Leisure section of the Sunday *New York Times*, there was the Santa Fe Opera.

It was an amazing thing, this monument to Western culture. Its amphitheater was a feat of acoustical engineering. The diva's vibratto was captured within a structure that had the effect of invisible walls; if given any slack, the warblings would take to the rolling desert hills at a gallop. The massive lean-to roof of the stage dipped inward as though ready to catch the sun as it settled down over the horizon: to hold it up for one extra, breathtaking moment, merely as a favor to the audience. It was an amazing thing. Opera set on stonewashed earth with Indians as close neighbors. Opera and not a limo within miles. Opera that landed like a spaceship to call forth that singularly otherworldly creature, the opera fan.

"Look," Bradley remarked to Paul Barnett. "The Martians. They've come."

It was amazing, he thought, that with all the voices buzzing in the vicinity of the terrace bar, Dorothy Cheswick's, exhumed from some buried turn-of-the-century drawing room, boomed out above the rest. True, it was no more amazing than his own case—he whose sudden appearance made heads turn. A path was parted by the panache that everyone said had been gone for far too long from the scene. Dorothy Cheswick claimed him first. Seeing her looming on the horizon, Bradley sent Paul away to get the drinks.

"How are you, you darling young man?" Dorothy exclaimed, planting a regal peck on his cheek. "We haven't seen you for ages."

Bradley took this calmly, smoking a cigarette and saving his energy. "I'm just fine, Dorothy," he said. "And you?"

"Surviving, as usual. You know my little joke: 'keeping our houses in order.' And what have you been doing? You know you've driven everyone crazy with your disappearing act."

"Well, I've been right here, Dorothy. I have a little place, a retreat, and for now I'm determined to keep it that way."

"Not licking old wounds, I hope?"

"No. I'm managing to keep myself entertained. I'm gardening. It's my latest passion."

"Well, good for you. But why be such a recluse? Why not call the garden club and have them schedule a tour? There's a new interest, you know, in landscaping for small spaces. I have to tell you, Bradley, I scoured the town for your phone number. I wanted to invite you to my opera gala, and not one soul could tell me how to get hold of you. You can thank Marissa and John for keeping your secret safe."

"Well, bless Marissa, and John too. I guess you don't frequent the La Fonda's men's room, Dorothy. Somebody posted my number there."

"My goodness, how rude. But you will come to my party tonight, won't you? My Steinway sits waiting for you to pound out a concerto. We all miss your dramatic playing."

"Sorry, but not tonight, Dorothy. I've been fighting a cold, and I think I should turn in early."

"Poor thing," said Dorothy. "Well, if you ask me, you look just splendid. A tan like yours should be illegal."

"Excuse me," said Bradley, distracted. "I've been ignoring the person who talked me into coming here. He's an old friend of my mother's. I think he has a hard time with crowds."

He signaled to Paul at the far end of the bar, and moved with a concerted effort to join him. As Bradley exchanged smiles, hellos, handshakes, a few friendly pats on the behind, he remained deaf to all comments and turned his back on everyone when he reached his date for the evening. He directed Paul's glance across the terrace. "You see those two men over there?" he said. "The one with the deep-set eyes and the Romanowitz nose, the other with looks to make Julio Iglesias blush from shame?" Paul looked and nodded. "Don't you think they both are looking over here as though they know they're putting something over on me?" Paul said he could see that. "Well, one of them is right," said Bradley. "Oh, God. Richard Gabrielli. How could he? John has stooped to the lowest of the low."

Before Paul could ask Bradley to explain, there came a brazen and forceful tap on Bradley's shoulder that made him spill some of his champagne from its flimsy and shallow plastic glass.

"Yoo-hoo," rang the voice behind them, which came from a woman who consumed square yards of precious space.

"Jesus," said Bradley with a start. "Marissa, you sneak. You scared me half to death."

She did not apologize. "Who's the stranger?" she asked.

"Didn't I tell you about Paul? He's a friend of my mother's; she sent him to check up on me. Tell him how fabulous I am, Marissa."

"How can I tell him that, Bradley, when you've been living like a mole? I suppose Dorothy already bawled you out about it. Hold out your hand, cutie." She passed him a sealed envelope containing the promised Valium.

"What's that?" asked Paul. "Cocaine?"

"I should stoop so low," Marissa said to him. "I have a conscience, which is something I wish I could say about John, Bradley. He's with that awful Richard. Tell me it isn't true that you asked him to dinner."

"Who, John? I wouldn't dare."

"No. Richard Gabrielli. John told me you asked him to dinner at the pool."

"Jesus. How did that one get around? He asked *me*, and I flatly turned him down. Don't you see him gloating? He thinks he's a paragon of sweet revenge."

"Well, thank God. I knew I knew you better than that. That John Aaron. He's playing a terrible joke on himself. He told me he brought Richard here to make you squirm with jealousy."

"Well, he's got that right, hasn't he? God, I hate seeing him like this, Marissa. I tried to prepare myself. I even called him, but I suppose you know all about that."

"It's hopeless, Bradley. Our John has gone off the deep end. Listen," she said as the terrace spotlights began to flicker, "can you meet me by the stairs at intermission so we can talk? Of course, John called me after you let him know you'd be here, and I think I should let you in on a few things. Nothing serious. You know John. Does he ever say anything he means?"

"I wouldn't be surprised if he told you he was plotting my murder after the day I've had," said Bradley.

"Come on, Bradley. He's a little meshuga, but he isn't violent, for God's sake. I have to go find Barry. You think you've had a bad day? You should know from Barry's bad day."

"What?"

"Later. Later, later."

Bradley grinned as he watched Marissa maneuver through the crowd, and he wondered how she avoided catching her voluminous hips on the band of someone's Rolex. "She's a dear about her weight," he said to Paul on their way inside. "Last Halloween she wore a long green dress as her costume and told everyone she was the state of Vermont."

"Why did you tell her I was a friend of your mother's?" asked Paul. "You seemed pretty darn candid about everything else."

"What's the difference?" argued Bradley. "What's the difference what anyone knows?"

"What about this John character?" asked Paul.

"It's none of your fucking business," said Bradley.

When Bradley noted whom he'd be sitting next to—a man in dirty denims in the company of a woman with limp, vegetarian long hair—he was thankful. They were a pair, he guessed, of nature's own, out because the opera itself drew them, or the scenery, or *something* drew them other than seeing who was there with whom. So he was emphatically upset when the rough-hewn stranger exclaimed, "My God. The infamous Bradley Roberson III," as soon as he sat down.

A harmless enough remark, thought Max Boorman, but instantly, and without so much as an inquiry as to how his name had been come upon. Bradley excused himself and headed for the men's room to take a Valium; he had not expected to need it quite so soon. Befuddled and feeling shortchanged, Paul Barnett leaned over and asked Max if he had ever known a person stranger than Bradley Roberson III.

"Is he strange?" asked Max. "I confess I don't really know him. But he hurt a friend of mine who still carries around his picture in his wallet."

"Not a John, by any chance."

"Yes, by any chance. Are you next in line?"

"Oh, no," said Paul. "I'm just a friend of his mother's."

"Well," said Max, "good for you."

To the lighthearted opening notes of *La Bohème*, the Santa Fe sun gave a nod of approval and disappeared into the desert hills, which billowed red, then velvet black, behind the opera stage. Nature and the music of Puccini worked in perfect unison. This spectacle was the only thing Bradley had looked forward to, but he was in the men's room now, and the men's room could have been anywhere, except for the wording of the graffiti that had caught his attention in the solitary stall: "Tenors are my favorites, but baritones will do. Please call Bradley . . ."

Bourbon, champagne, and breaded, stuffed trout were flushed away to enjoy the high life of the Santa Fe Opera sewage system. Emptied, Bradley was soaked with sweat and sobbing out the despair of a hunted man who had yet to face his enemy. He sat glued to the bathroom floor through the first act, afraid to go back to his seat. It could be the slob who knew his name. It could be anyone. He was certain now that the villain was not Robby Valdez. He sat clasping the torn envelope of Valium until he heard the sweet duet of the lovers Rodolfo and Mimi that closed the first act. Then he rallied to put himself back together for Marissa. Before the mirror, he fixed his hair with his fingers and pursed his lips in satisfaction that he was presentable. He smiled at himself in a way that frightened him, because it was so lifeless, so ghostly, this smile of a man whom no one loved, even when he tried to be so charming.

Still, he met Marissa only slightly shaky and immediately offered her a cigarette.

"Oh, that poor Barry," she began, for she rarely got right to the point. "Did you hear about his dog yet? Shot. Those goddamned Taos Mexicans. But I suppose that's what you get for being white and living in those mountains. I don't care what anybody says about it; Taos is an ugly town. I don't understand why he stays there. He should move here, where it's safer. Sweet Bozo. Such a dog."

"That's horrible, Marissa," Bradley said, ever amazed at her offhandedness. "Barry drove down here after that? How could he move? I'd be in shock."

"Sometimes, Bradley, in a crisis the instinct just takes over and tells you what to do. He did exactly the right thing in clearing the hell *out*. He threw practically all of his clothes in the car, too, not that he has that many, and he knows he can stay with me for as long as he wants. I told him, 'Barry, you've come to the right place for comfort. Just have a Jacuzzi and block the whole thing out.' "

Bradley smoked for a moment, like taking a few bites of sorbet between courses, and then directed Marissa to the matter at hand. "So," he said, "what's our friend John up to now?"

"Oh, that John," said Marissa. "I don't know why I'm telling you this, because he was just overreacting, naturally. Isn't that John? I thought it was lovely that you called him, and I told him so. I said that it was about time. But he wanted me to tell you never to do it again. He said that if you insist on bothering him, he'll sell out and settle in Honolulu. Can you imagine? Don't pay any attention, Bradley. He'd never leave here. Never. I'm just obeying orders."

If he had not been so tan, Bradley would have blanched, but blanching for Bradley was impossible. Instead he turned sallow, and the color change was enough to bring Marissa to attention. "My God," she said. "Did you mix?"

"What?"

"Your liquor. What have you been drinking?"

"It doesn't matter," Bradley said flatly. He gazed out into the blank space of a desert night. "Marissa, why do you tell me these things? Don't you know it upsets me?"

"Well, it shouldn't, for God's sake. You know John. He's such a griper."

"You don't care that it hurts me, do you? No. You don't even know. You just glide along reporting tidbits like between-meal treats. You have very busy hands, shaping your ridiculous pottery, but I think you have clay for a brain, Marissa. Are you at all aware that John hates me? That his hate is *real*? And do you know that I love him to whatever extent is possible for me? The futility of it all is killing me. Marissa, darling, I've *used* you. Do you know why you have my phone number? Only because you talk to him every day, and there's always the chance that one of your little news briefs will convey that he's ready to talk to me. And I'm going to keep on using you because I refuse to give up; I just won't. So you can turn right around and tell him everything I say to you. It will sink into him, even though you'll have forgotten it all by morning. You go tell him, Marissa, that his latest threat has made me decide to OD on Valium, drink myself to death, and leave me on his conscience. You tell him that is something that I don't think he can live with and that it's an absolute promise. Tell him to try to call me in the morning, and if he doesn't get an answer, he'll known what I've done. Can you remember all that? Now, one more thing. Just in case he wants to check on the chance that I'm bluffing, he knows where to find me: on the street without a name."

He left her with her lips tensed and her body drooping under several yards of pleated black gauze. He walked to the parking lot, stranding Paul Barnett, who searched for him on the crowded terrace.

At his car Bradley looked to the sky, which was perfectly clear—the kind of sky that can raise and magnify a buried sense of hope. But Bradley was too far gone for the antidote to work. Instead it turned on him, and under a sky so vast and starlit, the universe closed in on him and paralyzed what remained of his powers of reason. He decided he was done with human beings, because he obviously didn't have the skill to deal with them. He was an alien brought to earth by creatures who had tossed him into the mechanics of humanity without a set of instructions, because they, themselves, had fallen to earth without them. It was time to give up the act. He sat in his sedan, willing his feelings to disengage themselves from his body. But the petrification that would segregate him forever from mankind would not come. With all his time alone in recent weeks, loneliness finally hit him where it hurt, and he drove away from the opera with an aching heart.

WOODEN INDIAN MISSING read the headline of a small item in the *City Different News* the next morning. The wooden Indian was Sam, who had his first ride ever in a

BMW on opening night of the Santa Fe Opera. The bartender sighed when Indian Billy was carried down from the lobby to replace him. She was questioned for clues but never said a word.

Chapter Fifteen

As Sylvia Valdez sat up in bed watching a country music concert on cable television, she tried to put aside her worry. It was close to eleven, Robby's curfew time, which he never honored on the nights his father wasn't home.

She could hear her father snoring. Loud snoring was his sign of life these days, and she supposed it was a sound that kept him company in the bedroom. When her mother was alive, her parents had both been quiet sleepers. She hoped to be forever like her mother and never snore, because she did not want snoring added to the list of her husband's complaints about her. Robert accused her of being too soft with Robby, of whining instead of administering discipline. Worse, he now frequently charged her with turning Stevie into a mama's boy because she let him play with their neighbor and let Stevie into their bed when he was away on government business.

She had tried to convince herself that a six-year-old boy was past the point of innocence and that harm could come from being held by a mother's arms in the middle of the night. But she didn't believe it. She thought that when boys were ready to leave their mothers, they did it by themselves. And if they never left, it was just their nature; their mothers had nothing to do with it. The lesson of the Holy Mother was that it was a tragedy to have to push away one's sons. These thoughts consumed her as Stevie quietly sneaked out of the house.

Stevie had heard his friend Bradley pull into the driveway and had watched him carry a body out of his car. When the body's foot caught on the gate of Bradley's deadwood coyote fence and fell to the ground, the little boy's curiosity grew to the point where he dressed and headed for Bradley's garden. When he found his neighbor's doors locked and his knocking went unanswered, he pulled a lawn chair over to the recessed window, climbed up, and grabbed a viga from which he swung up onto the low, flat roof. Walking stealthily over to the skylight, he felt as brave and as secretive as a spy.

Bradley was at one end of the table with his head down. Opposite, a tall glass of bubbly wine sat in front of a wooden Indian. Maybe it was a magic trick, thought Stevie. Maybe Bradley was concentrating on magic to make the Indian pick up the glass and drink from it. When the magic didn't happen, Stevie grew afraid and worried about how he was going to get down from atop Bradley's squat house. He began to call for his mother.

Sylvia Valdez came running from next door, buttoning her robe on the way. "Where are you?" she called. "What are you doing out here?"

"Tell me how to get down," Stevie yelled from the roof.

"Stevie! *Mijo! Madre de Dios! Te va a caer!* You're going to fall!" Was the world going crazy? she wondered. What demon was playing games with her son? "*Mijo*. What are you doing up there?" she cried.

"Bradley has an Indian," called Stevie. "It's really ugly too." He went over to the skylight and peered in to see if either Bradley or his Indian had moved. But everything was still the same. Maybe the Indian was too old and

Bradley could trade him in for a newer one. Stevie rapped on the skylight and called Bradley's name. Bradley didn't budge.

"Mama," Stevie cried again. "I'm scared. Tell me how to get down."

"Madre de Dios," Sylvia whispered frantically as she surveyed the structure of the house. "Slide down to the top of the carport, *mijo*. You can do that, no?"

He did that easily.

"You see that viga there?" his mother asked, pointing at a protruding beam through the outdoor lights. "Grab on to it and let your legs drop, and then let go when I am ready to catch you." She ran over and reached up for him. Stevie dropped into her arms and slid down to the earth over the slippery, quilted nylon of her robe. When Sylvia loosened her grip, Stevie did not let go.

"Diablillo. Shame on you," she said, giving him a gentle spank. "What were you doing up there?"

"I was watching a magic show. But it didn't work. The Indian was too old."

Mrs. Valdez grabbed Stevie's shoulders and shook him. "*Ee,* Maria. I told you to stop talking like that! Don't you talk like that, *mijo*. What the devil is going on in there?"

Stevie started to cry, and this alarmed her more. She held him fast and braced herself to hear that he had seen an evil thing.

"Tell me, *mijo*," she whispered gently now. "What did you see?"

"An Indian." He sniffed. "A wooden Indian. An old one. They're at the table, Mama. Just still. I called, and Bradley didn't even hear me. He's so still, Mama."

"Maybe he just fell asleep. It's very late, you know. Maybe Bradley was just too tired, you know, to get himself into bed."

"I'm scared. He isn't moving."

"His doors are locked?"

Stevie nodded.

"That back door too?"

"I don't know. It's scary that way. There's a dark closet in there."

"Come, *mijo,*" said Mrs. Valdez. She grasped little Stevie's hand and led him home. Tucking him in bed, she told him not to worry; she would go and check on his friend Bradley. "You sleep now, and don't think about crazy things."

"Okay," whispered Stevie. He closed his eyes. "I'm going to dream about the Indian," he said as his mother quietly left him.

Sylvia was glad now that Robby wasn't home to make things ugly. Her husband, too, would have made things even worse, because of how he felt about their neighbor. Perhaps she should listen to Robert, she thought as she returned next door. Sylvia opened Bradley's back door, releasing into the night air a stench the strength of which made her stop in her tracks. She took a deep breath, proceeded through a sea of garbage bags, and went through another door, which led into Bradley's kitchen. The smell inside was not much better. Such filth, she thought; who could imagine such a thing?

What Sylvia at first made of what she saw upon entering Bradley's dining room was nothing less than the work of the devil. The Indian, a horrible thing, was staring right at her. And there, curled up in the Indian's lap, his head burrowed in its tattered, rag-doll arm, was her neighbor, Bradley Roberson III. How she hoped that this was not what Stevie had seen. Yet it eventually beckoned her forward in a rush of pity that left thoughts of the devil behind. Bradley's breathing was irregular, and she recognized it as the breathing of someone loaded with liquor. Even drunk, Bradley hadn't lost his looks; she saw him only as a beautiful boy clinging to his favorite ugly doll. A boy whose mother should be ashamed to have left him alone like this. For a few seconds she stroked his head. "Come, *mijo,*" she then said, nudging him. "Come. Get up and go to bed." She shook him hard, then resorted to slapping his face to get him moving. The blow made Bradley open his eyes, and he smiled at her stupidly. "Holy mother," he mumbled.

"Stop," she said. "Get up now. Get up. I'll walk you to your room if you show me where it is."

She helped him to his feet and with all her strength supported him as they walked to the bedroom. There he fell onto the water bed, and with a smile fixed on his face he immediately floated back to sleep. She removed his shoes and stared at him through the darkness. What happens, she wondered, to make a man like this? What evil has he done to have no friends? Bradley's phone began to ring. A friend, perhaps, who should know of this man's loneliness. She answered it.

"Well, who are you?" asked the voice of a woman.

"A neighbor. Bradley is sleeping. He is sick," said Sylvia Valdez. "Who is this?"

"I'm his mother. Aren't you sweet to take care of him? Listen, can you leave him a note and ask him to call me?"

Sylvia heard the woman dragging on a cigarette. "I'll look for some paper," she said.

"Is he really sick? I mean, wouldn't he have told me? It's probably just a handy excuse."

"I don't know about such things," Sylvia said briskly.

"About what things?"

"I don't understand you," said Sylvia. "I will let your son know that you called."

"Thank you. And please tell him to take care of himself. And, please, would you tell him that I'm miserable and I need for him to help me out of this mess?"

"I think you should tell him that yourself," said Sylvia. "I'm only a neighbor. Good-bye."

Sylvia pitied Bradley even more for being the child of

the woman on the phone; she seemed so much more a child than a parent. On her way out she pulled the garbage bags from their closet prison and set them by the side of Bradley's house. She felt it was the least that she could do for him.

When she went home, she checked on Stevie and found him smiling in his sleep. Automatically relieved, Sylvia smiled, too, but she would have had a great deal to tell her priest if she could have peeked inside her Stevie's head, for there was the wooden Indian, alive and drinking champagne. "Fabulous," Bradley Roberson exclaimed in the dream. "Really. Fabulous."

Mrs. Valdez turned on the television in her bedroom and stared at an old musical. With one ear perked, she listened for the sound of Robby's Chevy to come thundering up the dirt road of Camino Sin Nombre.

Chapter Sixteen

WHILE the thin fat lady was still having her day, John conceded that there was something to be said for public opinion: he never wanted to see or speak to Richard Gabrielli again. On and off through the evening they had talked about home design, Mexican artifacts, and whether the Historic Architecture Committee's recent leniency regarding the construction of multistory buildings signified the end of the Santa Fe look or the institution of an exciting new direction. John had found Richard to be pleasant, if not stimulating, company. But, then, at the opera's second intermission John left the issue of multistory buildings open by making a trip to the men's room. He returned to Richard Gabrielli with a new concern, namely Bradley Roberson III. Some slime, he said, must have needed the added impetus of graffiti to jerk off over visions of Bradley in the stall. Leering in a way that dispelled his handsomeness, Richard put John's theory to rest while coming forward as the slime of whom John spoke. His scribblings were all over town, he boasted. He meant for them, he said, to knock an asshole off his pedestal.

"What in the world did Bradley do to turn you into a toilet vigilante?" John asked, astonished and filled with contempt.

"He's a whore," Richard replied haughtily. "He's a hustler with a pole stuck up his ass who chases after rich, old, boring guys like you."

With his stomach tight and his hand clasped around a gin and tonic, John lurched into the crowd in search of a friendly face. He found sanctuary in the form of Max Boorman, who introduced him to white-striped Paul Barnett, and then to his companion, Deanie. Extending her silver- and turquoise-jeweled hand, Deanie told John he had the face of a patrician and must have been a Roman in a former lifetime.

"Your Bradley has disappeared and left poor Paul without a ride home," Max interceded. "But do tell: Were you a Roman, John?"

"I hope so." John forced a smile. "They had so much fun."

Paul and John eyed one another in trying to assess what each possibly could have in common with the other men to whom Bradley had been drawn. Paul guessed it was the money; John knew Bradley better and deemed Paul just another open target of a man unable to hide his age and gluttony for punishment.

"Do you want Bradley's seat?" asked Paul. "It doesn't look like he'll be back to claim it."

"You're my savior," said John. "I just found out that my date for the evening has a contagious brain disease. I don't suppose you know where Bradley went, do you?"

"You don't care, John," chimed in Max. "Remember? But I bet Marissa Goldman could tell you. Paul said she was supposed to meet him after the first act, and she was here looking for you a few minutes ago."

"I guess I'm bound to bump into her sooner or later," said John. He turned to Paul again. The white stripe in his hair was striking in an oddly pleasant way. "Did you come on a little too strong?" he asked.

"I don't remember coming on at all," Paul exclaimed. "On the contrary. I wasn't even sure what we were doing together once he came to meet me—over an hour late, I might add. He was acting like a nut. He made me sit with a gruesome-looking wooden Indian at the lodge bar, and he was more attentive to the Indian than he was to me. He kept lighting cigarettes for him. He was drunk to the gills, of course. Am I right that that goes without saying?"

"Maybe he's in touch with some ancient Indian spirits," the blissful Deanie remarked. "They play tricks on the people they like, you know. It's a test."

Max squeezed Deanie's bony shoulders, which were half covered by a flowery Mexican shawl with unraveling fringe. Deanie tilted her head up at him and wrinkled her nose. "Deanie's taking courses at the Holistic Health Institute," said Max. "She's getting her degree in aura balancing."

"What's that?" asked Paul Barnett from Oklahoma. "A new dance?"

John and Max suppressed a smile.

"Oh, it's just a kind of spiritual tune-up," said Deanie. "It's like getting your vibrations adjusted."

"As opposed to your valves," said Max, winking.

"Max really needs it," Deanie declared. "He's so out of harmony. So many people are, you know. Especially the Russians, but really the whole world. The whole world needs aura balancing."

"Hear, hear," said John. "I'll sit next to you, Deanie. I think I need *my* aura balanced. You can do your work on me."

"I'm not certified yet," said Deanie. "But you can sit next to me, anyway. You know, I think your aura is okay."

John gave Deanie a small, friendly hug. "That's good to know," he said.

There are many who argue that while the glorious music and vocal feasts of romantic opera will eternally stand among civilization's highest artistic achievements, the librettos of opera—steeped in melodrama and overblown simplicity—are merely relics of their time. For one to sob today when the large tenor sings to a pink bonnet left behind by the woman of his dreams is a likely sign, one might conclude, of deeply rooted neurosis. But in *La Bohème* were bared human feelings that had a contemporary ring. The third act portrayed the parting of lovers. The poet Rodolfo asked the stricken Mimi to leave him. At first he feigned contempt and accused her of flirting, only to break down and confess that she was beyond reproach. The truth of the matter, John knew, was that he couldn't abide her coughing. It kept him up nights. Because Rodolfo loved her so, he sang, he could not deal with her suffering; and therefore she had to go.

Was it any wonder that a man with visions of a murdered Carmen whenever some Florida swampland was lost to a higher bidder should equate poor Mimi's consumption with Bradley Roberson's inability to behave himself? After months of reverberating hurt, why not suffer sudden shame at having banished from his life a man whose only crime was his intolerable immaturity? As the lovers bid themselves a heart-rending adieu, John Aaron was visited by a vision of Bradley Roberson III lighting a cigarette for a wooden Indian. He blamed himself that such a beauty should stoop to such a pathetic statement of repugnance against the adult world. When he exited the amphitheater after the conclusion of the opera's third act, John was desperate for news of his estranged. It was an enormous relief to find Marissa standing watch for him on the balcony.

Marissa bounded up to him and pulled him aside. "Can I speak to you?" she said officiously. "You know, John, I have lived through two divorces. I lost my only brother to the Unification Church. But I swear, I have never felt so downright horrified and hurt as I do right now. I have had my emotions accosted, John. You were right about Bradley being the king of putzes. My God, are you well rid of him."

John knew this was the medicine he needed, and he squeezed Marissa's hand in hope of pumping out a few more doses. When she said they needed privacy, he led her down the stairs by the ticket booth. He sat on a middle step and slid to the far side to make room for her.

"So?" he said.

"He's insane," she spouted. "And it was just the last straw, that's all. First there was you and Richard. I had to defend you to at least a dozen people today. Where is that scumbag, anyway?"

"I don't know," said John. "I dumped him. He's earned his reputation; I should have listened."

"Too bad you weren't so quick to figure out your darling Bradley. But I should talk. God, to think that I stuck my neck out for him. To think I took him for a friend."

"Marissa, you're so good for my soul tonight."

"Well I really wish you would count me out of your

drama," she complained. "You don't even have a cigarette, do you?"

"I haven't had one for three years," said John. "Besides, you shouldn't smoke. One vice is fine, Marissa. Two can kill. Would you like a Velamint?"

"I want a cigarette, John. My nerves are shot. Between you, Bradley, and poor Barry, I'm telling you, John, I should start charging hourly rates for the crap I put up with. Barry won't leave the theater, you know. He's afraid a sniper will open fire on the terrace."

"Tell me what Bradley did that was so horrible."

"He royally insulted me. God, does he know how to insult a person. He told me point-blank that I was a carrier pigeon, that that's all I ever was to him."

"He's upset about something," said John. "He stranded his date, you know, not that the man misses him. Don't take Bradley so personally, Marissa. Take it from one who's learned the hard way."

"I know he's upset, but he shouldn't take it out on his friends."

"No one should. We all do. But isn't there more? You're so worked up. I always thought you were blessed with a fat person's iron stomach for ridicule."

"What do you know about a fat person's stomach, John? I don't think I want to tell you what else he said. It upsets me too much, even though I doubt he meant it."

"Darling, of course you want to tell me. You've been dying to tell me everything since you grabbed me upstairs. So are we done with beating around the bush now? Because intermission's almost over, dear."

Backstage, Rodolfo reapplied his mustache, and Mimi sprayed her throat, readying to die with the voice of a songbird.

"You should carry cigarettes, John. You don't have to smoke them, but you should carry them in case people need one. If I could have had a long drag, I would have told you already that Bradley said that he was going home to commit suicide. He said he was going to drink himself to death and suggested that you try to look him up to see if he's serious. God, why did I give him that Valium? Just three, though. He can't do it on three. John, I know it's just one of his sick games. And idiotic? It's idiotic insanity, John. He wants you to come running. Forget it, John. He wasn't serious for one minute. It finally made me understand why you won't have anything to do with him."

John concentrated on the cars passing on the highway to keep his faculties in order, to keep himself from letting loose his fury over a man he struggled to believe was undeserving of his unbridled emotion. Trying to conjure in his mind a tasteless piece of theater, he thought of Bradley succumbing to his Berlin mood.

"I'm sorry for even mentioning it, John," said Marissa.

"How drunk was he?"

"I couldn't tell. He just looked sick. A little green around the gills. I can tell you one thing, though. He didn't slur his words. His voice was as sharp as a tack, John. My God, you're not thinking of going to him, are you?"

"I don't know what I'm thinking. And even if I did, it's not your problem, is it?" he snapped.

Marissa rose up as abruptly as she could manage. "I won't have my head bitten off again, John. Not tonight. Not by you. I'm going back to Barry. I'd rather deal with his paranoia than with this. At least it has some basis in reality. God, where is anyone coming from anymore?"

John followed behind her up the stairs. "What am I supposed to do now?" he muttered to himself. "Forget all about it, I suppose."

Inside the amphitheater, Rodolfo's Mimi collapsed from consumption, and John felt the late-night air bite him in the back. He coughed. He sighed. He wanted his aura balanced. As the crowd filed out the exit doors for one last time, he groped in his mind for a means of ushering the drama to an end. He looked at Paul Barnett, whom he noticed was sticking close to his side, and in the man's white stripe he saw a flag of surrender. In a last gasp of resistance John hooked his arm inside that of the man from Tulsa and asked him home.

In the hot tub in La Barranca, two men paired by default each mustered excitement through secret fantasies involving their common link, Bradley Roberson III. They retired to John's bed where their bodies entwined only enough to suggest the reassurance that each of them needed, that one had only to point a finger to detect a gust of affection in the air.

After an early breakfast on the patio, John drove Paul Barnett back to the Bishop's Lodge, and when Paul left him, it was all John could do to prevent himself from calling out, "It was great being dull together."

He and Paul had awakened together at seven, and no passion passed between them; they merely exchanged the kindred smiles of resignation of men who shared the habit of rarely sleeping late anymore. It made John wonder if celibacy wasn't indeed better than facing such a mirror so early in the morning.

As he drove away from the Bishop's Lodge, John was invaded by the memory of how fine it used to be to awaken Bradley. It had always been such a treat to see that gorgeous head pop up from the first shock of consciousness and to hear that husky whisper ask what time it was.

"Ten-ish," John would usually reply.

"Cunt," Bradley would remark, and fall back on his pile of pillows. There had always been something so endearing about that instinctive resistance to enlisting in the regimen of waking hours, however unregimented they later proved to be. Then there had been the challenge of enthusing him, and the sense of victory that had come when a brainstorm that erupted out of John's early-morning cup of coffee proved inspired enough to make Bradley jump out of bed. A chance to see the sunset over the Grand Canyon in the dead of winter, the annual emergence of the giant Shalako *kachinas* at the Zuñi Pueblo: the boy had had a thirst for all things otherworldly.

Charging down Bishop's Lodge Road past the turnoff to La Barranca, driving only for the sake of driving, John remembered his and Bradley's ski trip to Arizona's White Mountains where there was a resort run by some enterprising Apaches. The ski lodge entertainment had been abysmal; an Apache foursome played oldies from the sixties on equipment Bradley guessed passed in and out of pawnshops. Bradley had been incensed by the audience's delight at such a pathetic attempt to mimick the dominant culture. He'd asked the waiter if there was another bar in the vicinity. The waiter told him of a place in the nearby Apache village, warning that things got pretty rough there. Bradley demanded to go.

The place was called the Blaze; John could smell it even now. Smoke, stale beer, and sour vomit. He recalled his own amazement that no one seemed to notice them when they entered in their après-ski casuals. They seemed to blend in, another ingredient in a pot of bubbling stew. Men sparred in one corner to a cheering gathering of spectators; couples danced by a jukebox in another corner. In a booth near the door a pair of octogenarians engaged in a long, passionate kiss to admiring applause.

Just at the moment they were beginning to digest the scene, a six-foot drag queen, decked out in a fringed buckskin dress and swinging a bag decorated with magnificent quill- and beadwork, came charging their way, calling out, "Oh, honey. Where have you been all my life?" Her name, she said, was Miss Kitty, after the only decent character on *Gunsmoke*. She pulled from her bag a bottle of perfume labeled "Aquarius," which she said was her sign. Miss Kitty bought a round of beer; later, now a threesome, they toured the reservation in the Mercedes, Bradley and the Apache queen singing "We're in the Money" at the top of their lungs and John trying to remember when he had felt so happy. Was it this shining moment that had prompted Bradley to light cigarettes for a wooden Indian? What could John do now but attempt to find out?

John knew the dry, old street, Camino Sin Nombre, that lay buried in the maze of the Historic East Side. You had to know old Santa Fe to know Camino Sin Nombre. As he headed there, fixing his gaze at the mountains, he did not scold himself for giving in but, with alarming clarity, saw why he had to risk the pain it involved. It was because the land didn't glow pink for him anymore. The mountains didn't tip their hats. They just stood there taking the sun like zoo elephants take their daily hosing. It was because in the midst of his quiet, self-pitying life after Bradley, he was reduced to taking the landscape personally, seeing it reflect his own colorlessness and the brittleness of his bones.

Yet John's Mercedes inched down Camino Sin Nombre so slowly that he could hear the crunching of individual stones beneath the wheels, and each crunch was like the jab of a needle to his spine. There was garbage stacked for pickup out along the edge of the street in front of every house but one. In the driveway of this dilapidated house, whose owner hadn't managed to take his garbage out in time, was Bradley's BMW. John would not have had it any other way. The surprise was that Bradley's garbage had made it outside at all. It was stacked high against a wall. John noticed the garbage before he noticed that the windshield of Bradley's BMW had been smashed to smithereens.

When he saw the windshield, John grew slightly nauseous from the thought that he had actually arrived at the scene of a crisis, whose severity he didn't care to consider. Relieved to see that the car was otherwise undamaged, he told himself that no BMW was safe in this town, that any symbol of rich Anglo infiltration was a potential target for desultory vandalism. Despite its architectural esteem, he never considered the Historic East Side to be the friendliest of neighborhoods. Even Dorothy Cheswick had been heard to mourn its quality of life when comforting guests whose tires had been slashed during one of her parties. As John instinctively transported Bradley's garbage bags to the street, their stench overwhelmed his temptation to blow things out of proportion.

"Hi," said a little boy who hopped off his bicycle in front of him as he stood by the road, brushing his soiled hands.

The cheerful voice of Stevie Valdez startled John. He had forgotten about neighborhoods with children. He would not have guessed that this was one of them. "Hi there," he responded awkwardly.

"Is Bradley up yet?" asked Stevie as he walked his bicycle behind John up the driveway.

John stopped in surprise to hear Bradley's name spoken by such a little boy. Surely Bradley was a movie that carried an R rating. "I don't know," he said to Stevie. "I don't think so. I just got here."

"He fell asleep at his table last night," said Stevie. "My mom put him to bed. Her slippers got all gunky because she stepped in his garbage. We're going to the mall to get some new ones, and she's getting me some more dinosaur books."

"That's very nice," said John, growing evermore anxious. "Does your mother often put Bradley to bed?" he asked.

"Uh-uh. Just last night, because I was scared. Are you Bradley's new gardener?"

"No," said John, utterly confused. "No, I'm not a gardener. I'm a friend."

"Bradley doesn't have any friends," Stevie proclaimed. "Except me. I'm his friend. And my mom's his friend."

John smiled warmly now. "Come over here, Bradley's friend," he beckoned, leading Stevie around Bradley's car. He pointed at the windshield. "Do you know anything about this?"

Stevie's mouth fell open, and he gripped the handlebars of his bicycle tightly, as if he braced for an escape.

"It's not so bad," John comforted, seeing the horror in the boy's eyes. "Windshields break all the time. Bradley's rich. He can get a new one."

"Someone hit it!" Stevie yelled. "Someone hit it!"

"But you don't know who, right?"

Stevie shook his head and then shook himself out of shock. "You're a detective, huh?"

"No. I'm not a detective. I'm really just a friend. My name is John. And what's *your* name?"

"Stevie." He pointed next door. "That's my house over there. And that's my brother's car. It's really loud. I like Bradley's car better, but my brother hates it. He says it's a faggot car."

"Nice of him," said John. He grabbed at his chin, then turned away. Stevie's eyes trailed John as he walked stiffly over to Bradley's fence. It seemed to Stevie that it hurt Bradley's friend to walk as much as it hurt his grandfather.

At the gate John paused, overcome with a perplexity that moved him to ask the little boy if his neighbor really had a garden.

"Yup," Stevie said, his face and voice turning proud.

John perused the mini-wasteland of Camino Sin Nombre and concluded that the little boy had a wild imagination. "I don't believe it," he said.

Stevie carefully leaned his bike to balance it on its

stand and marched his way over to the fence. To the side of the gate he spied a wooden moccasin on the ground and pointed it out to John. "This is the Indian's foot!" he exclaimed. "I knew it wasn't real."

What was suddenly real to John was that Bradley had actually carried a wooden Indian into his house in the night, and he tried in vain to see the humor in it. He stared pitifully at the moccasin until Stevie opened the gate and grabbed John's waist in fright when he saw what lay beyond it.

Bradley's garden had been dismembered. Its flowers were torn from their stems and strewn and stamped upon, their colors only a little more delightful now than if they had been the violet, pink, and yellow eyes of a sea of disembodied heads. Stevie burst out in sobs, and John automatically stroked his hair, comforting the boy not at all. Stevie ran, crying for his mother.

As he stood staring at the scene, John moaned at the shame of it, that the wonder of beauty should be assassinated before the eyes of such a little boy. Then he mourned the magic of Bradley's hands, so harsh to the piano keys but obviously softened to create from dust the lovingly scalloped flower beds that he could see were once the home of such delightful colors. John bent down and grabbed up some blossoms, tearing them into tiny pieces as he stood up again. His own anger shocked him, and he found himself wondering how he could have been so blind to the innocence that had once been the spirit of this garden. He sought a way into the house, wiping away a tear.

The storage closet that welcomed him inside the back door was still reeking from the trash that had burrowed there for so long. He could hear Bradley's breathing, which was loud and mixed with mumbling. It was the garbled sound of a feeble struggle to fight off the world, but at least it was a sign of life. John took his time about waking Bradley to have him face a mess that just might put to rest his playful regard of suicide attempts. In the kitchen, John headed straight for the windows over the sink and opened them as wide as they would go.

John's immediate task of opening all the windows in the house was temporarily interrupted when he stepped into the dining room and met the Indian that he immediately realized was stolen from the Bishop's Lodge. He examined the creature's pose in the dining room chair, the body slumped to the side, the head hanging down, the arms dangling in despair. "And what did he do to *you*?" John heard himself say. He found an empty bottle of bourbon on the breakfront. It smelled like the air had done the drinking, and John resumed his quest for windows. Even in the living room John could hear the breathing, and as he stood in one spot a few feet from the piano, the rasping and moaning built up to a deafening crescendo. John suddenly couldn't stop it soon enough.

In fact, Bradley looked despicably fine, albeit a little rumpled in his opera clothes. His lips were parched and parted slightly in suggestion that a wet finger come and moisten them. And John knew that this was the fear that had kept him out of the room so long: that he would want to do an idiotic thing like moisten Bradley's lips with a wet finger. John opened the bedroom windows and then fetched a glass of water from the kitchen. When he returned, he sat on the corner of Bradley's bed and glanced from Bradley to the floor, back and forth, poised for a getaway he couldn't bring himself to make. John's eyes were on the floor when Bradley's tongue licked his lips and one eye opened just a crack.

"What time it is?" he whispered.

John spilled the water just a little. When he turned his head, he was calmed somewhat by a clouded look of gratitude.

"Too early for the kind of day you're going to have," John replied with a solemn face. "You know, your room stinks. How's your head?"

"How do you think my head is? It's like a squeezed-out sponge. Is that water for me?"

John held out the water. Bradley gulped it down and held out the glass for a refill, his eyes alight with diplomacy.

John raised an eyebrow and took the glass. "Come see me in the kitchen," he said. "Is it conceivable that I might find something there to make for your breakfast?"

"Depends on what you'd stoop to work with," said Bradley.

"I refuse to work with moldy bread."

"Oh God," Bradley said, grabbing his head and curling up on his side. "I think I'll go back to sleep."

John thought this was a good idea. He thought he might like to do the same, at home, curled up in his own bed, alone and keeping himself out of trouble. As it was, he found some refuge in Bradley's kitchen.

"Did you meet Sam?" called Bradley from his bed. "I rescued him from a gang of Texas oilmen at the Bishop's Lodge bar. They were threatening to buy him for a mascot."

John didn't answer him. He didn't hear him, really. He was cracking eggs into a pan to fry them. He wondered if Bradley would eat them; Bradley preferred his eggs scrambled, but the milk was sour.

"John? Hey, you. Did you see my garden?"

The eggs sizzled, and John couldn't bring himself to break the news. "Bradley?" he called out.

"John."

"I can't remember if you eat fried eggs."

The answer never came, and the eggs were never eaten.

BOOK V

Chapter Seventeen

THE obliteration of a tiny garden and its lesson for Bradley Roberson III had ironic roots in American Indian history. After Kit Carson had maimed, murdered, and burned to the ground everything in his wake, including some peach orchards that had been tended for centuries on the floor of Canyon del Muerto, a Navajo chief had said of him, "For killing our women and children, for burning our homes, we can forgive him. But for burning down our peach trees we will never forgive him, for that was wanton destruction." The logic of an ancient worldview says that only nature is innocent.

John was removing the eggs from the stove when the blow of Bradley's silence struck him from behind. Turning, he froze in the doorway as Bradley looked out his bedroom window, his bare back rigid. Bradley's neck was taut, and the veins of his arms stood out like rivers on a bas-relief map as his nails dug into his palms.

"I couldn't tell you," said John. "I'm so sorry and so angry. It was a beautiful thing that you made. I never dreamed you could do something like that."

"Shut up," said Bradley through his teeth. "Shut up. Shut up." A slow march of teardrops traveled down his cheeks.

John waited, anticipating a tirade that would be unleashed the moment so much as a breeze disturbed the stillness. No breeze came, and he waited a long time.

Then Bradley turned, and John stepped inside the bedroom. Though Bradley's face was wet, John kept himself from reaching out to him.

"John?" Bradley's whisper cracked the wall between them like the first blow of a wrecking ball. John shook his head.

"John? Do you think I'm an evil person?"

"I don't think so," John said, feeling something crumble. "No. You're not an evil person."

"But I hurt people. I hurt you."

"We all know about your moments, Bradley. I have mine, too, you know. It doesn't make us evil. It makes us obnoxious." He smiled. Bradley sat on the floor and cried.

"I'm all fucked up, John," said Bradley. He wiped his face with the fine Italian shirt lying beside him.

John stood his ground; there was Bradley on the floor, blowing his nose into a hundred dollars' worth of fabric and begging for authority. "I know," he said.

"Who's doing this to me, John?"

"Fuck. I don't know. Do you want me to say God? It's not God, Bradley."

"I'm a shit."

"So what's this now? You brought this on yourself?"

"Don't make fun of me. I'm telling you I deserved it."

"For what? Because of how you treated me? This is not some divine court executing my sense of justice, Bradley. Let me tell you about Richard Gabrielli. Last night he thought I'd get a kick out of the fact that he's been scrawling your name on every public men's room in town, and I turned my back on him. Cruelty and destruction are not my idea of justice, Bradley."

"Richard Gabrielli? Richard Gabrielli did that? To *me*?" he said. "What did I ever do to him? All I did was turn him down for dinner. I guess I wasn't very nice about it. But, my God. He must really take things to heart. That's it, John. He took it to heart, and I didn't even notice. That's just it, John."

"That's what?"

"*I wasn't paying attention.* I never pay attention to anything."

"If you say so."

"Fuck you, John. I'm having a revelation, and you're being condescending. Don't you see what's going on here? Somebody is out to get me for a reason, and I don't have a clue what it is because I wasn't looking. I'm on automatic. I go one way, and there's trouble, so I go another way, but eventually it all blows up in my face, and I'm always surprised, because I never pay any mind. I'm telling you, John, not everybody's garden is all torn up in Santa Fe this morning. *My* garden was singled out, and there's a reason for it."

"The garden's not the end of it—your windshield's smashed too. If you insist that you're being paid back for something, you must have done a really bad thing, Bradley. What was it? Did you tattle on the Mafia? Did you come on to somebody's little brother?"

Bradley got up from the floor and sat down on the bed. He rested his arms on his thighs, clasped his hands together, and swung them between his legs. "Oh, God," he said.

John sat beside him and reached for Bradley's hand; it was like holding a rock. "Bradley?" he asked. "Did you come on to somebody's little brother?"

"I wasn't paying attention."

"That little boy? Stevie?"

Bradley looked up. "How do you know Stevie?"

"He came over when I was outside. He told me his mother tucked you in last night. You didn't come on to somebody's little brother and sleep with a married *woman,* did you?"

"Of course I never did any of that," said Bradley. "But

I suppose it could be interpreted that way, if someone got things all twisted up. My God. The two most innocent relationships of my life have gotten all twisted. . . . It *had* to be Robby. That's Stevie's brother. Robby hates me."

"I know. Stevie told me."

"What else did Stevie tell you? And how does he know that Sylvia tucked me in? I didn't even remember that until you said it just now."

"To tell you the truth, I'm not sure he knows. It was hard to follow him," said John.

"Well, isn't this fabulous? I've got a little six-year-old kid who worships the ground I walk on, and his mother thinks I need taking care of. Well, that's great. Now I've got a teenager who wishes he could kill me."

"And you deserve it, of course."

"I deserve it because I'm so stupid that I never stop and think about what's going on. Now, how am I supposed to handle this?"

"How about calling the police?"

"Call the police on my neighbor? That's very intelligent, John. Then I can sell my house and go alienate somebody else. Maybe I can move next to some redneck's horse ranch and have my house stampeded like Elizabeth Taylor's in *Elephant Walk*."

"I don't have any other suggestions."

"You shouldn't. Things like this don't happen to you. You know how to stay out of trouble."

"Says who? I'm here, aren't I? Wasn't I supposed to find you on death's door or something? Despite my better judgment, I came to help."

Bradley stared at him. "You *are* here. Jesus, do you see what I mean about my being on automatic? I didn't even think it was strange when I saw you here. 'Sure. John's here. Sure. Why not? Marissa did her job like a good girl.' Did it occur to me it was a little odd that you were in my house? John, I swear, there's no hope."

"There's the present tense," said John. "It's as good a place as any to start paying attention, I suppose." John stood up and walked over to the window to take another peek at the garden. "So what's to do?" he said. "Why don't you take a shower and get dressed?"

"Are you saying you forgive me?"

"No. I'm saying I'm not thinking about it. Frankly, I'm trying like hell not to have any thoughts at all right now." He smiled sadly at Bradley and looked out the window again.

"You want to go home. Please don't go home, John. If you go home, I'll just sit here. I'll never get anything done."

"The little boy was very upset," said John. "Why don't you shower and get dressed and go see how he is? I got the impression that it was his garden too."

"Stevie saw it? Oh, God. Poor Stevie."

"He was so excited to show it to me. Do you know who he thought I was? He thought I was your gardener," said John.

Bradley smiled a little. "He doesn't know about you and plants," he said. "God bless Stevie. He doesn't know much about anything."

"You should go see how he is. And yes, I am going home. But call me later and I'll help you deal with your car. Call me when you're ready to take it into town. I'll lend you the Audi if you promise to drive it sober."

"That's a heavy condition, John."

"Well, it wouldn't hurt to think about toning down the liquor—that is, if you really mean to start paying attention to things. Go see the little boy before your morning glass of bourbon. I'll see you later, darling."

"You won't stay here with me for just a little while? I need protection."

"Well, so do I," said John. "And guarding you in the shower would be hazardous to my health. I'd like to cut out of here while your breath is still foul, if that's okay with you."

Bradley smiled and said, "I'm glad you haven't changed."

"Well, I'm not. I'm going home to call my shrink."

Walking outside, John was greeted by yelling and shrieking: mother and son, he guessed from the quality of their voices. He admired how the Hispanics sustained the rising and falling cadence of their speech even as their emotions got out of control. Jesús Acosta had never lost it, even in his ugliest moments. Each summer John went to the Jose Greco room at La Fonda for an evening of flamenco; his amazement never waned at seeing the dancers who'd mastered the pounding of rhythm into floorboards. The Hispanics were people with a constantly audible pulse; they went to sleep, he suspected, to a heartbeat lullaby.

John heard his own heart pumping now, and his head throbbed along with it. The strong beat of life might be bred into other people, but to him it felt more like a costume forever splitting at the seams. He had grown up in a house where a dancing heart had meant that death was priming for attack. Still, he had managed to supply the calmness Bradley had so obviously needed inside, so perhaps this pounding was not his father's death toll visiting but life congratulating him by kicking him awake.

He drove away from Bradley's house confidently. This time he would be smart. This time he would watch for signs, hold up the crucifix the moment he suspected that Bradley was about to bare his fangs. He would steer clear of dangerous patterns like Bradley's plea for him to stay. This time he would leave Bradley to fight his inner battles alone, if only to stop deluding himself that he was the cause of them. Smart, thought John; he would be smart, and sooner or later, for better or worse, it would all come clear.

Bradley took his shower and put on a bathing suit, just like he did every sunny morning. He was afraid to go outside but not enough to think not to dress for it. Putting water on the stove for coffee, he lit up a cigarette. When he opened a beer, John seemed to be standing there behind him telling him to think again about the present tense. The time had come to face the world with a clear head. Pouring the beer, he carried it into the dining room for Sam. Now that he had liberated Sam from gawking tourists, wasn't it only fair that Sam do his drinking for him in exchange? Maybe Sam could have his headaches too. Maybe Sam also could answer the phone and, if it was Cassie, tell her Bradley was out.

Lighting up another cigarette, it struck Bradley that his dining room was different. After a few drags the difference presented itself: A cigarette smelled strong and distinctive in a room where nothing had smelled distinctive for weeks. He checked the garbage closet: empty. John must have done the deed: John, or maybe Sylvia. Sylvia, John, and Sam, he thought. Who were they, anyway? The ghosts of Christmas past, present, and future?

The phone rang.

"Didn't that woman tell you I called?" Cassie greeted him.

"What woman?"

"That neighbor woman you had answering the phone for you last night. She said you were sick. She said she'd leave a note. You do sound a little raspy. Are you taking care of yourself?"

"I've been better. Listen, can I call you back, Cassie? My home was vandalized last night."

"No, you cannot call me back, Bradley," Cassie said. "You always want to call me back, but not this time, sick or not. My *life* is being vandalized. You've got to tell me what I'm supposed to do with this fucking asshole you stuck at my side. The man has worn out his welcome."

"You want me to fire Franklin? I can do that, Cassie. Anytime you say."

"Yes, I want you to fire him. Maybe you can find someone a little more considerate of your generosity. Someone who won't follow up a trip to China by using your money to hire houseboys. There's someone new in our house, Bradley. A Cambodian. Aren't there any rules about flaunting boys under my own roof?"

"Franklin hired a houseboy? Are you kidding?"

"Poor Tricia's stuck with nothing to do except lose money playing gin with me while we watch the soaps. The two boys are out shopping right now for sirloin rat, or whatever it is those people eat."

"Well, tell him to get the hell out of there. Tell him you'll have him arrested if he shows up again. Tell him anything you want to."

"*Me*? Why me? Why do I have to handle this? You made this mess. I want you to come home."

"I can't do that, Cassie. Honestly, I can't get away."

She began to sob. He had never heard her sob like that before. She had cried so discreetly when his father left them. Bradley had always ascribed to Cassie the incorrigible stamina of the objects that surrounded her—the paintings, vases, furniture, and clothes that supplied her happiness. Of course he knew of her pain, but hadn't she always seemed to manage it so well?

"God, Cassie," he said. "I'm sorry you're so miserable. I just can't come home right now. Honey, that would simply do me in."

"Well, I'll come there, then," she said between sniffles.

"Of course you will," he said. "But not now. Cassie, it's just the absolute wrong time. I don't expect you to understand, but I'm on the brink of getting my act together here. I mean, I really mean to try. John's talking to me again. Cassie, nothing will work out if you're around. I know you know that."

"You know what you are, Bradley?" she cried. "God, why do I even bother calling you? I can put up with anything, can't I, if I put up with you, my darling prima donna? I'll put up with Franklin and his irresistible little friend. What goddamn difference does it make? I'm going out to get my hair done. They can kill me with rat poison, but at least I'll look good when they throw me in the trash." She hung up.

Bradley rubbed his temples. After a while he went back to the dining room, took a fresh bottle of bourbon from the cabinet, poured out a glass, and after some hesitation, set it before Sam. "Even her walk, Sam," he told his houseguest, "is infected with the twitch of the morally ill." But such statements didn't help to quiet his head. He moved quickly toward the bathroom and gagged over the toilet from despair. Then he ripped the *Evita* theater poster from the bathroom door and tore it into pieces.

The next bourbon got as far as his lips before he slid the glass across the table to the wooden Indian. Maybe he had miscalculated, overlooked a reason why Cassie was owed. Surely she must have tied his shoelaces a few times, and she *had* read to him. He remembered that. She read him Kay Thompson's *Eloise* books. She relished the line, "Ooo. I absolutely *love* the Plaza." She had read to him even after he turned four and let her know he could read by himself. She had let him stay home from school whenever he wanted, and stay up as late as he wanted. They'd watched late-night movies in bed together. He remembered crawling under the covers and all the way to the foot of the bed, frightened by Vincent Price. "It's just a silly movie, Bradley," she had said, giggling. He admitted she'd been capable of wisdom.

There was a knock on the door. "No rest for the

wicked," he said to Sam as he rose to answer it, hopeful it was John. But it was Stevie and Sylvia, both with the faces of condolence callers.

"Hi," Stevie said, holding out a bunch of broken blossoms he'd gathered from the pillage. Sylvia held out a bunch of holy roses.

Sylvia Valdez had heard the noises, she said. And after Stevie had come home so upset, she could only assume that her wild weed had turned into a wild animal in the night. Robby would admit to nothing, but there was poison in his blood. Her own mother had seen the signs. "You watch this one," she had said when Robby was a baby. "This one was born to make you weep."

In the living room, Stevie fumbled at the piano. Sylvia sat at the table next to Sam. She would have her husband take away Robby's car keys, she said. She had demanded them herself, but Robby would not give them to her. He had taken off again in that ugly car of his. "More poison, that car," she'd said. She asked Bradley if it wasn't right to take it away. She could think of nothing else to do.

Bradley chain-smoked as she talked. He wanted to tell her that none of what she said had anything to do with him.

"Sylvia?" he interrupted finally. "Can I ask you to go home? You can leave Stevie here, but I really don't want to hear about Robby anymore."

"I'm so ashamed," said Sylvia. That was all that her tales of Robby the Terror had added up to; she had no hint of his motivations.

"I understand that," said Bradley. "When is your husband coming home?"

"This afternoon."

"Listen, tell him it's all right. Tell him I won't sue or anything like that."

"Robby should clean up your garden," said Sylvia.

"Stevie and I can take care of the garden. Robby shouldn't be involved."

"*Ee.* He will kill me. Robby will kill me," said Sylvia.

"Not before he kills me, obviously. Please go home now and let me talk to Stevie. The poor kid must be so confused."

Sylvia asked if there was a vase for the roses. Bradley got up and emptied the blue Tiffany Favrile of wilting peonies, picked days ago from the garden. Sylvia said that it was thrilling to see her roses in such a beautiful thing.

"You want it?" asked Bradley.

"I couldn't."

"You took care of me last night, or so I've heard. You always take care of me."

"I couldn't take it from you. Not now," said Sylvia.

"I'll just have to send it over with Stevie, then," Bradley insisted. "Sylvia, listen. You are only Robby's mother. You aren't his keeper. There are limits to a mother's responsibilities. Listen, I hear you spoke to my mother last night. You could stand for just a little of her to rub off on you, you know. She won't take responsibility for anything."

"You don't know what it's like to have a devil in your house," Sylvia persisted.

Bradley took the roses from the vase and handed it to her. "It's time for you to go home," he said.

The house was quiet. Stevie sat outside. The garden transfixed him like a natural disaster, and he hummed a desultory melody that cast shades of Cassie before Bradley as he knelt beside the little boy and nodded for Sylvia to go.

"Do you know what you're going to see here tomorrow, kiddo?" Bradley spoke very softly. "Piles and piles of dirt, that's what. I'm going to rake up all the dead things and get rid of them, and the dirt will look just like new, new and ready for something else. And you and I will go to the nursery tomorrow and get loads of beautiful new plants. Sound like a good idea? I want you to think hard about which colors would look best together out here, okay, kiddo? Think hard and tell me what you come up with when I come get you tomorrow."

"Tonight maybe I'll dream I can kill my brother," said Stevie. "My mom says he did it."

"Well, your mom doesn't really know who did it, and neither do I. She only thinks she knows. And I bet we won't ever really know, because that's the way it goes. We're lucky it was just a garden this time, you know. Sometimes it's people that get all torn up."

"My mom says it's the devil."

"Well, I don't know about the devil. What is that, anyway? Your mom knows a lot of things, but she can't tell you what the devil is, I bet. And I don't know what it is. You know what I think? I think the whole world is an orchestra, and this conductor is trying to lead just too many instruments and too many musicians at once. There's too many different people trying to play, and he can't keep up with them, and they can't keep up with *him*, so the music just doesn't come out right. Do you know what I mean?"

Bradley led Stevie inside to the piano, where he sat down and played some Schönberg. The discordant sounds made Stevie put his hands over his ears. Bradley sent him home with a gentle rub of the head.

Bradley continued to play, once his audience was gone. With every note that signified the way the world worked, his head let out a little scream.

Chapter Eighteen

THE Fourth of July passed through Santa Fe with a perfunctory municipal salute. There was a pancake breakfast on the Plaza and fireworks at the high school, but no parade. Parades came later to commemorate another revolution, the one the Pueblo Indians lost to the Spanish in 1692. On the private front, however, the Fourth of July proved as good as any other excuse for a gala party. It was a lucrative day for the catering business, and servers were busy at poolside, dodging splashes of those who found the Fourth a matchless day to swim.

John Aaron had been invited to a picnic on the Pecos River and to two parties: one in town, the other at an interior designer's hideaway in the foothills of the Sandias, north of Alburquerque. They were men-only affairs, and outrageousness was the prevailing mood of each cluster of citizens for whom the Bill of Rights held no real guarantees. John had sent his regrets to the out-of-town hosts and told the local hosts that his attendance was iffy at best, depending on the progress of an ailing friend. If his friend revived, however, he said they might have in tow a wooden Indian who was apt to consume a great deal of champagne. "What Santa Fe party would be complete without Indians, wooden or otherwise?" John was told. "We just hope he's not a pig with the cocaine."

Sylvia Valdez, preparing *carne asada* for a family gathering in Albuquerque, washed the pork off her hands. For two days her husband had been living with the farmers of Doña Ana County. After listening to the chile growers of the Southern Rio Grande Valley explain why canning factories were for crazies who needed assembly-line work to keep from playing with themselves all day, he was very much looking forward to a cold beer and the baseball game on television, and afterward a chat with his friends on the Santa Fe City Council. The last thing he cared to hear about was his next-door neighbor, his wife's matinee idol with the mental maturity of the six-year-old who seemed to hang on Bradley's every word.

The same six-year-old was now interrupting his mother's cries of shame with the arm movements of a frenzied orchestra conductor. "This is what God does, Papa. He makes Robby play ugly music." This did it for Robert Valdez. Grabbing Stevie's arms, he forced them to the child's side; the action brought tears to Stevie's eyes as readily as if his father had pressed down on the handle of a water pump. "Cut it out," shouted Robert Valdez. "You're making me nuts!"

Sylvia ran from behind the kitchen counter. "Don't you touch him," she screamed. "Don't you yell in this house. Don't you leave us with that *diablo* named for you and walk in here and treat us like animals, like we're upset about nothing. Your namesake is an animal. He drinks himself crazy. He smashes up your neighbor's car and tears up his yard. He acts like he doesn't have any parents. I heard it all! I heard it all last night, but I don't say nothing, because what could it be? Just that he is maybe smashing some bottles, that he is maybe banging into walls, because *he* is your son and he smashes things and bangs things all the time. But now it's not just nothing. Robby is attacking the homes of sleeping people. *Ee.* Some son we have. *Gracias,* Maria. *Muchas gracias por uno hijo muy amable. Sí, señor. Tu hijo es muy simpático. Escupo en la cara de tu hijo!*"

Stevie ran and stood against the refrigerator with his

hands over his ears, staring at the *retablo* of Saint Francis on the wall.

Robert Valdez threw himself on a chair at the table and shifted his eyes from his wife to his son. His father-in-law was snoring on the couch, and he envied the failing hearing that let the old man sleep in peace while the walls caved in. "Where is Robby now?" he asked.

"Where should he be? He's riding around in that car of his," said Sylvia. "That car, that confiscated Chevy you were so proud to get from your friend Montoya. *Escupo en esa coche.*"

"You spit at everything, no? *Tu escupa en mi cara*?" Robert Valdez asked his wife.

"*Siempre escupo en la cara de la violencia. ¡Detesto la violencia!*" Sylvia began to cry again. Stevie ran to her, and she took him on her lap. "This one will not have a car," she said.

Wasn't it like her to blame everything on cars? thought Robert Valdez. Absentmindedly he put a hand on Bradley's blue vase, unable to resist a pretty thing. He looked over at his wife's face. When she cried, the sunken lines around her eyes puffed out, making her look as lovely as he knew she felt sad. He reached out for her hand and leaned over to rub Stevie's head. Why did it have to be so confusing to come home? he wondered. What had he done to make the child shrink from him? "How's my basketball player?" He smiled gently. "Are you going to show your *padre* a thing or two this afternoon?"

Stevie stared at him, biting his lip. Finally he relaxed, as his mother dried her eyes.

"Do you want to go with me later to get the car washed?" Robert asked Stevie. He dug in his pocket and pulled out a fistful of change. "I've got a lot of quarters for the vacuum hose," said Robert Valdez.

Stevie smiled. He was indeed his mother's son, Robert

thought, seeing how handsome Steve's face became when his eyes were bright.

"More car talk," said Sylvia Valdez.

He groaned. "I'll deal with Robby, *mi vida*. If he did what you say, he won't do it again. You hear me on this, *cariña*. But it's not my fault. You listen to me. It's not our fault, yours or mine. We can't keep him off the streets. He's a kid, and the kids live there." He sighed. "But I guess it's gone too far, no? I'll talk to him. I'll see what's going on in that head of his; I'll see if I can straighten out his twisted thoughts. Hey, you, Stevie. Help me out, *mijo*. What's all this talk about ugly music, eh?"

"Bradley told me," Stevie said. He spoke with confidence as his mother stroked his hair. "He told me about the force that got Robby and the ugly music. He told me about all the instruments."

"A very interesting man, this neighbor of ours. So, Sylvia, did he call the police?"

"He doesn't want police," said Sylvia. "We have an animal who tears up his beautiful garden and plays mean tricks on him on the street, and all Bradley wants is peace and quiet."

"A man would call the police," said Robert Valdez. He reached over and patted his wife's face. "A man would do something," he said. "He wouldn't be afraid of making trouble for his neighbor. He might care about you, but what does he care about Robby? What does he care about me?"

Sylvia sent Stevie from her lap to pick some roses for the beautiful vase Bradley had given them. Clutching her husband's hand in both of hers, she told him she was glad he had come home; Robby was too much for her, and there was nothing she could do. She returned to her work, and Robert rose, heading to the bedroom. "Let me know when our problem comes in," he said. His sigh indicated disappointment that his wife chose to remain in the kitchen.

"As if you wouldn't hear him yourself," she said.

Robby walked in a little after four o'clock, while the baseball game was on. Sylvia and Stevie were at the mall, which relieved Robert Valdez no end. Robby punched his father in the shoulder as he said, "*Ee*. The man is home." Robert saw how his son bounced as he walked, as if he owned every patch of surface touched by his shoes; he watched him check his face in the hallway mirror, flaring his nostrils, as if to acknowledge that he was a god who breathed fire. Robert Valdez stood up, lingering in the hallway as he pondered how to break through to the son who stood marveling at himself.

"So you were late getting in last night, eh?" Robert began.

Robby turned, not coolly enough, his father judged, to have innocence on his side. "So what?" he said.

"Your mother thinks you were up to no good."

"So what's new?"

"So what were you up to?"

"Nothing. *Nada*. Cruising with friends. That's all I do."

"Have a few beers?"

"Yeah."

"Hassle the Anglos?"

"A little. I had a little fun, that's all."

"Is that what vandalism is? A little fun?"

"What vandalism, man?" Robby's eyes shot out as though he had been stung. "You got some detective following me or what?" He might as well have confessed.

Robert approached his son, removing his hands from his pockets as he walked. At what age did men get smart about deception? he wondered. "Get off your high horse, you fucking big shot," he said. "Somebody attacked the neighbor's house last night. Your mother thinks it was you."

"She thinks everything is me. She thinks I got horns growing out of my fucking head, man."

"She thinks she can prove it. Or were they a coincidence, the noises that she heard?"

"Maybe she was dreaming. Let her fucking prove it, man. I didn't do anything," said Robby.

Robert Valdez grabbed the front of Robby's T-shirt in a ball with his fist. Swatting Robby's face, he pushed him through the doorway of his room.

"Fucker," Robby cried. "You fucking Anglo-lover."

Robert kept hitting until he could see Robby's face begin to swell. "Suppose you give me those car keys," he said, sitting down on the bed in disgust.

"No way, man," Robby yelled.

"Suppose you do it before I start digging for them, eh? If I do that, you better protect those big balls of yours, *hombre*."

Robby reached into his back pocket and threw the keys on the floor. "You wanna know what my friends say about you?" he cried. "It's fuckers like you that let faggots rule this place, man."

Robert Valdez swung his leg over Robby's desk chair, leaned against the back of it, and eyed the poster of a baby-faced actor with a cross dangling from his ear. So now there was something to talk about, he thought; they had reached some common ground.

Garbage bags stuffed with floral debris lined the walk to Bradley's doorstep. He and John had labored all July Fourth morning to clean up the yard. Now, after a simple lunch of chicken basil and avocado salad that John had made at home (Bradley's kitchen being short on spices and utensils), they sat in the sun with Indian Sam. Only the latter quenched his thirst with beer and not iced tea; a fresh pitcher sat shaded by Bradley's oiled legs, which were stretched out for a full hit of ultraviolet rays.

Robert Valdez called a hello to John from the gate, stopping several feet from him as he recognized the real estate developer. They had sided together at a zoning meeting in favor of selling several acres of the northwest quarter to a corporation proposing a year-round resort. Eyeing Indian Sam and then John, Robert Valdez thought about what deception some people got away with in a business suit. Bradley called out a greeting, and his neighbor mumbled a reply, hunting for something on which to settle his eyes besides two essentially naked men and a wooden Indian who held, slightly suggestively, a bottle of Dos Equis between its legs.

Robert Valdez was a stocky and sturdy man. Bradley noted his round face, the round belly that stretched his summer sport shirt out over the Indian buckle of his belt, his thick arms, and the Navajo silver watchband. Bradley observed that his blue running shoes, covered by overly long beige pants, looked new. Bradley took his time examining his visitor before rising to ask what he could do for him and offering a beer. Robert Valdez kept his eyes moving. Bradley's tan body, with the little strip of red that covered his privates, embarrassed him more standing than seated. "I understand there was some trouble here that involves my son Robby," he muttered into the air.

"So Sylvia says," said Bradley. "But as you can see, we've got the matter cleaned up now, pretty much. Did you say you wanted a beer or not? It's a little hard to hear you."

"No thank you, no. I've got my family waiting for me. We're heading down to Albuquerque."

"How's the high-tech industry catching on down there?" asked John Aaron from his chair. "I hear companies are slow to follow Digital's lead."

"It's happening," Robert Valdez responded, glad to be offered a harmless topic. "Slow but sure. It's the water problem, you know. You'd think the state was about to dry up and blow away."

"And Arizona gets the Colorado River project," said John. "We should rig a pipeline to Scottsdale's swimming pools."

"Damn right," said Robert Valdez. He returned his attention to Bradley with some hesitation. "I understand you're not pressing charges," he said.

Bradley sat down again and crossed his arms and legs, determined to seem casual in the face of a visitor who seemed pained by his own breathing. "On what proof? Anyway, the damage is done," he said. "I know Stevie and Sylvia were all upset about it. Why prolong anybody's agony?"

"No point in it, I guess, except that a boy could learn a lesson. But I guess I can handle that end of it."

"You have your hands full. My parents did, too, but they let the shrink deal with it."

"I guess it's never easy raising kids," said Robert. "'But now especially it's tough. Some of these punks see a town changing, and it turns them into warriors. There are plenty of types around who convince them that breaking the law is the way to go. But I'm his father, so I guess I'm accountable. Despite what the news would have us think, there are still parents who feel responsible these days. Have they assessed the damages to your car?"

"I assume so," said Bradley offhandedly. "But it's insured. It's no big deal."

"Fair enough," said a more relaxed Robert Valdez. "I was wondering if he could do any work for you. He'll have a lot of idle time. I've loaned his car to someone in my office. It wouldn't hurt for Robby to bend his back a few hours a day. Frankly, my son Stevie could do with a little less of that, no? There's a day camp out at El Gancho that's going to teach Stevie how to swim while my wife learns to play tennis. He won't be bothering you much more this summer."

Bradley reached for his iced tea and gulped it down, the agitated movement of his throat expressing the strength and rhythm of his anger. John got the pitcher ready to pour him some more.

"I don't want Robby here, Mr. Valdez," Bradley said. "I'm not exactly prison-warden material, and I won't have my house used as a place for a juvenile delinquent to do time. Although I do appreciate your intentions; they're very biblical. But I'm sure you can appreciate it that Robby and I will probably never grow on one another. We have what might be called a natural clash. I make him violent and he makes me nervous. It might be better to steer him away from me and toward his little brother—under adult supervision, of course. But then you might see that Stevie is as uncomfortable with him as I am. Mr. Valdez, do you know the line from Voltaire, 'We must cultivate our garden'? Tell that one to Robby, Mr. Valdez, and just ask him to keep away from mine."

Robert Valdez gave Bradley a concentrated look as he thanked him for his advice. "I'll bet you went to a fine eastern university," he said. "I myself went to UCLA . . . on the GI Bill."

"I skipped college," Bradley offered with a shrug. "I went to Juilliard."

"Never heard of it."

"It's a music school."

"That's right. You play the piano. Is that where they taught you that bullshit about God being an orchestra conductor?"

"Not directly, no. Listen, Mr. Valdez, as you can see, I have guests here."

"Don't mind me," said John. "'I'm not having any

problem entertaining myself." He was still holding the pitcher. "Can I give anybody some tea?"

"No thank you," said Robert Valdez. "I'm on my way home now." He turned away and scanned the dirt plots around him. "It's a little late to get things started," he said.

"I'll figure something out," said Bradley. "Don't worry. I have a lot of idle time on my hands. Just like Robby."

"I'm sorry this happened," said his neighbor. "I'm really very sorry for my son's actions. Nobody deserves this." He stepped away. "Well, good luck getting it back in shape," he remarked as he left.

Bradley turned to John with a sneer. "Very manly of him, don't you think? Too bad he couldn't stay." He stood up and disappeared into the house, returning with a glass of bourbon, which he gave to Sam. "Sorry," he told the Indian. "I've been ignoring you."

Throughout the course of the day John had watched Sam go through two six-packs; each beer can was set to rest in his lap several minutes before its contents was poured out on the dirt. He realized that Sam's switching to bourbon out-of-doors implied something serious. Bradley stared at the Indian for a while. Recalling his own credo that sunshine and bourbon don't mix, he picked up the glass, then picked up Sam, and moved the party inside. After getting the Indian settled, Bradley crashed his body down on the Taos sofa.

John had to bring in his own chair. "I think Mr. Valdez did very well," he said to Bradley. "You know, coming over here was a big step for him. He could have just stuck a check in your mailbox and figured he was done with it."

"I wish he'd done that," said Bradley. "I could have ignored it. I wish all that came out of this business was an undeposited check."

"The man said he was sorry, Bradley. He admitted his

son did it. I think that's something. I bet he extends his apology by not reporting you to the Bishop's Lodge for Indian-napping."

Bradley sat up suddenly and grabbed his feet, rubbing them as though he were trying to dig out a stain with his thumbs. "God," he cried. "Shit, John, my feet are itching."

"Too much sun, probably."

"Ouch. God."

"Calm down. Go soak them or something."

"What the fuck is going on?"

"Allergic reaction to macho?"

"It's not funny."

"I didn't say it was. Shall I rub them for you?" John raised an eyebrow. "Darling?"

"I'll go soak them."

John watched Bradley leave the room. Alcohol withdrawal, he thought, but he didn't want to jeopardize Bradley's resolve to stay sober by mentioning it. He'd seen him through two meals and several hours of anguish, as all the drinks had gone to Sam. He doubted that Bradley's methods would take hold, but as an act of good faith, he had loaned him the Audi; it was best to leave that as his only statement on the matter.

Having to be so painstakingly cautious was draining John. Over the two days they'd spent in one another's company, John felt himself change hats from Bradley's visiting nurse to something between priest and psychiatrist. Priest, because a psychiatrist would have earned enough to make a monthly payment on a vacation home, if you totaled up the minutes that Bradley had held his ear with outpourings of bad memories. Psychiatrist, because with the endless streams of complaints and confessions Bradley made about his life, about his mother and his father, John still did not feel privy to the depths of Bradley's soul. Bradley merely insisted repeatedly that he was born without one.

The night before, when John had asked him to play something at the piano, Bradley had refused. He could only play for himself now, he'd said; he'd gotten used to it and he liked it. Months before, music was the only thing that had let John in during the frequent periods when Bradley had shut his body out. Now Bradley seemed to tell all and guard all at the same time. Two days of contact and already John felt the minutes mounting into a pile of hard work. John looked at Sam; at least he had some competition to liven things up.

"He won't let Stevie come over anymore," said Bradley as he came back into the living room. "Sylvia, either. Robby was just an excuse. That asshole came over to size up the situation. He wanted to snoop. He wanted to see everything." Bradley carried a towel he'd soaked in cold water. When he sat down on the sofa, he threw the towel over his feet and moaned.

"He's never been here before?" asked John.

"Never. And he won't come again. None of them will come again."

"You don't know that for sure."

"Yes, I do. He'll lay down the law. He's already laid down the law. You heard that business about day camp. He couldn't have made himself any clearer. He's officially declared me a bad influence. You'll see. I'll call over there tomorrow and ask when Stevie can go to the nursery with me, and I'll be told he has to go shopping or something. I'm sure the guy thinks I've corrupted him already. Not to say that I haven't. God, look at me. I've got my feet all wrapped up like an old man in a nursing home. I'm falling apart, John. Stevie *shouldn't* see me. Every fucking minute he spent with me I was falling apart. Of course he should go to camp—he's six years old. What the hell was a six-year-old doing paying daily visits to some weirdo in his private sanitarium?"

John tried to humor him. "Such corruption," he said,

"gardens and Beethoven. You're right; there should be a law against people like you."

"They're both so sweet," continued Bradley wistfully. "Stevie and Sylvia are the sweetest people I have ever known. Did you notice Stevie's hands? His fingers touch the keyboard like blind people touch faces. He was never going to play very well, though; he doesn't know anything about power. When I was his age, I think I knew everything about it. If you don't know power, you don't play the piano. You play an instrument that takes a lot of effort but makes a little sound. Stevie should play the oboe."

John waited. "How are your feet?" he said finally.

"Better. But my hands are itching too. Maybe it's you. Maybe it's just having somebody else sitting in my house. I love my little house, John. I should pay more attention to it. Paint the walls or something. Stroke it. Let it know it's been good to me."

"Well, if you're so allergic to me, I guess I'd better leave. But it isn't your house that's putting up with you, you know. I am. Some swell time I'm having too. 'What did you do today, John?' Oh, I just had a terrific time keeping Bradley's glass full of tea and sharing lunch with a wooden Indian. That should make me the envy of the whole goddamn town, shouldn't it?"

Bradley pulled off the towel and halfheartedly threw it John's way, missing him by several feet. "Is that what this is all about, John? Is that why you're back? So the vultures can start feeding on us again? Well, fuck you. I *was* going to apologize, you know. I was going to tell you that I really like seeing you in my house. It feels comfortable."

"Well, all right, then," said John. "Let's forget about it."

Bradley went and got his cigarettes from outside and lit one up. "I'm not allergic to you. That's not why I'm itching," he said. "Probably my body is just telling me it's there. I haven't been paying very good attention to my body, either, as you well know."

"As I well know," John concurred.

"Can I get you some iced tea?"

"That would be nice."

There seemed something very sweet in Bradley's bringing him his tea, a plea for patience, an admission that serving people was new to him.

"Is it okay if I take a nap now?" said Bradley. "I'm very tired."

"Why shouldn't it be okay?" asked John.

"Because I have to ask you to leave. I have to ask you to leave, and I don't want you to take it personally."

"I won't."

"Any of it," said Bradley.

"Any of what?"

"Just any of it, that's all. I know you want more out of this, but I can't give it to you. As long as you understand that, this will all be okay."

"This is supposed to be new?"

"Just my being honest about it. I can't give, but I want you to love me. I just can't see that there's anything in it for you. You know what an asshole I tend to be. I want you to think, John, about what you can and can't live with before you decide whether or not you want to see me again."

"Clever boy," said John. He stood up and went to the bedroom to change out of his bathing suit.

Bradley followed him. "What's that supposed to mean?" he asked from the doorway.

"It means that your so-called honesty is nothing more than a way to absolve yourself of any guilt. It's just an extension of your selfishness."

"You don't understand," said Bradley. "I didn't mean it that way. Why are you turning it all upside down? All I'm trying to say is that it's fine if you walk away from me. I'll be miserable, I'll hate myself—but frankly, John, I don't think you owe me the time of day. There's not a soul alive who does."

There is nothing so nerve-wracking as being prodded to give up on someone you have daily tried and failed to give up on, especially at that instant when your heart has acquiesced to a life sentence. John slowly buckled his belt and heard himself mutter something about a party in town he was planning to pop in on. There was going to be a drag show plus dirty movies on a giant video screen. He didn't suppose Bradley would want to go, would he? Bradley said he didn't know how long it would be before he would have any interest in parties, although it would be good for John to go himself.

"Well, I'll call you later," said John. His face was drawn, as if he'd been out in the sun for hours, though the sun was not to blame.

"I'll be here," said Bradley, who grabbed the Audi keys from the kitchen counter and went out with him. "I'm just going to get some ice," he said outside.

"You'll be arrested driving around like that," John called to him. Men with bodies like Bradley's should be required to wear shirts in public, he thought.

The day before, John had called his therapist to confess that once again, he was hopelessly in love. When he was told that they obviously had to reexamine Bradley in the context of a shadow figure who represented what John condemned most highly in himself, he was somewhat irritated, although he couldn't have said what he would have liked the doctor's reply to be. She told John to start a journal and record in it his physical and psychic reactions to all of Bradley's words and movements. As always, he should pay special attention to his dreams. After listening politely to these instructions, John canceled all of his sessions for the summer. Asked why, he replied that he wanted to try a fresh approach to his feelings, to let them breathe a little magic before picking them off in the shooting gallery of analysis. "Haven't we done Bradley as shadow figure to death?" he asked. "And isn't it a miracle that he's popped up again full force? I think it's amazing. I think love is an amazing one-syllable word, and I don't want to break it down into a bunch of deadly multisyllable complexes."

Four months ago he hadn't felt that way, he was reminded; four months ago he had claimed to be bracing for a heart attack, threatening to leave his internist for refusing to agree that he was suffering from asthma, hypoglycemia, and the early signs of epilepsy. Four months ago, his therapist politely continued, he had paranoid dreams of being cornered by a growling pack of Dobermans. "How are you going to end up after this round with your friend?" she asked. "With your house under heavy guard and you climbing into bed at night under an oxygen tent?" John bid her good-bye and slammed the receiver down on her warnings.

Now, one day later, when he drove home from Bradley's house, John felt his pulse rate accelerate, and he broke out in a sweat. He was hopelessly in love. It was not the love, however, but its hopelessness that had attacked him. That was what Bradley had been trying to tell him, that it was all perfectly hopeless. The only room Bradley could make for him in his life was the kind he made for an extra chair; he would be lucky if Bradley remembered to dust him off once a week with a kiss. Could he bear it? he wondered. His pulse normalized when he stopped questioning, when he accepted his fate to bear all.

His feelings for Bradley ran herd over him, and he doubted he would ever win back the controls. Not that Bradley himself had much to do with it. John didn't need his therapist to explain that the source of his love was his own need; his was an unoriginal story. "It's the same old mystery," he told himself, "and the plot still sucks."

Once home, he called Marissa. Before he could come out with much beyond hello, she bombarded him with her own tragic tale. She had been in the midst of biting off the head of a Godiva tennis racket, thoroughly engrossed in Danielle Steele, she said, when a bloodcurdling scream made her drop her book, gulp down her chocolate, and run to the guest room. There she had found her guest, Barry the dog mourner, rocking back and forth on the bed, sweating profusely and chanting, "Bozo. Bozo. Come here, Bozo."

What could Marissa do but take the poor man in her arms and give him refuge like a shelter for the homeless? Barry accepted her charity by burying his sorrow in her ample, long-neglected flesh, and as Marissa cried from rapture, Barry beckoned one last time for Bozo to come running home. Marissa's body was as cozy as a featherbed, and finally turning his back on the gates of dog heaven, Barry lay peacefully on top of her until her pained moaning from a leg cramp jolted him to attention.

"Oh, Father Sky and Mother Earth," prayed the novitiate Indian from Perth Amboy, New Jersey, "return your child's soul to the living from the burial grounds of the sacred dead." These were Barry's final words before leaping out of bed, throwing on his jeans, stuffing his backpack with the frenzy of a timed game-show contestant, and driving away into the night.

When Marissa saw that Barry had left his sacred prayer feathers lying next to her on the guest room nightstand, she was reminded of her own absentmindedness. She had climbed into bed without her diaphragm, which, when last examined during an attack of yearning months before, had not yet disintegrated from lack of use. Marissa considered that Barry had fled his nightmare only to leave her to contend with her own. But soon her hurt gave way to nostalgia. She wished she could bronze his very earthy scent for a keepsake, and she stroked his prayer feathers with the care of a lover's hand.

"Darling, think of it as though Barry had brought all those Indian spirits down from Taos and you joined them in a little dance. Could it be you were selected by a mountain god to bear his baby?"

"Stop it, John. You sound like Bradley."

"Do I?"

"You saw him, didn't you? You went to his house."

"Guilty as charged."

"And how is he?"

"Sober for the last forty-eight hours, if you can believe it. By the way, you were wrong about him. He wasn't alone and miserable; he's living with someone."

"You're kidding. He's a swine, John. A liar and a swine."

"It's purely platonic. His friend is a vision, darling, straight out of one of Barry's cosmic dreams. It's an Indian, Marissa—an Indian is keeping Bradley sober. This is a fact, so maybe what I said about Barry is not so farfetched."

"You're in it deep again, aren't you, John?"

"Darling, did we ever doubt I would be?"

"Well, I won't be your shoulder to cry on this time around. I'll never forgive him for what he said to me the other night. I swear, John, I thought you'd learned."

"Life is not a school, dear. It's a prison. And I'm a hardcore case, locked up once again in Cell Block BR-III."

"Well, stay out of maximum security, for God's sake, or you'll end up hanging yourself."

"A hunger strike is more my style. Do the planets line up right for us having lunch tomorrow?"

"Oh, why not?" said Marissa. "A girl has to eat."

It cheered him that in the midst of his predicament he had risen to the occasion and comforted someone who appeared to have it worse. A horrible thing, to be insulted like she had, after she had been so generous. He knew how it felt. He used to like how it felt. It was nice to know he no longer did; perhaps he had learned something, after all.

John spent much of the afternoon in his writing studio contemplating what other type of studio he could possibly turn it into. He couldn't imagine that he would be writing anymore, now that the door had been closed on his distance from his main character. Perhaps he should take up painting or woodworking; but such hobbies required enormous commitment, and he had always been miserable with his hands.

"Help me, Max," he said over the phone. "I'm a rich man in search of a new toy. I'm putting my word processor up for sale."

"How much?" asked Max.

"What do *you* want it for? I thought you'd turned your back on modern technology."

"If Updike uses one, they can't be all bad. I'm thinking of writing a fantasy: Rambo Meets the Brothers Karamazov."

"A definite six-figure advance. But really, Max, I'm looking for hobby ideas, now that writing's out of the picture."

"Have you ever tried fishing? Great trout streams in the Pecos."

"Too seasonal," said John.

"Ballet?"

"Ouch."

"Maybe you'd like my new one. Beading. Deanie bought me one of those Indian looms that we used to have in Cub Scouts. We made watch fobs then, but I'm going for the big time: headbands, belt buckles, change purses. I'm going to put Hong Kong out of business."

"Threads make me nervous," said John.

"Besides, I don't think you should sell your word processor, John."

"I guess I shouldn't. Maybe I should try a novel about my friend Marissa. She's just had a spiritual encounter with an Indian from New Jersey."

There was something to be said for Marissa's advice, John decided; he could see it was dangerous to make Bradley the center of his world. Calling the host of the in-town party, he said he would be over as soon as he showered. "Is there anyone intriguing in the crowd?" he asked. An architect from L.A., thirtyish and very successful, was sniffing out real-estate possibilities, he was told. He was looking for some prime property on high ground suitable for a passive solar home for himself: his third home, his first solar. John had just the right acreage off the Old Las Vegas Highway near El Dorado. "Maybe I'll take him for a ride out there," he said, "if he has his checkbook with him."

John stayed at the party longer than he should have. He realized this when he found himself in a guest room with the architect who, all too willing to negotiate a deal, was frantically opening drawers and cabinets looking for rope, or a reasonable substitute, like an extension cord. He liked being tied hand to foot like the carcass of a deer, the architect said; this fantasy stemmed from early childhood when he had been traumatized by the movie *Bambi*.

John told the architect that he didn't want to sell to him, after all. The land he had in mind was too near the hunting grounds for mule deer, and he didn't want to be held accountable for a fantasy gone haywire in the shooting death of an L.A. man with a pair of antlers affixed to his head. He checked his watch and excused himself, saying he was about to miss an important date with a phone freak who was calling him at home. It surprised him to realize that he had not dialed Bradley's number in the last twelve hours; this he took as a healthy sign.

When John pulled into his driveway in La Barranca, the headlights caught hold of a wicker basket and a giant bag of Puppy Chow. There was a distinctly non-Aryan mutt in the basket, a cute thing, part sheepdog maybe, part who-knew-what else? The quivering creature was a little shorter than John's forearm. Attached to its little red collar was a note on paper that smelled like it had been dunked in Paco Rabanne pour Homme. "Not an ounce of German blood in him. Darling, some of us just need a little housebreaking. Thanks for being there," it said. John sighed; picked up the dog, the basket, and the food, and carried them into his writing studio. There he laid the entire Fourth of July edition of the *City Different News* over the terra-cotta tile floor and fixed a saucer of warm milk. This done, he picked up the phone and dialed.

"What time is it?" answered Bradley in a groggy voice.

"Three-ish," said John.

"Cunt," said Bradley.

"I just wanted to thank you for the dog. I'll be thinking of you tomorrow when I'm cleaning up his shit. That's all I called to say. Good night, *liebschen*."

"Arf, arf," said Bradley, "and sweet dreams to you, too, *mein Herr*."

BOOK VI

Chapter Nineteen

IN summer, some tourists came to Santa Fe for many things, and some came only for one. Spiritual seekers came to be adopted for a time by the ancient Indians and Spanish. Buyers came for that special painting or piece of furniture. They had a suburban Dallas breakfast nook that simply cried for a Spanish colonial table, a Houston hearth that wouldn't be warm without the crowning of a gilt-framed Indian brave crouching by the firelight. In mid-August the hotels and motels were booked solid by aficionados of Indian crafts. On the Plaza, at the galleries, and in private houses, people flocked to celebrate the continuing artistic legacy of the American Indian. Indian Market parties always included an artist who received no fanfare on the reservation but found himself a temporary Santa Fe celebrity.

In early September conquistador costumes were pulled out of closets and marched around the Plaza on horseback. On a podium in front of the Palace of the Governors, a mariachi band played cumbias and salsas for dancing in the streets. It was a time when Anglo women dared be seen in public wearing lace mantillas and frilly Mexican dresses, or snakeskin cowboy boots over skin-tight pants of silver lamé. With massive consumption of tamales and tostadas and beer, bodies crashed against each other in the Plaza, and out of earshot a random symphony of shattered glass was performed by those like

Robby Valdez, who were still caught up in the spirit of rebellion.

The history of the Fiesta was as obscured as what it was meant to celebrate. It was once a pageant commemorating the victorious arrival of DeVargas, who, having squashed the Indian Revolt, secured Santa Fe once again for Spain, by arriving in town in a green velvet suit. (It was said that DeVargas gave hot chocolate and tortillas to the defeated Indians as a show of peace.) Fiesta was revived after a long lapse in 1916 by the Chamber of Commerce as a tourist attraction for which most of the town's Spanish population could not afford the price of admission. In the 1920s, Santa Fe's Anglo artists won their fight for a free Fiesta and devised what became and has survived as the high point of the revelry. The artists gave birth to Zozobra, Old Man Gloom—a grotesque effigy over forty feet tall, condemned each year to be burned at the stake. Taunted by the whirling torches of fire dancers and the chanting of "Burn! Burn!" Zozobra moaned over loudspeakers as puppet strings manipulated his arms into a languid, futile dance of struggle. Old Man Gloom went up in flames; the crowd cheered. It was September, and as the tourists had gone and the skiers had not yet come, Fiesta celebrated Santa Fe's reclamation by people of all races who actually lived there.

Bradley Roberson III was fixing up his home. His garden, never replanted, had been left to nature, and little tufts of weeds, chamiso, and other grasses sprouted up like botanical accidents on the surface of the moon. Bradley bordered his patio with potted cactuses and hung wind chimes from the vigas, which protruded like stubs below the roof line. The chimes, he told John, took the air's erratic pulse (against which he often found himself monitoring his own).

The stereo, which had previously been given little rest,

was often silent; when it was on, it more tweeted than woofed. Satie, Bradley told John, had become his favorite composer because he weighed his notes sparingly, "like chemical powders poured out onto a gram scale." Lush was out, it seemed, and dry was in.

Bradley was conscientious about his garbage now, storing it in sealed metal cans by the side of the house. As he had essentially stopped cooking, his refuse was made up of little that could offend; with the lid slammed down on his drinking, he had given in to his craving for chocolate and "any junk food that crunched." When John didn't take him out to eat, he lunched on potato or corn chips and completed the meal with a Cadbury hazelnut bar. Breakfast was his health meal: chopped dried fruits and almonds kept in abundant supply.

Bradley now often awoke at sunrise, filled with a restless passion he harnessed in the obsessive renovation of his house. He would sit Sam down among his materials, a can of beer beside him, and leave him an unveiled monument to the depths a man could sink. Plaster dust and paint spatters accumulated on him in layers. By the time the walls of the living room had been worked to the texture of a stone-polished earthern bowl, Sam resembled the sort of ghostly Indian spirit that could be blown around the house by gusts of wind.

And through the summer months John worried as Bradley worked. Had sobriety squelched Bradley's sense of humor? Was the outlandishness on which he and so many others had feasted like gluttons gone? Would Bradley no longer be fun as he ceased to be snide?

By the time of the Fiesta, Bradley had moved paint cans, drop cloths, trowels, and plaster from his living room and set to work on his dining room. This sent him out to eat a lot, always with John, who viewed every order of club soda, Coke or iced tea as an indication of Bradley's determination to clean up his act, though he wished Bradley would remove sex from his list of dangerous substances. Still, it was enough to be invited back into Bradley's private sphere. This meant, among other things, being party to the Indian medicine show on Camino Sin Nombre. Indian Sam (about whom Max and Marissa were sworn to secrecy) had been proclaimed a religious icon, paint spatters and all. John listened to Bradley tell of his ritual meditations before sainted Sam, who helped Bradley excavate his innermost thoughts, and before whom Bradley prayed "for the impossible—for clarity."

One night Sam's guidance reintroduced Bradley to the lover to whom dying BJ Roberson had fled, the poet who had stopped Bradley out on the street near Juilliard years before. The man whose poor timing had foiled his efforts to reconnect son to father crept into Bradley's thoughts in a wholly different guise; he was not heartsick and pleading for empathy but sinister, tinged like the underbelly of a lizard. Bradley imagined a pillow being lowered by the poet's strong arms as his father lay below in a postcoital swoon.

"What is it?" Bradley asked Sam, his spirit guide. "Do I hate the poet because he robbed me of the chance to do the asshole in myself?"

"Too complicated, city boy," the Indian replied.

"So where am I in this?"

"Innocent," said Sam.

Bradley wept for BJ, whose soul had been sent packing before his son's birth, and he cursed him for being such a coward. But looking at it dispassionately, Bradley saw he had been little more than a witness of BJ's misery. That he'd been a child forced to be such a witness was truly his misfortune; but misfortune, he realized, was far easier to set aside than blame.

Trickier, and far more wrenching, were his sessions with a woman Sam introduced as the Goddess. She took many forms. Each time she appeared in Bradley's field of vision she was different: a porcelain statue, a tightrope walker, a golden-haired girl. But in whatever exquisite form she took, she always did the same thing: fall from a height. The statue falling from a pedestal, the tightrope walker from the wire, the little girl from a high-flying swing. Sam and Bradley watched her fall, but neither extended his arms to try to catch her. Once, as the little girl sailed off her swing, Bradley began to move forward, but Sam restrained him.

"She'll break her bones," said Bradley.

"Crush you," cautioned Sam.

About two weeks after the Fourth of July, Bradley sent a bilingual telegram to Eighty-sixth Street with the following directive: "Refugee Camp Closed. Stop. Move It or Die." Response was immediate: Franklin Petrie and his houseboy quit the Roberson home. Bradley then found himself on the phone, forced to defend the idea that he'd acted in Cassie's behalf, only to be told that he had loused up a fairly happy little family. Cassie swore that she would pine away not only for Franklin but also his Southeast Asian lover, who danced so wonderfully for them after dinner and sang such lovely songs. Bradley's rage came as quickly as had Cassie's forgiveness. "I hear the Peace Corps has an aching need for manicurists in Indonesia," he quipped. "Can you file other people's nails, Cassie? Or can you only do your own?"

"I'm all alone and you're being sarcastic. Just what am I supposed to do now, Bradley, while you're off wandering in the desert with the Jews?" she complained.

"Well, why not go to Egypt, Cleopatra? Put kohl on your eyelids and parade down the Nile. Flash your pearl-like teeth before the camera at the pyramids. You kissed Franklin; surely you can learn to kiss an asp."

"I can learn to kiss anything that's more comfort than you. Jesus God, Bradley. Just who am I supposed to go with now that you've thrown my traveling companion out into the street?"

She had presented a problem that required some thought. "I'll send Tricia with you," he said finally. "She'd be willing to go, I guess, if I give her an extra month's paid vacation. No reason she shouldn't get out of New York and see the world through your rose-colored glasses."

"But what about the house?"

"The house can sit on its ass," said Bradley.

"Empty? Bradley, that's too sad."

Sam was right, he told himself. What was there to do but to let the Goddess fall?

Frankly, John Aaron did not count himself among those Santa Feans who sought visions from distant worlds via shards of ancient Indian pottery placed under their pillows; indeed, after unsuccessful acupuncture treatment for a bad shoulder he tended to denounce all healing methods not covered by Blue Cross. But when he would happen upon Bradley with his eyes glazed, muttering phrases such as, "The Goddess is doomed, the Goddess is crashing," John had to acknowledge that the extraordinary effect a wooden Indian was having on Bradley Roberson III was worth an investigation of its marketing potential. He acknowledged, too, that the best service he, himself, could offer Bradley was to extract him from Sam's clutches as often as possible and so help him to preserve his sanity.

One glorious summer morning, he convinced Bradley to return with him to the cliffs near Santa Clara where the two of them had gone a few days after Bradley's introduction to New Mexico. The first time, as they'd hiked, Bradley had hung close to the sun-warmed rocks, shrinking against them at times, as though in stepping out from them a few inches, he would be swallowed up by the empty spaces that loomed around them. And inside a cave where echoes scurried like rats' feet along the walls, fear had turned Bradley very passionate. With his nerves gnawing a hole in his stomach, Bradley had clung to John, feasting on John's own hunger.

John lured Bradley to the cliffs so many months later with the bait of ancient spirituality, though he, himself, yearned for more earthly pleasures. Once they started on up the trail to the caves, however, John noted with dismay that Bradley was more concerned with keeping the puppy from stumbling over its clumsy paws than with keeping his own balance or protecting himself from spirits unseen. Finally they found their old cave. After spreading out an elaborate picnic Bradley sat staring through the shadows at John. Haunted by his own memories, John was baffled at this remote Bradley, who seemed to have left his energy at home, bottled up in one of his empty paint cans.

"Do you know Eliot's *Prufrock*?" Bradley said. He proceeded to recite the poem in its entirety, relishing the words, "roo-oo-oom . . . , go-o-o . . . , and Michaelangelo-o-o." Their sound vibrated musically through the dark cavity where an Indian family had lived hundreds of years ago-o-o.

"Times change but not people." John had learned this adage from his father, who had felt it to be a great lesson in life. Yet there, in an old Indian cave set off from people or time, John began to quiver from the chill of the changed person before him. He waited for some sarcasm, for a bitter curl of the lip, a haughty dismissal, but none came.

"Can I kiss you? Please?" he asked.

Bradley held out his arms hesitantly, but John's excitement was eroded by a kiss as abrasive as sandstone.

"What's happening to you?"

"I wish I knew," said Bradley. "But, God, there you go again, taking it personally."

Bradley leaned over to rub noses with the puppy. "Sweet nose," said Bradley. "I think I'll bite it off and eat it whole, you little monster."

John turned a stone around in his hand, trying not to feel so hatefully jealous of a little dog. His frustration made Bradley smile. It had been a master stroke to give John another pet, he realized; the dog distilled John's emotions, as Sam distilled his own memories.

John persisted in refusing to name the animal, unable to call out Bozo or Pokey and have some four-legged creature come drooling his way. (Bradley had offered as a possibility Perro Sin Nombre, the Dog Without a Name, but this suggestion met a less than enthusiastic reception.) Some definite ideas loomed before John as he watched the puppy being showered with more affection in an hour than he himself had been shown in a month, but these he kept to himself.

Back at home, John meditated on possibilities. Every morning the name that came into immediate use was Fucking Shit, because of what John faced when he walked into his studio. He would stick the poor thing's nose in its namesake, wallop it on the behind with a rolled-up magazine, drag it outside by the collar, and tie it to a juniper tree. This is what it had come to, he mused: laying a fresh edition of the *City Different News* on the floor and allowing an animal to come back in and share his first cup of coffee, his quiet time. Mornings were reserved for trying to come to grips with his feelings for Bradley the Dog Giver, but there was no way to contemplate the nature of love when an animal was whimpering. Every morning the puppy would give him only a few minutes' peace. Hiding under the studio desk to atone for its sins, it inevitably came slinking up to John, head lowered, tail wagging with pitiable despondency. John tried in vain to concentrate while the puppy sniffed and nibbled at his feet, undaunted by the gentle kicks that punctuated John's frustration. John would yell, the puppy would whine, and John would ask, "Can't you leave me alone, dog?" The tail would wag from the excitement of having been addressed, making John sigh and pick the puppy up, then sigh again when he realized that he had drawn the animal to his chest. "I suppose you think you have all the answers," John would say; then the puppy would make John laugh by licking his face before squirming to explore what was on the table. Annoyed again, John would toss the puppy off his lap. "Pest," he'd say. "I suppose you hate me now." To this the puppy responded, as programmed, by wagging its tail, begging to be picked up again because it liked John's lap and the way John rubbed its neck with his knuckles. The same pitiful act, again and again, and it always worked. John drank his morning coffee with the puppy on his lap. As for why his love for Bradley grew with so little fertilizer, he could never figure out a goddamn thing.

Finally, after John had come close to beaning the animal on the head one time too many, he bypassed the ASPCA hot line for the counsel of dog lover extraordinaire Max Boorman.

"Max," he queried over lunch at the Palacio patio, "what would you think of a man who daily contemplates the murder of a helpless mutt?"

"I'd think he was capable of the vilest acts of human history." Max chewed his wad of gum emphatically.

"But I'm not a vile person," said John. "I just hate dogs."

Ramon the waiter came with their drinks. He was as cheery as ever, though he had discovered some time ago that Santa Fe freed tourists from all the demands of home, including the calculation of fifteen percent tips. His regulars heard frequent complaints of his being shortchanged, and John, for one, always obliged him with an extra percentage to compensate.

Max clinked his glass of bourbon against John's gin and tonic. "That innocent little animal doesn't have a fucking thing to do with your personal problems, John. Give the thing away if he's bringing out the worst in you. Let him make some worthy person happy."

"God, would I love for you to take my dog," said John. "But I'm stuck with it, unfortunately. It's supposed to teach me a lesson."

"Pertaining to whom, I wonder? Care to give me a numeral for a hint?"

"Bradley's the one who should have it," said John. "He loves the thing. You should see him roll around on the floor with it; it borders on sexual abuse."

"So give it back to him."

"I'm not supposed to do that," said John.

"Why the fuck not?" asked Max.

"Bradley's heavy into symbolism these days. He'd say I was rejecting him."

"And how would he feel about caninicide? Because I wouldn't put it past you to kill the little thing one of these days."

"'Oh, God. He'd get enough mileage out of that to take him to Mars. But here I am in hell."

"Until you learn to love your dog, I reserve my sympathy," said Max.

John watched Max wolf down his lunch with the finesse of a Hun. Here was a man who took life in stride, living his angst vicariously through the characters in the Russian novels that he held so dear to his heart. The man didn't do a lick of work to speak of and never took the time to savor someone's efforts in the kitchen; still, John had to admit he looked good. Max was fat, but, damn it, he was full.

Marissa Goldman, too, was full and getting slightly fuller by the minute. Her countdown for her late period had begun in the middle of July. Every morning she would call John and say, "Not yet." When August came, John suggested she get a scientific reading—if not for her sake, then for his, because the suspense was murder on his blood pressure.

A baby conceived by a man of mystery, John mused, who had come down from the mountains to attend the opera while mourning his murdered Bozo, would truly immortalize the season as the Summer of the Dog. In mid-August, Marissa called to say that a little Aries baby was indeed on the way.

"Can you think of a worse combination, John?" she asked. "A bull and a ram? Oh, why can't life be kinder? Must I have a child destined to lock horns with me at the drop of a hat? Where's the Libra of my dreams who can be our referee?" Then she wept, not for being cheated by the stars but because she was so happy.

"I'll do my best to help out," John said. "Or will a Capricorn make it worse? Oh, God. You know, darling, a baby is just what you need. We've all been saying it for years. Have you told Barry yet?"

"I can't reach him. His fucking phone's been disconnected. You know I haven't heard a word from him since he left me. I thought he would at least call for his prayer feathers. Some Cheyenne or Blackfoot or Redhead medicine man gave them to him for protection. Maybe he's dead, John—maybe he got eaten by a bear because he didn't have his goddamn prayer feathers."

"So call one of his friends in Taos to track him down. It's a small place. Somebody will know where he is."

"But what if he gets the idea that he should take the baby away to raise it in some godforsaken cabin in the mountains? This baby is mine, John. I don't want it stalking through the forest in pursuit of sacred deer."

"A child should know his father, Marissa," John said. It surprised him how excited he felt at the thought of a baby joining his circle of friends. It was his one tragedy, this absence of children. The course he had followed had so estranged him from babies that he doubted he'd know what to do with one if it were handed to him. Back when he was married, he'd toyed with the idea of becoming a father, yearning to give a child a tour of the best of humanity. Beautiful places and things, art, theater, beautiful parks and buildings sprung from mankind's magnificent spirit: all that he'd had to discover on his own, because his own father had been blind to everything but man's waste. There had been a time when he would have given anything to prove his father wrong, even a new generation to change his father's heart. But for its divorced fathers, Santa Fe was more a center of visitation rights than of custody. John's fantasy had withered under the desert sun that made children appear like mirages before him, or sometimes posed them as the handiwork of a primitive culture.

Around town the joke buzzed: "Marissa Goldman's pregnant," and its answer, "How could they tell?" John was not alone in scorning such cattiness.

At August's end, Marissa opened the door for a courier bearing two dozen long-stemmed white roses and an envelope whose contents shook her nearly as much as the confirmation of her pregnancy itself. It was a surprise delivery from Bradley Roberson III, who had been incommunicado during this summer of surprises.

> Dear Marissa,
>
> What tales you and I can share about our respective Indians, wooden or white! Your news thrills me, but I thought it inappropriate to call you after all this time, in light of how horrible I was when I last saw you. I beg you to chalk it up to the depths of bad taste, which, however hard I try to bury, alas, continues to seep to the surface with the slightest lapse of vigilance. To think I never thanked you for sending John to me—a thing that by now he has surely cursed you for, my dear.

A few days after I heard about your pregnancy I had a vision of you and your baby, Marissa. As is my routine, I asked my Indian, Sam, what he thought about it. This was his reply: "Shit."

I have learned to take my Indian very literally in these cases, Marissa, to match his words exactly with the image that emerges in my mind's eye. So I thought about this quirky thing, the image of Madonna Marissa and the word *shit*, and what emerged from my unconscious is a memory I'm meant to share with you only. So, here you are again, darling, resurrected as my confidante.

I was five, or maybe six, so Cassie was about twenty-nine (my age now, ironically) as I remember it. It was a time when we still viewed one another as allies and relished every minute we spent out of our oppressive house. It was winter, and we bundled ourselves up to go skating at Rockefeller Center. She had on a white fur coat and hat, and though it was a bitter-cold day, she warmed me up just by gripping my hand. On the ice, every time we split apart, I felt the cold bite me, and I struggled not only to keep upright but also to keep from crying before I could link up with her again. Also, I remember looking around the rink and feeling incredibly happy that my mother was so beautiful and warm, while so many other women seemed cold. Because we were so determined to stay joined, Cassie and I dragged each other down a lot, and we'd just sit there, blocking traffic and laughing. Other skaters smiled at us, and I remember thinking we were warming them up. After one fall a very handsome man skated over, joined in on our laughter, and helped us to our feet. The three of us formed a chain and continued around the rink. I was in the middle, thinking, I have two blankets now—a short-lived luxury, because soon

Cassie switched places with me. "You don't need to be in the middle," I protested. "You have your furs on." She said we'd take turns, but I didn't think that was fair, and I started pestering her that I was cold and wanted to go home. She kept talking and laughing with this handsome stranger until I got so obnoxious that it was impossible for her to enjoy herself. I bore a grudge against her for the longest time—well, you can imagine.

I can't help but think, Marissa, that it was on the ice that Cassie began to curdle before my eyes, at a moment when witnesses might have sworn that we were the most loving mother and son around. In this, I don't think she's much different from the other mothers of this world. Their children pick the oddest moments to turn against them. My heart goes out to you, dear, because no mother is safe from an onslaught of derision from her child. And this is what Sam has induced me to tell you: You have our sympathy.

Needless to say, darling, it's one lucky baby that will have a mother like you, because underneath the busybody I so cruelly chastised at the opera is a woman who is warm and caring (to a fault, your child will say). You held my hand, didn't you? But at my coldest moment, all I saw was the shit. . . .

Marissa put the letter down. It was the last sentence that made her forgive Bradley's insults of the past and ponder her own future. He'd written: "Now you know how tainted are the hearts of children."

Chapter Twenty

EVENTUALLY the city of Santa Fe began to recover from the Fiesta and the tourists who departed to their respective homelands. In the fall, the social season dried up as abruptly as the Santa Fe River tended to do in its announcing the end of the Spring thaw. Finding a decent parking place near the Plaza ceased to be a challenge (and maître d's obliged gladly when one called at eight for a table at nine). On Camino Sin Nombre, a certain black Chevy reclaimed its old spot in the Valdez driveway.

Throughout the summer Bradley had heard in snatches of conversation that the Valdez family was undergoing a transformation that placed him well outside their sphere of concern. At the tennis club where they now owned a family membership, Stevie had learned how to swim in a few short days and thought nothing of running to the end of the low diving board, halting there to grab his nose before leaping into the water while he waved to his mother. Sylvia's social circle had expanded beyond her sisters to encompass several wives of her husband's fellow politicians; at home, Stevie's grandfather was teaching the boy how to whittle.

"He's working on something for you," Sylvia had told Bradley outdoors one day, "but I'm not supposed to tell you. You will get it on your doorstep, his little surprise."

"So you'll let him come that close?"

"Why wouldn't I?" Sylvia asked, and Bradley probed

her eyes for confirmation of his suspicion that Stevie's dropping off a gift and running away was seen as a harmless exception to an otherwise hard-and-fast rule that the child steer clear of him.

Sylvia cut off their chat with a hasty excuse, her face clouded. Her husband had said that people who give beer to wooden Indians were maybe meant for institutions and needed watching by professional people. She didn't fully agree, but perhaps Bradley was indeed too exotic an influence for an impressionable little boy. She had begun to worry about Stevie's dreams after he had spoken to her excitedly of wooden Indian armies riding across the desert on the backs of dinosaurs.

From time to time Bradley would catch glimpses of Stevie showing off on his bike, daring to ride with no hands or making a hairpin turn. Though Stevie would always wave at him, the boy never approached to say hello. That Stevie's smile of greeting was not as broad as in the days when he scraped his knees on the surface of Camino Sin Nombre forced Bradley to wonder further what dangers the child had been warned about that had made him so distant.

Around Santa Fe news buzzed about Bradley Roberson III and the renovation of his once miserable house on miserable Camino Sin Nombre. John Aaron was the only one who had seen it, but he had reported on every detail, as if delineating the perfect body of a dancer who had let John experience him one limb at a time. With such precision, he marveled, had Bradley alternated Apache baskets with nineteenth-century colored pencil sketches by Plains Indians in captivity on his living room wall! How perfectly he had molded the niches on each side of the patio doors and how dramatically he lit them, so that there were shadows like clouds cloaking the kachina dolls that were set inside the cave-like nooks. And how magnificent were the rugs he bought, all forming a pleasant harmony of natural dyes and geometric patterns that only the Navajo can execute. The house would be truly perfect, said John Aaron, if Bradley would just take down the horrible rip-off Warhol portrait of his mother that blew the impact of his painting arrangement in the dining room.

It was with an almost visceral pleasure that Bradley had removed the favorites of his father's stock of Impressionists from their ornate Roberson frames and highlighted them with simple borders. (His joy, however, had been undercut by Cassie's excited phone call upon being once again bequeathed his leftovers, a Dégas ballerina among them.) Seeking pain—or atonement—he had pulled a long neglected work of art from the bottom drawer of the breakfront and, after framing it in dazzling gold leaf, assigned Cassie's portrait a place of honor on his dining room wall. Wistful memories of gardening with Stevie Valdez fell away as Bradley stood ruminating before the addition to his severely pruned art collection.

"Now I know you're out to drive yourself crazy," John announced as he entered the dining room to face a Cassie with violet eyes; magenta lips; pink, orange, and yellow hair; and puce eyebrows. Her electric smile hardly shorted out the message that her eyes conveyed: that a gorgeous face was no passport to freedom for a woman in a cage.

"Sit down," said Bradley, "and feast your eyes on my living nightmare."

"What are you doing? Vying for my masochist-of-the-month trophy? For God's sake," said John, "give yourself a break."

Bradley sighed. "God, what stock I come from. No wonder the Valdezes think I'm the Antichrist."

"Leave it to a Jew to fetch the Antichrist for a bite of lunch. Or should I leave him to his worship?"

"I know what's going to happen," said Bradley. "I can feel it in my bones. My house is finished; my walls are reinforced, and here I sit in my renovated fortress. I need to have that portrait here, to remind me that life is one invasion after another—from the moment the tiny sperm breaks through the wall of the tiny egg. She'll be here, John. It's only a matter of time."

Everyone wanted to know when Bradley would be throwing an open house to show off his hard work. After all, Santa Fe *was* an endless celebration, and with its revelers arriving from the hinterlands like penguins waddling onto the beaches of Waikiki, there was a certain legitimacy afforded to those who adopted Dorothy Cheswick's credo: "Our houses should publicly speak to the heart of why we're all here."

But Bradley had no plans to open his house to the public. He considered having John and Marissa over for a quiet dinner, but even this seemed too big a breach of the intensity of his solitude. In fact, even John's wandering through his few rooms, extolling every detail, made Bradley edgy. He knew John's appreciation should make him happy rather than nervous, as should the thought that John would one day come to think of the place as a second home. Meanwhile, though it distressed Bradley for his possessions to form the linchpin of their union, he remained loath to change the situation.

In the middle of September Sylvia Valdez received in her mailbox a rough sketch of the house next door with this caption: "I know the adobe's still a mess outside. It's next on my list. But the inside is my own little piece of heaven. Can you come for coffee Thursday at eleven? ——Yes. ——No." When the card was returned with a yes, Sam, who had been neglected for so many days that the liquid in his glass had solidified into an amber shell, was promptly poured a triple shot of bourbon.

Sylvia dressed for the occasion. Coffee at Bradley's required a pair of modern jeans, full at the hip and tapered at the ankle, and a big shirt with a bold and jazzy print. On her feet were ankle-high boots, black and laced, with pointy toes. The tennis club membership had brought her fashion, just as the summer had brought a valiant drive to pull her little family together.

"*Ee*. This is nice," said Sylvia, entering Bradley's living room through the patio. Her eyes toured his walls, floor, and the *banco* under the picture window with a show of interest but became downcast in examining his straight-backed, rough-hewn antique chairs.

"So, is it Santa Fe?" asked Bradley.

"Oh, yes," she said. "It's very Santa Fe."

"Coffee's waiting," said Bradley. "And *biscochitos*. I didn't make them, though. I bought them at Maria's bakery."

"Maria's is very good," said Sylvia. "I buy *semitas* there when I'm feeling lazy. Stevie likes them better than mine."

"He'll know better when he grows up," said Bradley. "Come on in," he said, ushering her into the dining room. Sam was at the table; Bradley was polite enough to seat her two chairs away from him. "You remember this guy," he said diplomatically. "I don't know why, but I love him more the messier he gets. He makes it hard for me to feel sorry for myself."

"Why do you have a drink in front of him?"

"Nostalgia, that's all," he said, shrugging. "You know, Sylvia, I haven't had a drop since that night you put me to bed. In a way I suppose I have Robby to thank. I think about Robby a lot, you know." He poured the coffee and set a small plate of cookies in front of her.

"How is he, anyway? I see he got his car back."

"His reward for a B minus in summer school. He got a television too," said Sylvia, "but only because my husband saw how hard it was for him to do the work. Robert remembered how hard it was having to read Shakespeare, himself. So the B minus made him very proud. I don't really know what to think about this reward business. *Ee.* Nobody gave me a TV set, you know?" She reached uneasily for a cookie.

Bradley wished she could relax. "No one would try to reform in prison, Sylvia, unless there was a promise of parole. Listen, when I was fourteen, I knew that I had millions of dollars in my name, all because somebody died. Somebody dies of cancer and Bradley Roberson III becomes a multimillionaire before he's old enough to go to work. Some might say that having a father like mine was like being given a winning lottery ticket. But what about how it feels to win before paying your dues? The thing is, if English is a tough subject for Robby, and he can suffer through it enough to get better than a passing grade, then maybe he deserves to win the lottery. It's legitimate bribery. You can't expect him to see too far ahead for himself; all Robby knows is that he's a sixteen-year-old with lots of things he'd rather do."

"He's just lucky he had a father who can afford to buy him things," Sylvia said with some distaste. "But in a few years where will he be? *Ee.* What will he be—a grease monkey? His father fought a war and learned what life should be. Me, I would like to see something make Robby stop and think—and it won't be a television set. Anyway, Señor Bradley, when you were sixteen, were you driving around and making trouble and breaking your mother's heart?"

Bradley smiled ruefully. "When I was sixteen, I had worse ways of making a monster of myself, Sylvia. I hurt a lot of people, when I thought to bother with them at all. From what I can see, Sylvia, one of the only differences between Robby and me is that he lives in the world and I lived to escape it. He's part of the rhythm of what's going on here. I've heard complaints in any number of restaurants about kids like Robby, and the drunks, and the traffic, as if none of those things belong here. I've even heard complaints about the style of the gazebo on the Plaza. People expect some kind of quaint, ancient paradise, but brutality is looming around every corner. Damn it, Sylvia, this town needs a little brutality to survive. If you didn't have Robby Valdez pulling flowers out of the ground, maybe this place would just space out into oblivion. Robby has a social function, Sylvia, and I suppose I'm jealous." He paused, hating her patient tolerance of his sarcasm. "Do you really think I didn't break my mother's heart when I was sixteen? My mother camouflages her feelings like an old-fashioned striptease, Sylvia, and whenever I think she's dropped a fan and I've caught a glimpse of something, you'd better believe I take a potshot at it. I have taken many potshots at my mother's heart and hit the bull's-eye maybe one hundred percent of the time. Darling, compared to me, your wild little Robby's an amateur."

Bradley pointed to the portrait on the wall. "This," he said, "is my Madonna Cassie. Tell me she looks like the mother of a saint who has had her heart left in one piece."

As Sylvia examined Cassie's portrait Bradley realized that he, himself, should have resorted to feathers and fans. He suspected his estrangement from his neighbor was now complete.

"You know, when you agreed to come over here, I got you something," he said with quiet sadness. "I know you're dying to get out of here, but sit just a minute while I get up and get it for you. Please."

"I don't want anything," Sylvia said. "You gave me that vase, remember? That's more than enough."

"But that vase was just something I didn't care about that you happened to think was pretty. What I got you is really for you, Sylvia. Anyway, you can't reject it because it doesn't belong in here."

He opened the top drawer of the breakfront and pulled out a small, very thin package wrapped in white tissue paper and tied with a pink ribbon. Handing it to Sylvia, Bradley said, "Don't open it now. Just take it home."

"*Madre de Dios*," said Sylvia Valdez. "You make a big show about giving me a gift and now you don't want me to open it in front of you? Are you afraid to see me smile or something? *Ee*. It's all a crazy business."

Bradley nervously checked his fingernails, and then smoothed his hair while looking at Cassie's portrait as intently as if he were facing a full-length mirror. Turning, he said, "Actually, Sylvia, I do want a favor from you. You said before that my house is nice, but I want you to tell me what you really think about it. It's important to me, Sylvia, though the reason is just a crazy business, as you say."

She looked down at her package, wondering what sort of person paid to hear what other people thought of him. What sort of person felt it necessary to have his hair and nails perfect for coffee with a neighbor? "I'd say you should stop shutting yourself up in a place where nobody will want to come," she said at last, dutifully. "This house is very nice to look at, but it feels like a place where people are not welcome to sit down. *Ee*, it's like these galleries here. It's like everything has a price tag, except nothing's for sale. Maybe you should do some simple thing like cooking, so your house will smell like somebody lives here. Me, I don't ask myself things like am I in the world or out of the world or what does my neighbor think of my house? I don't know. You put all this time into your house, Bradley, but you know, I think you didn't love doing it; it didn't come from your heart, but maybe from some need to impress people. Now, that Indian of yours is a big, ugly thing, but when I found you that night, you were curled up in its lap, hugging it, and that must have come from the heart. But if you love this ugly thing, why don't you take care of it? When you love something, Bradley, you think about how is this person feeling today and maybe I can do something to make him feel better—it's not you who are in the center of things. I've been sitting here trying to figure out why you wanted me to come over, but now I see what's going on. You give me a thing. You don't give *you*. Your words weren't meant for me; they were all for you. The only time I think you ever gave you was when you were with Stevie. Then you shared something, maybe because you were living in the world of a little boy. What I think of this house is that you should make it a place that can be shared with someone—and not just someone to watch you."

"That's enough," said Bradley softly, but Sylvia was finished. "Tell Stevie I say hi, won't you? Tell him I hope he's having a good time at school. Are you going to the club for lunch? It's getting to be that time—and I have to go to meet someone."

She looked at him, remembering how tan he used to be. Now he'd gone all white, but he was still such a handsome thing. "You could buy yourself a clock, you know."

"It's a rule with me: Time should be left to take care of itself."

"You really are a crazy person, Bradley. But that's the thing about this town. You said it, I think. We get all the crazies here. *Ee,* at least it isn't boring. I'll never say to you that you are boring."

Looking at Bradley's slumped shoulders, Sylvia could barely make herself leave him. Her own home seemed unusually warm when she returned to it. With her father sitting at the kitchen table slurping up the *carne asada* left over from supper, she unwrapped her present from

Bradley Roberson III. It was a painting on a sheet of tin, slighty rusted, but its image was clean: a sweet portrait of the Virgin of Guadalupe, framed with dabs of red and white unmistakably meant to be roses.

"*Mira, Papa,*" said Sylvia. "*Un regalo de nuestro vecino.*"

"*¿Ese maricón?*" her father queried suspiciously.

"*Sí. El maricón, pero un hombre muy bueno, aunque es medio loco.*"

"*Claro que es loco,*" said the old man, who had no fondness for homosexuals, neighbors especially.

"*Es posible. ¿Pero, quién sabe? Me cae bien ese joven. Así me parese. El es maricón, pero no me importanta eso. No me cuida.*" It was not her place to judge; she only knew that she liked her neighbor, Bradley Roberson III. She bit her lip and shook her head in wonder at her gift. Then she leaned it up against the blue Tiffany vase that yet formed the centerpiece of her kitchen table.

Chapter Twenty-one

THE L'Etoile de West Cooking Celebrity Search, a contest that had been advertised on handbills distributed outside gourmet shops and croissanteries, had drummed up few interested in joining the too-short roster of volunteer chefs. (John joked that Bradley should submit one of his omelet recipes and title it "Huevos de los Muertos," for assured inclusion in the restaurant's star lineup.) Admitting their conceptual flaw in thinking Santa Fe teemed with creative souls anxious to be applauded while donning aprons, the owners revamped the celebrity angle of the restaurant. Two weeks preceding the October grand opening a press release appeared in the *City Different News,* boasting generous plans to decorate L'Etoile's walls with the works of unsung artists and host book-signing parties; authors would receive full profits but what the restaurant needed to recoup its costs. The opening itself would feature an unknown photographer's "cowboy hunks" series called Risqué Rodeo, along with a poetry reading from *Living with the Lizards,* a staple-bound publication from Jemez Mountain Press.

The news release provoked an angry letter to the editor from Dorothy Cheswick, who wished the owners ill will for having fired local adobe artisan Epifanio "Joe" Salazar and replacing him with a crew of ski bums who wintered in Vale, Colorado. "If this illustrates a dedication to local talent," she wrote, "no doubt their walls will soon be crowded with pictures hailing from New York and Houston."

As a regular on the owner's dinner party guest list, John felt obliged to ignore Dorothy Cheswick's call for a boycott of L'Etoile de West and humored Bradley into joining him at its October debut. "I hear," he said, "that through their Boston connections they got Julia Child herself to approve the menu. Plus, a fashion designer, whom they claim shall remain nameless, donated a congratulatory case of California champagne."

Bradley's appearance at a public event, his first in many a moon, provoked numerous whispers at L'Etoile's well-laid tables. "The ghost walks," someone said, leering Bradley's way. Another raised a wineglass and gave John an acknowledging wink: "I see John's airing the furniture again." The insults, however, were inspired less by Bradley's habitual absence than by his blandness. In the past he could be relied on to put forth observations as engaging as his tan. Now, with not a trace of his old incisiveness (or tan) he had lost his novelty, and in a white suit amid whitewashed adobe walls, he was no more vibrant than an unpainted sculpture poured from a plaster of Paris mold.

His fans, weary of inquiring after what he was doing with himself only to be told flatly that he was lavishing in a perpetual state of uselessness, turned their attention elsewhere. Not even his most recent unlisted phone number, changed thanks to the continuing creativity of Richard Gabrielli, could add fizz to a mystique gone flat. But the once fervent attempts by passing acquaintances to engage him in small talk were replaced with a collective cold shoulder that relieved Bradley. Only the intrusive stares of Richard Gabrielli, awarded with the rare social invitation for his freehandedness with ¡Viva Mexico! discounts, managed to provoke Bradley's dismay. Overall, he found it most pleasant to be able to relish in peace the Alaskan Salmon Trout at a L'Etoile corner table with John, who complained that his entreé was drowned in lemon juice.

Bradley's own culinary debut, Chez Roberson, might have been rated "uneven" had its samplers extended beyond his intimate circle (to which John and Marissa held exclusive membership).

The spinach-and-feta strudel *hors d'oeuvre* was lovely, served with a fine fumé blanc (for John) and a glass of Perrier (for Marissa). Bradley drank apple cider, saying it was very "of the season." Handing Marissa her plate, he insisted she try out his new Italian divan, its downy cushion white, its base fancifully curved and "deliciously chrome." When Marissa lay down, sighing as if she had landed in the arms of a dream lover, Bradley set a present on her voluminous chest: a revised edition of *Baby and Child Care.*

"It's good to have a well-rounded approach to the little people," he said blithely. "Cassie tells me I was a Dr.

Spock baby, but I doubt she's remembering right. If it's true, then I wish the man a painful death, if he hasn't had one already."

"My God," said Marissa. "Bradley just said the name Cassie, John, and I didn't see smoke coming out of his ears."

"He's trying to get her married off to a movie buff," said John. "The poor woman's hardly seen the light of day in the past month. Just how do you go about making eyes at someone with *The Seven Samurai* performing mayhem on the screen, I wonder?"

"God, no Kurosawa for *her*. Her latest hunting ground is the 'George Cukor Remembered' series," offered Bradley.

"She manhunts at the movies?" asked Marissa.

"At an adult extension course at the New School. I decided it was about time she got a college education," Bradley said. "She seems to be enjoying it, and she's meeting men left and right. I guess that with a movie running, somebody can feast his eyes on her for two hours and get hooked before she opens her mouth and reveals that her head is stuffed with kleenex."

"So it's working?" Marissa asked.

"Well, she had a setback after *Pat and Mike*. I had high hopes for the guy too: a rich banker in his late forties, divorced and childless. His ex-wife was an alcoholic, and he finally 'stuck her away in a vault.' Cassie's words. But—and here's a lesson for you, John—he had this golden retriever that he took on all these hunting trips, like to Scotland, where he shoots quail. He had some special arrangement with overseas governments that let him sneak his dog through quarantine, so you can imagine how influential this guy is internationally. Anyway, according to Cassie, this dog was quite the gourmand. No dog food for him: prime rib, venison steak, and snacks straight from the dining room table, which even Cassie thinks is pretty uncivilized. She knew better than to complain about it, though; she didn't care to risk having a steak knife flung at her across the table or maybe even being threatened with a gun."

Bradley paused, suddenly solemn, and lit up a cigarette. An inquiring look from Marissa raised in him a conscious effort to perk up again. "How do you like my little Greek things?"

"They're not as creative as your omelets," said John. "I still think your omelets are cooking-contest material. Maybe someone will announce open auditions for a 'Santa Fe Egg' book. You could call them Eggs con Brio."

"Stop the egg talk," Marissa said. The white divan seemed to highlight a pale green hue in her complexion. "God, I hate being in the room with eggs these days—eggs, hot dogs, or Cherry Coke. I gag at the smell of Cherry Coke."

"We're both happy to hear that, darling," said John.

"A little respect here, if you please. Anyway, I want to hear more about the banker and his dog," said Marissa.

"I dropped the subject, Marissa, and it will stay dropped," said Bradley. "I decided to preserve what little dignity my mother can't manage to preserve for herself. Not preserve—resurrect. I have a mission to resurrect what little dignity my mother has shoveled down the tubes over the years. What happened with Cassie, the dog, the banker, and also a couple of slices of raw tenderloin is nothing George Cukor would have found any humor in. Now she's signed up for 'Lana Turner and Gloria Swanson: Vamp Queens or Camp Queens,' so maybe she'll find some William Powell to carry her through New Year's Eve. Otherwise I may just have to bring her here for the holidays."

"John," Marissa exclaimed. "I think we really are witnessing the beginnings of détente."

"Ronald Reagan spoke three words of Russian on national television," John said. "Anything's possible."

"Can we talk about something else?" Bradley begged. "Like Halloween, which is a mere two weeks away? I don't have the *faintest* idea who to be. Maybe I'll just put a pumpkin in Sam's lap and let the evil spirits of the night do their work while I read *The Berlin Stories* in front of the fire."

"You will not do that," said Marissa, "because everyone will be secretly dying to see what you come up with. And who can be morbid on Halloween? Did you hear that Barry sent me sacred blue cornmeal from the Hopi Reservation? I'm supposed to throw a pot to put it in and keep it by my bed so that the baby and I can sleep with its protection. And let's not forget the pine needles from a tree struck by lightning. With all this stuff I'm getting in the mail, I've decided to paint a king-size sheet with token natural disasters and go as Mother Nature."

"Who will you be, John?" asked Bradley. "Father Time?"

John poured himself a third glass of wine, ignoring Bradley's reference to his forty-seventh birthday, which was tastelessly imminent. "I thought that maybe we'd come up with something together. Nijinsky and Diaghilev, for instance."

"Oh, gag me," said Bradley. "How about Wagner and King Ludwig II? You'd make such a great Wagner, John. We could pin a Star of David on a velvet beret and you could sing an aria from *Parsifal* in Yiddish."

John actually found the idea somewhat appealing. "If only I knew Yiddish."

"Well, you have two weeks to learn."

"When's dinner, Bradley?" asked Marissa. "The hors d'oeuvre just can't hold me, *boychik,* now that I'm officially eating for two."

As for Bradley's main course, the best that could be said about it was that it succeeded in making Marissa Goldman chew slowly. Trying his hand at molé stew, Bradley had put too much unsweetened chocolate into the mix and had let it simmer, without stirring, for too long; thus, bitter mortar clung to the meat. Bradley apologized, urging John and Marissa to imagine that they were eating in a Mexican restaurant in London.

John sipped the exquisite Château Lafite-Rothschild he miraculously had all to himself. Lately Bradley had been generous to the point of philanthropy, as though he thought expensive wine would fill a coffer in an otherwise wanting soul. Often when John would turn maudlin over his sensual deprivation, Bradley would use the wine as an excuse, claiming that John's flesh was weak only because he was drunk and it was his own fault for not having controlled himself.

When the phone interrupted his addition of fresh strawberries to slices of amaretto cheesecake from Desserts ¡Ole!, Bradley swore under his breath. Two of the three legitimate possibilities as to who could be calling were sitting in his dining room, and the one who remained had the power to dampen whatever enjoyment could be squeezed out of the rest of the evening. Bradley opened the refrigerator door, drawing the receiver from the kitchen counter to his ear. From the note of cheer in his mother's hello, he prayed that the banker had offered to donate his dog to science as an act of restitution. Cassie's latest experience had been such a blow that her voice had developed a constant quiver, as though she had shed the vestments of hope. He considered it a small victory that her pain affected him, as her giddiness did now.

"Three guesses who just called me," Cassie sang into the phone.

"Dog Lovers Anonymous?"

"Nope."

"The Chairman of the Board of Citicorp to ask why you were wasting your time on his underling?"

"Nope. One more, Bradley."

"The president offering you an ambassadorship to Monaco."

"Franklin Petrie." Her squeal reminded Bradley of a cartoon cat whose tail had been plugged into a wall socket.

"Come again?"

"Franklin Petrie, on his knees," crowed Cassie. "He loves me, Bradley. He said he was an absolute idiot for fucking up a good thing. He said we're fated, and he doesn't want to fight destiny anymore."

"And you believed him? Oh, God, please don't tell me you actually fell for it. Cassie, he's scum. He's the worst thing I ever did to you. I have years of repentance left for setting you up with him."

"I think you never really got to know him, Bradley," Cassie countered. "You hardly spent any time with him—talking, I mean. Remember, Bradley, I lived with the man; I know how sweet he can be. I know he's a Dr. Jekyll and Mr. Hyde. Who isn't, darling son of mine?"

"*I'll* tell you what he is, Cassie. He's broke. That's why he called you and said those things. He wants a handout."

"He has enough money to take me to the theater. Orchestra seats too. And then to dinner and dancing at Windows on the World."

"Very broke, Cassie. Can't you see he's spending his last nickel in hopes of a high return on his investment?"

"You think it's impossible for someone to love me, don't you?" Cassie said. "You can't see that someone I *lived* with could come back for the sheer reason that he misses me. Maybe he doesn't love me, Bradley, but he could miss me. How do you know it wasn't you that stopped him from falling in love with me? You and what you think of him."

"Well, then, why not just leave me out of this altogether? But do me a favor—no, do yourself a favor. Suppose he gives you this wonderful night on the town and then goes to bed with you and you have an absolutely fabulous time, and then when you're all sated, he asks you for money or asks you to ask me for money—"

"Stop it."

"No. Listen. All I'm asking you to do is to test him by refusing to give him a penny. Will you do that? You don't have to make a scene—just turn him down, *if* he should ask you for something. Is it asking too much for you to try to protect yourself, Mother?"

"No." Cassie spoke like a child who'd been reprimanded.

"Will you do what I said, if the occasion arises?"

"Yes."

"Promise?"

"Yes."

"Good girl. Now I have to go; I have dinner guests."

"Who?"

"John and Marissa. Cooking dinner for three is all I can handle, partly because of phone calls like this one, Cassie. They upset me."

"You always make me apologize, Bradley. I'm so tired of it."

"I'm just telling you the truth. Mothers and sons should be truthful with each other. Just be careful, darling."

Hanging up, he battled the gloom that bore down on the arch of his smile with the stress of concrete blocks. Mustering his most insouciant tone, he called out, "Cheesecake, anyone?" twirling into the dining room with a tray.

Happy with wine, John attempted to lift Bradley's spirits with a couple of verses of "You Took Advantage of Me."

Marissa, more distressed than Bradley by Cassie's phone call, silenced him. In thirty years, she realized, the baby she was carrying might see fit to address her as she had just heard Cassie Roberson being addressed. The idea of having an abortion suddenly loomed in her mind as an option she had been a fool to overlook in the excitement of considering that a child would fill a void in her life. She stared Bradley down. Could motherhood actually be like the dropping of the atom bomb, as he'd suggested, with no hope of escaping its fallout?

"Why do you blame her, Bradley?" she asked. "You talk to her like she's a hopeless invalid, for God's sake. How can you let her feel so unloved?"

Bradley spoke matter-of-factly. "I blame her because she is incapable of looking at herself in the mirror and seeing anything but a painted doll waiting to be sold into a happy home. But you know, I have finally managed to feel sorry for my mother, Marissa, in spite of the fact that I don't love her the way I should. I realize it's probably not her fault she's such a victim. Darling, if I knew how to help her, I would, but it seems all I can do is see that she gets purchased by somebody who'll give her a better deal than she's gotten so far. At least I've stopped blaming her for my own little victim's complex. Anyway, what would you do if you were assigned to be the guardian of a person like her?"

"Do you ever ask *her* how you can help?" Marissa spoke in earnest. "Have you ever tried to find out what set her on a path to self-destruction?"

"If I find out the exact hour of her birth, will you do her astrological chart?"

"Don't be such an asshole. I asked you a straightforward question."

"Sorry. Well, her father was an amputee and her mother was a two-bit whore at a truckstop. True white-trash angst. Now, this would turn some women into country-western singers."

"Would she have given birth to a Juilliard student if she'd stayed where she was?"

"Is that what she did it for? Make a loveless marriage for the sake of a lousy pianist whose father gave Juilliard enough money to keep them from throwing his brat out on his ear? So I could have ended up with a life of guzzling beer in a pool hall. So she got out. Big fucking deal, darling. It didn't do a fucking thing for her; not as far as I can tell."

"She obviously hates herself."

"My, we are getting *profound*. What are you after, Marissa? Is a child responsible for his parents' self-hatred? My own salvation is more than I can handle, as we all know."

"I'm sure she wants that for you, too, Bradley. She must love you," said Marissa.

"If love is dependency, she loves me enough to drown me."

"From what I know, she raised you by herself, didn't she? She didn't have much help from your father." She avoided Bradley's eyes now, her thoughts drifting inward. Her hands pressed her belly as though they were testing for overripeness in a melon.

"Marissa, for God's sake, you're nothing like her. With you there to love it, your kid won't suffer. Listen, Cassie was scared to death of me, Marissa. I was like some warden assigned to control and punish her, constantly speaking in a foreign language and confusing her. But, God, when I was a little boy, Marissa, I absolutely worshiped her. She was so beautiful, and her voice had a soft drawl that was like music. I loved to watch her dress; she was just magical. Naturally my father freaked out at the little queen who was out of the closet at age five while he was still in it at thirty-five. I got pulled out of Princess Cassie's magic kingdom, and when my father died, and I finally had the go-ahead to make it back, all I found was this scavenger who followed me around, hoping to snatch up a bisexual courtier at Studio 54. She had programmed herself for certain misery. God, I never forgave her. But she hadn't changed; I was the one creating the illusion. I got her all wrong."

"I was taught that there *were* no illusions, from the beginning of time." John had tears in his eyes.

"But you still had them, John," said Bradley.

"Did I?"

"Tell me you didn't believe your father had a handle on the truth of the universe."

"That was before I realized he'd never had wine like this." John toasted the picture of BJ Roberson, in sad salute to fatherhood.

"Get serious," said Bradley. "How about the illusion that he loved you?"

"I'm almost twenty years ahead of you in soul-searching, Bradley. I don't think I need another round of it. You, dear, are my only lingering torture."

"To which you cling for dear life. You have the illusion plague, my dear, and I'm your medicine."

"Let's not get presumptuous, Bradley. I'm glad it's so cut-and-dried for you, but I've stopped trying to figure it out. And, you know, I sleep better. When you get to be my age, Bradley, I hope *you*'ll sleep better. Once you realize that daily joy and sorrow don't have a hell of a lot to do with how you pull the strings, you'll stop crying out in your sleep. And you'll be a hell of a lot happier when you realize that the worst of it, which in your case might be poor Cassie, is absolutely out of your control. It's time you let her fend for herself, Bradley. Set up another trust fund for her if you have to, but otherwise it's time you dropped the whole fucking thing."

"But she's my job," Bradley cried out. "John, she's all I'm trained for."

Bradley's collapse at the end of the table drowned the sleeve of his white silk dinner jacket in tears. John glanced at Marissa, motioning her to stay put. Finally he got up and went over to Bradley, taking him in his arms. After being gently kissed and stroked, Bradley quieted down at last. "Witness," John said, poking him in the ribs, "the desperation of the unemployed American worker. Marissa, we have to help this poor kid find a way to make an honest living. Do you think anyone would take him on as a cook?"

"Fuck you." Bradley was smiling now.

"If only you would, you twenty-carat street urchin. If only you would."

Chapter Twenty-two

WHAT was there for an adequate pianist with a smattering of drama and dance on his Juilliard transcript to do for a living in Santa Fe, New Mexico? Waiting tables or manning a gallery were possibilities that Bradley dismissed out of hand, for such work involved cajoling people he might otherwise maneuver to avoid on the street. His allergy to machines that flashed error messages every time one pushed a wrong button prevented his considering an announcement of computer training for modernized hotel reservation systems. He put a checkmark by an ad for a tile grouter, as his own work on his kitchen counters evidenced an innate grouting ability. Remembering how he'd hated digging plaster out from under his nails with a straight pin, however, he erased the check.

"It's no use," Bradley said to John, who popped in to suggest that the first light snow of the season was worthy of celebration. He'd brought along some fine herb cheese and crackers to share before a piñon fire. Bradley greeted John's cheerfulness by throwing down the *City Different*

News in disgust. "I think it's time to pack and put my passport back into circulation," he announced. "How do you suppose the job market is behind the Iron Curtain? Think they'd hire me to stand in a museum with a sign around my neck saying, 'Lemon off the Capitalist Assemblyline'? Today I told Cassie to sell off our art collection so she doesn't have to keep bugging me for money. I told her to have a ball. Next she'll be telling me she got a job at Sotheby's."

"Something will turn up," John assured.

"Right. Like that shoo-in slot at the piano bar at Marietta's."

"They didn't expect you to audition with a classical repertoire."

"So who gave them the idea that I was Hoagy Carmichael? You?"

"Do something with him, Sam," John said to the wooden Indian on whose lap was stacked two weeks' worth of classifieds. "I give up."

"Sam can't help me. He's been on welfare all his life," said Bradley.

"I still don't see what's wrong with Marissa's idea about your being her apprentice. She gets tired these days, and Barry's too busy shaking his Indian maracas in the direction of Los Alamos to lift a finger. God, I wish he'd leave her in peace and crawl back into the woods. Anyway, you loved gardening. Clay isn't that much different than dirt, as far as I can tell."

"Why does she give me the distinct impression she thinks I'm a charity case?"

"Maybe because you act like one, darling."

"Honestly," Bradley exclaimed. "I think I'll apply for a Russian visa. You're putting me in a Moscow mood."

A Berlin mood was closer to the truth; Bradley's stubborn determination to resist his old patterns was all that kept him from boarding an airplane to stew in self-pity as a failure. His will was cracking.

Two days after a conversation that had made him feel like hurling Bradley off a Sangre de Cristo mountain crest, John bounded through Bradley's door with a triumphant grin. The stereo blared Lotte Lenya as John announced that he'd learned, in the waiting room of his orthopedist, how arthritis was forcing Herman Petrovich (formerly Peterson) to retire completely from his role as accompanist for children's and adult beginner dance classes at Madame Petrovich's School of Ballet. Naturally he had put in a good word for Bradley. The hours were less than ideal—eight to ten A.M. and three to five P.M., weekdays; nine to noon, Saturdays; and the pay, at five dollars an hour, was all the school could afford. However, John reminded Bradley, for anyone in the arts to find work that corresponded with his talents was a true rarity. One need only consider that there were more actors masquerading as waiters than counter positions at McDonald's around the globe.

Bradley didn't mind the low pay; if anything, he felt that his piano playing should command less. Yet once his day took on some semblance of a schedule, his existence as a working man unfolded as the equivalent of a sandwich without filling. His former idleness had steeped him in a depression that suppressed his appetite; now he grew distressed over the weight gain that resulted from the overly long lunches that bridged the void between his hours at the Petrovich piano. During his meals he took to writing Cassie regularly, exclaiming in one of his reports to her that before securing a front-row seat at Madame Petrovich's, he had never known that mornings could be so entertaining. "The dancing ladies bring me presents of gratitude for my smiles and applause," he wrote.

Mrs. Meyers (wife of a landscape photographer with aspirations to be the next Ansel Adams) brought me a green-chile-and-cheese croissant this morning and promised me a fresh one every Wednesday. Maisie Duncan—newly divorced, very sad, but very pretty—brought me her famous (she says) piñon-nut brownies, and Elaine Lovejoy—a Gothic romance writer who says dancing helps the rhythm of her prose—brought me homegrown basil from her herb garden. There are two men in the adult morning class, but neither of them speaks to me.

The afternoon classes with children—girls all—are more depressing. All those expectations, that earnestness; will any of these penguin-shaped prepubescents ever make the corps de ballet of Detroit, let alone New York or San Francisco? But time will teach them, I guess. Anyway, who am I to say that none of these little darlings will defect to join the Bolshoi in their prime?

Bradley's letters to New York went unanswered, however, as Cassie herself was in the midst of the most highly charged activity that she could recall since her days as a typing student in Richmond.

It turned out that what Franklin Petrie wanted after all was not money but an endless quantity of cocaine that only vast amounts of money could procure. Cassie had withheld from Bradley that through her venture into the art business, via sale of his inherited paintings, she was managing to support Franklin's habit. Her reward was frequent and frenzied sex, as pure a high for her as the cocaine rushes that kept Franklin functioning. But the thrill was soon to fade.

On a miserable rainy night in early December, Cassie announced to Franklin that multiple orgasms would warm her up enough to go fetch what he needed, which she doled out in puny lines. This strategy resulted in a busted lip, a black eye, the vandalism of her boudoir, and the theft of her engagement ring, the only diamond BJ Roberson had felt obliged to give her. Franklin left without what remained of the kilo purchased with a miniature Renoir and hidden behind the toilet in the master bathroom.

"There's not a soul to blame for this," Cassie told the emergency room resident at Lenox Hill. "No," she said, correcting herself, "there are two *soles* to blame. I should have known better than to run up the stairs in a brand-new pair of shoes." Fighting off tears, she explained that her mother had taught her to break shoes in on a gravel road before wearing them to a dance, because if you didn't, you were sure to embarrass yourself and jitterbug your way to a busted fanny. "Even after you've turned fifty, you should follow your mother's advice, don't you think, Doctor?" The doctor silently sewed up her lip, dressed her eye with gauze and tape to keep it quiet, and decided it would be useless to ask her any more questions.

What's a busted lip? What's a black eye? Just a bang-up ending to a bang-up time. That's what Cassie said to herself as the taxi took her home. As to the loss of her ring, well, she had seen an evening soap-opera heroine lose a ring like that and bounce back just fine. Besides, she thought, the ring had probably scared off what could well have been the best of her potential suitors. Wasn't that how it was these days, that diamonds turned off men of character? What depressed Cassie was the fact that she might still be marred by Christmas, which would mean that she had a Chinaman's chance of finding someone to spend the New Year with.

Then came the shock of seeing her face in the mirror. One beautiful eye did not turn more beautiful to compensate for the ugliness of the mass of gauze and tape that kept its partner in the dark. Her eyes had always carried each another, she realized; they were like Siamese twins with the same pair of legs. Seeing her stitched lip made her think of a black widow spider finding a home to make her mouth a carrier of its poison. Who would get near her; who would dare? Panicked, Cassie pulled open the drawer of her vanity, drew out her little cloisonné box, and dug around for the remaining dirt from home as frantically as Franklin had rubbed her gold-beveled hand mirror for straggling crystals. Only after she sat dead still, finger in her mouth, her tongue having licked her finger clean minutes before, did it dawn on Cassie what she had done: She had exhausted her protection against all the vile forces in the world. She had rejected the fleeting temptation to board a plane for New Mexico, certain Bradley had given her such a reputation that Santa Fe would welcome her like sharks greet swimmers off the coast of Australia. With this newest shock, however, she swallowed what remained of her pride.

Bradley, groggy from sleep, deciphered through Cassie's sobs and pleas for salvation that his mother had fallen, most likely beyond repair. He told her he would fly out to pick up the pieces as soon as he could get there. Hanging up the phone, Bradley turned to John and announced that Cassie had at last met her demise and that he was leaving in the morning for New York to deliver her to Santa Fe to die.

"I think that Indian has done damage to your brain," John replied. "Since when does a hysterical phone call in the middle of the night confirm a terminal condition?"

"I don't know." Bradley sighed sadly. "But that's what Sam is telling me, and I'm too tired to argue."

A few hours later, having left John to set up accommodations for Cassie at Marissa's (again an empty nest, since Barry's sudden departure for Machu Picchu), Bradley sat in his first-class seat, striving to work himself into a New York mood. It was hard to brace himself for the scene that awaited him: the mixture of Cassie's powerlessness and his recently relinquished tyranny that it seemed she required to survive. If she loved him, if indeed she had ever loved his father, perhaps it stemmed from her inward recognition that the life of a battered serf offered safety.

The maid had done her best to restore order to the house on Eighty-sixth Street, but upon entering, Bradley noted how his absence had freed its pall to be converted into a chaotic assembly of neglected relics. The paintings Cassie had seen fit to dispose of left gapes like missing teeth on the walls, and Cassie's attempt to rearrange the heavy furniture creatively had created a warehouse effect. Cassie's room was darkened, but through its ever-present smoke emerged a sound haunting in its familiarity: the humming of the woman who still unburdened her soul with light, random melodies.

Cassie smiled impishly at Bradley from under her satin quilt. "What a gloomy face, just like your father's," she said. "Sweetie, I hoped you'd walk in laughing." She smiled as broadly as her stitches would allow, shedding more light on the disaster. "I mean, it is ridiculous."

Bradley moved closer. "Mama, how awful." He stared at her. Overcome, he opened his arms, "I feel so bad." He rested his head on her Dior-draped bosom and cried.

"It's just the shock, Bradley," Cassie said, trying to comfort him. "Last night I was so scared, I forgot what my mother used to tell me. 'Cassie,' she'd say, 'A woman has to keep on going no matter what happens, hold her breath and wait it out.' I forgot to hold my breath, and look how I've upset you."

"I hate this house. I hate what it's done to you."

"Houses don't *do* anything. I sure am tired of this one, though."

"God, I'm so sorry." Bradley began to search for solace in the softness of her quilt, but it failed to muffle the unforgiving pounding of his heart.

"Didn't you try to tell me about Franklin? I guess you

did leave out that he's a drug-crazed maniac, but forget about it, sweetie. It was fun while it lasted. For heaven's sake, let's just get out of here and cheer you up. I'm ready for the Mardi Gras. Is it like a Mardi Gras in that town you're in?"

"Truly," said Bradley, finally infected by his mother's smile. "We saints parade with room to stretch in Santa Fe, New Mexico."

Cassie's unbandaged eye squinted as Bradley helped her from his car in Marissa Goldman's dusty driveway. "Can't they turn the sun down in this place?" she asked her hostess. If Marissa's heart had begun to go out to Cassie Roberson the evening Bradley had served her up for dinner on Camino Sin Nombre, it completed the journey that day, melting at the sight of the battered face that Marissa's lips brushed with a welcoming kiss.

"You'll adjust," said Marissa cheerfully, putting her arm around her guest, who arrived in a traveling suit of pink-and-green paisley.

"All this light is making me dizzy," Cassie said. "Or maybe it's the air. Am I wrong or is the air a little strange here?"

"Strange enough to have moved your son to get a bona fide job," announced Marissa. "Honestly, Cassie, I can't believe it. When my friend John first told me he'd met a man from New York who traveled for a living, I thought he was out of his mind."

"Traveling is a wonderful occupation," said Cassie, still squinting. "I think playing piano in a drafty dance studio is going to give Bradley back problems, and let me tell you, there is nothing more tiresome than a man with a bad back."

Was this real? Bradley wondered. Was he actually leaving his mother with a woman who thought a Jacuzzi would take care of the world's problems? The very idea of the two of them becoming inseparable had frightening implications: It meant Cassie would still be at Marissa's when the baby was born; Cassie would play a part in the formative years of another human being. With a shudder he realized that Marissa's baby was arriving in his own birth month of April.

After fretfully helping Marissa get his mother settled in the guest room, Bradley escaped in his BMW, speeding to John's house in La Barranca. Ordering John off his office phone, he proceeded to rage in a voice so angry, the dog yet without a name scurried out of the room.

"How could you let me make such a terrible mistake?" Bradley screamed. "Why didn't you stop me? Do you know what happened over at Ste. Marissa Hospital? My fucking life passed in front of me, that's what. Why didn't you warn me that those two would leap into a conspiracy to do me in?"

John Aaron sat back in his desk chair with a smile. "Just when life was starting to get dull," he said brightly, "things are picking up again."

BOOK VII

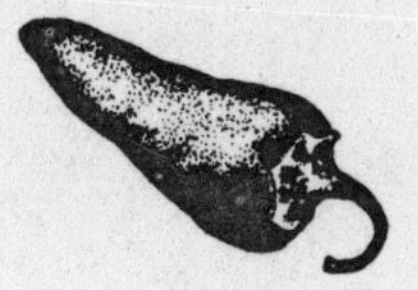

Chapter Twenty-three

A heavy snowfall gave a lift to the holiday season, or so insisted the most dedicated Santa Feans. The snow truly did lend a special beauty to the *farolitos,* the candles set inside of paper bags that lined the rooftops and streets of the Historic East Side. It was a new Bethlehem bearing the cachet of Dorothy Cheswick and her committee. A fresh snow, the flicker of candles below, and the stars above that were sewn into a flawless fabric of darkest blue: here was a picture postcard Santa Fe Christmas.

Bradley set *farolitos* out along the driveway of his house. Inside, Sam held in his lap a handmade card that had been put in the mailbox by Stevie Valdez. (As Stevie had drawn a picture of an Indian beside a Christmas tree, Bradley assumed it was Sam for whom the card was intended.) It was sweet of Stevie to draw a tree beside what was merely a symbol of the past, to pair a sign of life with something so lifeless. Bradley responded via mailbox with a wooden Santa Claus ornament; he was sure Stevie still believed.

Sylvia hadn't spoken to Bradley since the day he'd refused to sign her petition to stop The Madonna Parade, an art exhibition organized by coastal emigrés who hoped to make their mark on the Santa Fe scene. "Free the Madonna! The Madonna is for everyone!" and "Free the Madonna—take Santa Fe kitsch out of the kitchen" were among the slogans that ran in teaser ads in the *City Different News.* Sylvia was certain Bradley would share her outrage; though he wasn't a Catholic, he understood that the Madonna was a sacred thing that shouldn't be made fun of like that. She knew he felt this, she said, every time she looked at his beautiful gift of the Virgin of Guadalupe. The last thing Sylvia had expected from Bradley was a harsh lecture on the importance of free artistic expression in a free society and the evils of censorship. She had not expected to hear that, nor did she care to hang around and listen to it. She turned from Bradley with a dazed look in her eyes, nearly colliding with the source of his foul mood as she came up the driveway.

"Aren't you cold?" Cassie Roberson asked Sylvia Valdez, who had ventured over in a long-sleeved cotton shirt. Cassie was happy the temperature had dipped enough for her to wear her furs without feeling like a fool.

"I just live next door," Sylvia replied. "*Ee*. Your coat is beautiful."

"Thank you. And you have such a nice barrette in your hair. There's a lot of that silver and turquoise around here, isn't there? I'd get some for myself, but it doesn't match anything I own. Is Bradley home?" She stabbed out her cigarette on the dirt driveway under the sole of her rust pump.

"Yes," said Sylvia. The woman reminded her of the *borracha* from Fort Worth who ran around popping her head into everybody's pictures at the March of Dimes Gala. Then she noted the familiar eyes, blue and flashing, and the voice that echoed from long ago over Bradley's telephone. "So you're his mother?"

"Ssh," said Cassie, putting her finger to her lips. "You know, there are people in this town who'd ignore me if they knew."

Cassie Roberson had been surprised to see that Bradley's name raised looks of disapproval when she was introduced to the scene at this winter's favored gathering place for discerning palates, L'Etoile de West. The restaurant's name suggested elegance to Cassie, who dressed for her Santa Fe debut in a black-and-pink-striped scoop-necked Ungaro that lit up every highlight in her freshly retouched hair. Cassie was escorted into L'Etoile by the hairdresser who had combined a number of tints to create the formula many would come to refer to as Cassie Roberson red. Marissa followed behind like a lady-in-waiting in a parade of royalty before the masses as Cassie held her head high, her black eye patched with a heavy coating of foundation instead of gauze, her lips ablaze with fuchsia. Observing a collection of fashion understatements in what she had been told was among Santa Fe's chicest establishments, she was instilled with a feeling of superiority. My goodness, she wondered, had anyone here ever heard the name Chanel?

An architect was moved to rise from his bar stool and kiss her hand. "A humble welcome," he said, "to a woman whose style puts us all to shame."

"How is it you're so delightful," another man responded upon being told her name, "when your son is such a bore?"

"He wasn't always," she replied. "Honestly. He used to be a lot of fun. Bradley's getting to be more like his father every day. I don't know if you heard about him, but Bradley's father laughed just once that I remember, and that was the day he met me." She turned to Marissa. "I think Bradley has finally inherited his father's misery."

After one week in Santa Fe, Cassie Roberson became the most popular new attraction since the day her son had landed fresh from New York. After suggesting that Santa Fe needed an army of fashion police, she joined the ranks of the quotable, and the love affair came full circle. Her hairdresser adoringly imitated the way she wrinkled her nose up at poorly tended coifs. When, after a day of shopping, she announced that she was passing up the choices of transforming herself into a rodeo queen, a Mexican wedding cake, or "some glitzy version of Indira Gandhi," the owner of PerSuede proposed marriage. A jewelry maker asked her to model his line of rhinestone oil-well pins (a bust in the Texas market but a hit in Paris). And Hank the Indian, provoking the purchase of a clunky turquoise necklace out of heartfelt sympathy, accepted Cassie's money with an honored bow.

But even Cassie's biggest fan, Marissa, was disturbed when one of Cassie's most persistent new admirers turned out to be none other than Richard Gabrielli. Three days after meeting her, Richard had seen fit to present Cassie with a Mexican blouse so lovingly embroidered as to make her eat her words and approach the world of ethnic clothing with an open mind. After two full-course dinners with Richard Gabrielli, Cassie Roberson flowered into a señora worthy of riding horseback in the Fiesta parade.

"He says he's just so sick of men," Cassie confided to Marissa after her first night out from under her hostess's wing. "They were just his meal ticket to a decent way of life, after all, and, honey, do I ever understand where he's coming from." Worse, Cassie believed Richard Gabrielli had been sent from heaven as a sign that her life was about to take a good turn.

His mother's boyfriend factored into Bradley's regret over refusing to sign Sylvia's Madonna show petition. Standing in the wings, shaded by portraits of the Virgin that John swore would have been rejected by matchbook-cover correspondence courses, Bradley seethed as Cassie made her Santa Fe debut as an art critic, Richard Gabrielli at her side.

"Do you call this art?" Cassie was saying. "I must have been to a thousand galleries all over the world, but I can tell you that art is a polite way of describing whatever the hell is hanging on these walls."

"Hear, hear," said Dorothy Cheswick, making a note to add Cassie Roberson to her Christmas party guest list. "I can tell that Bradley got his refined taste from you. But, forgiving this unappetizing display, how do you like our Santa Fe, Mrs. Roberson?"

Cassie looked Dorothy up and down, thinking how nice it would be if the woman could find someone to bring out the softness in her eyes. "How come everybody talks about this town as if they own it?" she posed. "It's nice enough, but I, for one, believe a city without a decent department store has no solid foundation."

When Bradley learned that Dorothy Cheswick had officially labeled Cassie "a breath of fresh air in a season that sorely needed it," and that certain individuals were upgrading Richard's reputation to the status of a closet prince, he took leave of John and the Madonna show and went home to bang on his piano. The banging had sneaked up on him days before, causing a reprimand at Madame Petrovich's for breaching the air of grace that had earned the school its reputation. It was hoped that he would work out whatever had caused his playing to degenerate in time for the resumption of classes after Christmas; otherwise, he was informed, they would have to replace him. Bradley, unwilling to lose his first job ever, banged as hard at home to get the rage out of his system. Sam looked on, in jeopardy of losing his honorary position as the household's sole drinker. Bradley had as yet resisted joining him, pouring his watchman a stiff half quart of bourbon per day.

Bradley was banging on the piano when John stopped by to check on him before Dorothy Cheswick's Christmas Eve celebration. Cassie, who had bought a new dress with money provided by a new trust Bradley had established through the sale of the New York town house, had just left him. Her modeling had failed to result in a concurrence with Richard that she looked smashing in green.

"Sure you want to stay home?" John's invitation was halfhearted; of late Bradley had been a poor excuse for company.

"I think I'll feel more festive if I'm alone." Bradley barely turned from the keys to acknowledge John in the doorway.

"I wish I weren't at such a loss as to how to bring you out of this."

"A one-way ticket to Beirut for the loving couple might do the trick."

"I don't know why you're so upset. Your mother and Richard are leaving you alone. Should I stop by after the party, Bradley, or should I just go home?"

"Up to you."

More banging ensued, and John had to speak. "Did you ever consider that this might have nothing to do with Richard—and that you just can't stand to see your mother happy?"

"Do me a favor," Bradley snapped, "and keep your lay analysis to yourself, won't you?"

"My dear crown prince," John said with a sigh, "you're just no fun anymore. It may be time to change you like a burned-out bulb."

Bradley turned his back on him. "Up to you." His voice was barely audible.

"And Merry Christmas to you." John slammed the door. Grinding his teeth until his jaw ached, he walked out into another beautiful snowfall.

Chapter Twenty-four

A few days before Christmas, Cassie Roberson had presented Marissa Goldman with a pound of Godiva chocolates. Among other gifts for her loving hostess were a bottle of Paloma Picasso perfume, a subscription to *W* (meant to encourage postnatal weight loss), and some tips for child rearing. The perfume lasted long enough to have Marissa's child's first memory of her mother be the smell of Paloma Picasso mixed with clay; the candy lasted two days. The *W* subscription was not renewed, but the child-rearing tips stayed with Marissa forever.

"Children of a violent nature should be made to watch hours of television," said Cassie over coffee one day. "It quiets the brain. I think if it weren't for television, there'd be constant riots in the streets of every nation of the world. Bradley could have used a lot more TV himself."

Cassie adopted the tone of her favorite health class teacher at Culpeper High, whose job it had been to encourage her girl pupils to say "no" in the woods. "If your child talks back to you, just laugh in his face. Let him think that every insult that comes out of his mouth is the silliest thing you ever heard. And for God's sake, don't tell him anything really true about yourself. They love to point the finger, and you don't need to hear it from your child. I've only managed to keep one secret in my life, and I'll tell you, it has kept me alive. A woman without a secret is a goner from the start."

Marissa rubbed her belly, admonishing the being restlessly kicking inside to pay attention. "Can you tell me what it is?" she asked Cassie. "What is it that made you survive the wars?"

"Oh, it's just a little thing. Something that God whispered to me one day in Virginia when my daddy whacked my mama with one of his crutches and then lost his balance and fell on top of her. 'You can go on ahead and laugh, Cassie,' He said to me, 'because none of this is real.' And for God's sake, Marissa, try not to let him see you cry over everything that upsets you; this brings on depression in a child. My mother hardly ever cried, and I hardly ever get depressed, so there you are."

Dorothy Cheswick's party had the same lovely wreaths she'd had created every year, a constant that made everyone, including John Aaron, very happy. Twenty circles of pine were decorated with dried chile peppers and Navajo silver buttons. Her Christmas tree, cut from the mountains, was spectacularly dressed in ornaments made by artist friends. Some were made of clay, others of papier-mâché, wood, or silver; some were miniature paintings. Dorothy aimed to get everybody very drunk, as the ornaments were to be auctioned off to raise money for the summer theater (which had had a catastrophic season). Five full bars were set up around the house to save people from having to wait in line for refills, and gallons of champagne, Scotch, bourbon, and bowlfuls of her famous Eggnog Santa Fe, spiked with fine tequila, abounded.

Those who had met Cassie Roberson on a number of occasions would concur that she was always bubbly in a way that made one hard-pressed to know for certain if she were drunk or sober. But when Richard Gabrielli conducted her out of Dorothy Cheswick's house, it had been clear to one-and-all that he was unequivocally drunk. Later everyone would share the blame for not force-feeding him coffee before allowing him to head outdoors and down the road. The news about the accident reached a stunned crowd shortly before one A.M. Richard was lucky to be alive, some said, but everyone agreed that the guilt would be enough to kill anybody.

In a letter to the editor of the *City Different News* Dorothy Cheswick confessed that she took "full responsibility for the death of one of Santa Fe's most charming new arrivals, the lovely Cassie Roberson." She had failed in her responsibility as a hostess, she affirmed, "by not hiring a driver and one of those splendid mini-vans to see people safely and efficiently to their homes. Richard Gabrielli ran the light at Paseo and Washington, but it was *I* who should have applied the brakes."

Robby Valdez, on the other hand, had the assurance of the Santa Fe police that none of the blame for the accident rested with him. He was told by a sympathetic officer that the New York woman's death was not a sack of stones he'd have to drag around for the rest of his life.

"Robby Valdez," whispered Bradley as he sat in a stupor at Santa Fe's only hospital.

"Poor kid." The policeman who had been elected to tell Bradley of his mother's death shook his head. "Not a thing he could do. Breath was as clean as a whistle." He processed orders to cremate a body that had made Bradley double up, gagging, at the sight of it before reaching out to stroke its gashed face and crushed chest. "*Ee*. That Gabrielli sure ain't gonna sleep, though. Don't care how much dope they shoot him up with . . . Hey, my poor buddy, here comes your friend."

"Robby Valdez," Bradley said as he looked up at John with eyes that begged for absolution.

"Darling," said John as he pressed Bradley's head to him, "it wasn't his fault."

"It's me!" Bradley cried out suddenly. "I'm Robby Valdez!"

"No," whispered John Aaron as he helped him to his feet. "No, darling, you're not. See me? It's just John here, come to get Bradley. Darling, it's time to go home."

At Sylvia's insistence the real Robby Valdez joined her in paying a condolence call to their next-door neighbor. Robby had prepared himself to say what his mother had asked him: that he was sorry for all the grief he had caused Bradley in the past, that if there had been any way in the world to prevent what had happened, he would have done it. This statement was on his lips, but when Marissa Goldman answered the door and he saw Bradley Roberson being soothed like a baby in an older man's arms, the most Robby could utter was, "I'm really sorry, man."

All his visitors registered surprise when Bradley raised his head from John Aaron's shoulder and asked Robby and Sylvia to please sit down in his two, new, comfortable chairs.

Looking Robby in the eye, Bradley asked, "Do you still hate me?"

Robby turned to his mother, who had no words to give him. "I never hated you, man."

"Liar." There was no venom in Bradley's voice. "Give me an honest answer; then I'll tell you whether or not I still hate *you*."

Robby wondered about a man who could be so direct while clinging to another man. "I guess I don't hate you."

"Do you wish I'd go away?"

"It's your life, man."

Bradley waited, eyeing him.

"I have to think about it," Robby added.

"So tell me: Do you care what I think of you?"

Robby Valdez shrugged.

"I guess so." Sylvia patted Robby's hand protectively.

"I think . . ." Bradley paused, turning to stare out the window over the *banco*. The stars seemed to mock him with their winks, giggling like Cassie over his solemn moment. Finally, with a little brightness in his eyes, he turned to Robby again.

"What?" the boy asked.

"Just that I'm older than you." With that Bradley put his head down on John's shoulder and began to cry again, his shoulders shaking from intermittent eruptions of laughter.

"He thanks you," John said to Robby Valdez.

"Hey, now," said Robby, "that doesn't make sense."

"It doesn't matter," said John. "Now I think everyone should please leave us alone. Marissa, dear, I know it's hard, but you need to go too."

"What about tomorrow?" she asked. "Is there anything I should do? Cook a meal or something?"

"I'll call and let you know. For now you and your baby should just get some sleep."

After everyone had gone, John moved Bradley and himself into bed. Bradley's tears slowed, falling off the tip of his nose, drop by drop, onto John's chest. John watched the trail; each drop that fell was like an electric shock causing him to tighten his hold. Bending to kiss Bradley on the forehead, he waited for the moaning, for the prelude to more sobbing, but there were only quiet sighs.

"I'm an orphan," Bradley whispered.

"You always were," said John.

"Why do I feel so warm? It's like I'm melting. God, but it feels so slow."

John stroked Bradley's hair.

"Poor Sylvia," said Bradley. "Imagine. All those Hail Marys. It will all be fine, though. It will."

"What are you talking about?"

"Robby. Now Sylvia Valdez has two good sons. Here's

my prayer for the holy mothers of this world: May they have only good sons."

"Ssh," said John.

"Maybe Sylvia would set up a shrine," Bradley went on. "Our Lady Who Helped Save Robby. Do you think Sylvia will want some of the ashes?"

"No," said John. "I think she would find the idea very cruel, because it is, you know."

Bradley thought of his mother's remains and was stung hard once again by the pang of mourning. He pressed his face into the crease of John's arm and wept.

Bradley pressed his eyes harder against John until he saw stars dancing, mocking him again behind his eyelids. "We'll give her to Sam," he said hoarsely, nuzzling his way up John's arm to a warm shoulder.

"Give who to Sam?" John felt a warm breath against his neck.

"Cassie. In an Indian silver box."

"Ssh." Suddenly John felt a nip of teeth. "Ouch! What are you doing, for Christ's sake?"

Bradley forced John's mouth open with his own.

"Do you really think now is—" John began, but the sight of Bradley smiling down at him silenced all concern.

"Tell me. Is there anything I can do for you, darling?" Bradley asked. The question moved John to tears.

They loved, and as the water bed rocked them, pain floated away on the tiny, packaged sea. The air dried and then chilled them. Bradley drew his comforter way up over their heads; under it the air was pungent and exciting, transforming a moment so prone to flee into a tangible, astonishing fact.

Outside, the air was just as pungent. Logs of piñon wood had been burned in countless houses, and though the fires had all died by then, for it was close to dawn, the sweetness that had risen from the chimneys lingered, as it would until the fires burned again. It was the constant smell of Santa Fe in the winter, available in souvenir shops as incense stuffed in little plastic bags sold with burners molded in the shape of Indian beehive ovens. There are not many memories that can be carried away like that, so handily compressed in a pellet to light up when the mood strikes. It is a rare memory that is so renewable when it fades—when the air is cleared of smoke, its source reduced to a tiny pile of ashes.